Spider Girl

Also by Peter Lear

Goldengirl

Spider
Girl
Peter Lear

The Viking Press   New York

Copyright © Peter Lear, 1980
First published in 1980 by The Viking Press
625 Madison Avenue, New York, N.Y. 10022

Library of Congress Cataloging in Publication Data
Lovesey, Peter.
    Spider girl.   I. Title.
PZ4. L89914Sp   [PR6062.086]   823'.914
80–14713
ISBN 0–670–66274–7

Printed in the United States of America
Set in CRT Electra

Spider Girl

1 Alone in the cellar of a derelict apartment building in New York's East Village, Sarah Jordan watched a spider on a web. It had not moved in twenty minutes. Nor had Sarah. She had waited. Her eyes had adjusted to the faint light provided by a flashlight with a red bulb.

The male spider ventured a foreleg toward the next strand. Sarah kept as motionless as the female waiting in the crevice between two bricks where the web was anchored. The ritual had resumed.

The male's approach is infinitely cautious. He negotiates the web in a series of delicate movements and spins a special thread on which to coax the tenant female. He telegraphs his presence by tapping the signal thread that leads to her lair. She studies the vibrations. One fault in the rhythm, one spasm of panic, and she reacts as if he is prey, she kills him savagely.

Sarah, twenty-three, wore cord pants, two double-knit sweaters, and a leather jacket for this. The dirt and darkness of the cellar did not trouble her. She combated the cold with layers of clothes, things more practical than pretty, thermal underclothes, and woolen socks that reached her thighs. She kept her red-gold hair tied in a brown silk scarf her father had thrown out three years ago. He did not know she had hooked it out of the plastic Salvation Army sack. Probably he would not notice if he saw her wearing it. In Queens last summer he had passed her on the street. She had shouted after him, and he had

1

continued walking as if she were some streetwalker calling him Daddy out of malice.

The gutted blocks of the Lower East Side were ideal locations for Sarah's work. The arsonists and vandals had practically destroyed the ecology. Here it was, rising from ashes. The spiders were pioneers.

The male diligently worked at the thread he had inserted in the web, strengthening it to take the weight of the heavier female. Abruptly he plunged downward and was suspended on a line below the web. This was not an accident. The female had emerged speedily from her crevice.

She moved straight to his silk bridge and examined it. In a moment she let herself hang from it in a submissive attitude, legs loosely bent.

The male, when he saw this, toiled slowly up his line and climbed onto the web. He approached her with stealth until only an inch separated the pair. The next move would be crucial. There was a point when caution would succumb to passion. A crazy, perilous scramble to coition.

From another world, someone said, "Chicken."

The voice of a child, thick with the contempt of one scrap of half-formed humanity for another.

"You're chicken. Scared. Go call your momma, Henry Dickinson!"

"Lay off, will you, Ruby?" put in another. "We don't know if he's chicken. Give him a chance. You'll do it, won't you, Henry?"

Sarah now recalled some children playing on the next block. They had been swinging Tarzan-style on ropes suspended inside the shell of a burned-out house. She had walked another block east to find a place free of disturbance. It was bad luck that they had come this way. She could hear the scuff of their feet directly overhead.

There was no movement on the web.

"Tell her you'll do it, Henry. Show her you ain't scared. Each of us guys had to do it sometime."

"He's scared out of his shoes. Anyone can see that."

"Ruby, will you get off his back? Listen to me, man. You want to join the Demons, right? Okay. Prove you ain't chicken by going down there in the dark while we shut the door and count to a hundred. Stick it out and don't holler and you're in."

"He won't do it. He's terrified of the dark."

"Who asked for your opinion, Janet Delac?"

"There could be rats down there."

"Spiders."

"Spooks."

"Jeez—that's just the point. You ready, Henry?"

A thin voice asked, "How do I know you will open the door when you reach a hundred?"

"You have to trust us, don't you, jerk? If you want to join us, you have to trust us."

"Okay. Start counting."

"Not till we shut that door."

Already Sarah had reached for the switch on the flashlight. If that terrorized child was coming down into the cellar, the blood-red bulb would likely shock him into hysteria. The discovery that the cellar was occupied could bring on a fit.

She heard the door being tugged open. Gray light burst in. Her heart pounding, she looked for someplace to hide.

"All the way down, Henry. No standing on the top step."

"I heard you."

The door slammed.

Sarah had backed into the darkest corner, to the left of the stairs. The cellar was rectangular, without recesses or furniture to give cover. She pressed against the wall, feeling its chill even through her layers of clothes. She could see without difficulty. Please God, the boy's eyes would take time to adjust.

Upstairs they were counting in chorus. She heard him descend the stone stairs. His steps kept time with the count, as if that gave him courage. Twelve, and Henry Dickinson was in view.

He was black, not much above four feet tall, and wearing a light-colored T-shirt and jeans. From the way his hands groped in front of him, she knew he could see very little. After reaching forward with one foot to make sure he had reached floor level, he stopped, looked over his shoulder both ways, folded his arms, and began to whistle. There was no tune in it.

Sarah breathed more easily. The boy was facing away from her and the count had reached thirty.

At forty-five, Henry Dickinson stopped whistling and inclined his head slightly to one side as if he could make out something ahead. He unfolded his arms and rubbed the side of his neck. He took two steps forward.

In front of him was a pile of coal. On it, in the place where Sarah had left it, was the flashlight. He reached forward and pressed the switch.

He must have known what it was, but he was startled. He gave a strangled shout of surprise and stepped away.

If he turned around, he would see Sarah for certain.

He did not turn around. He lifted one foot off the floor and pulled off his sneaker. Gripping it tightly around the heel, he raised it above shoulder level.

It was not the red bulb that had alarmed Henry Dickinson. It was the small male spider, now alone on the web.

She could not allow it to happen.

Without a word Sarah was on him, one hand taking the wrist that was poised to deliver the death blow, the other clamping his mouth. So impetuous was the action that the back of the boy's head crushed into her breast and she gasped for breath.

In as calm a voice as she could raise, and with her hands still gripping Henry Dickinson, Sarah whispered, "It's okay. No one's going to hurt you. I didn't want to scare you, but I couldn't let you kill the spider. Promise you'll keep quiet and I'll tell you the reason. I want you to let go of the sneaker to show me you heard and understand. Okay?"

He dropped it at once.

She released his wrist. "Now, shape up. I'm nothing to be scared of. Just take it easy and we'll talk." With her hand still lightly over his mouth, she moved around to face him. Then she withdrew the hand.

Henry Dickinson's forehead had creased and his lips were pressed into the shape of a dime. His toes located the sneaker. Without taking his eyes off Sarah, he lifted his foot and helped the heel inside.

"You hate spiders?"

He made no reply.

"Just don't like being down here with one?"

A shrug.

"I'm going to let you in on something. If anyone tells you they have never been scared by a spider, they're lying. Don't buy it. I've seen a gorilla scream for his life when a spider appeared in his cage. A full-grown gorilla, Henry. People are no different."

He didn't look too impressed.

"It's natural to hate spiders, but you can get to tolerate them. You can even get to like them a little. Not long ago I was terrified of them. I really mean that. I wouldn't go to bed at night before I had checked every part of the room—ceiling, walls, floor, under my pillow—to make sure I wasn't sharing it with a spider. Yet here I am in a dark cellar stopping you from killing one. Isn't that crazy?"

Henry Dickinson nodded.

Sarah continued talking to the child, trying to make him understand what made this spider's life indispensable, but with one part of her mind she was listening to herself. Something was wrong and she could not think what it was. "Every living thing abandoned this place. Fire drove out everything. The heat and the smoke and the destruction turned it into a desert. If nature wants to reclaim the place, she has to start over. This web tells us that the process has begun. It means a female spider has decided the cellar is habitable. She has spun her web, and now she waits in that crevice there, between the bricks. She's a colonizer, Henry. Her instinct—you know what that is? —her instinct tells her that one of these days a fly will come by and get trapped in that web and provide her with food. But something else has happened. This one, you can see, is a male. He has found the web and he knows there is a female here. You see the thread he's moving along? He built that himself on her web, to interest her. But that's dangerous work, because if she mistakes him for a fly, she'll kill him. The moment she appears, he drops down on a thread, just to be sure. If she hangs from the silk bridge he made, he figures he could be welcome, so he climbs up again. I've been watching a long time, and she's already come out once. He won't give up. And when he gets there, if he's careful, she'll let him climb on her back and they'll mate. That's nature replenishing itself."

As if he had not heard a word, Henry Dickinson said, "The counting stopped. It never reached a hundred."

Sarah felt a tremor of concern. That was what she had dimly perceived through her discourse. The children upstairs had gone silent.

"You can bet they put the bolt down," said Henry. "Punks!" With the cool of an old campaigner he went slowly up the stairs and leaned against the door. "You can't trust no one."

He kicked it twice, shook his head, and rejoined Sarah. "Want to try?"

It was solidly made. The fire had soiled the paint job but left the structure unimpaired. She could not move it. "Maybe if you yelled," she said, and realized as she spoke how futile the suggestion was. Henry's friends obviously had gone.

"How long was you figuring to stay, lady?"

She smiled. "Do we have any choice?"

"They'll be back before dark, I guess. Do you have long-life batteries in that flashlight?"

"I have no idea."

"It's kind of faint. That's why I mentioned it."

"That's deliberate. The spiders wouldn't care for a bright light."

"Don't get the idea I'm scared of the dark, lady."

"It hadn't crossed my mind. Actually, I was thinking of things I should be doing this afternoon."

Of lunch with Vicky. *She* wouldn't fret when no one showed up at the campus cafeteria. Theirs was a casual arrangement, something that had more or less become slotted into Tuesday yet could as well be Thursday, when they both had the same hour free. Vicky had majored in philosophy and was writing a doctoral dissertation they had never discussed except in the most superficial way, because they had so much else to talk about. They shared a healthy contempt for men that Vicky fueled with weekly bulletins on the experiences of the two girls who shared her apartment. Sarah had met one of the girls and knew the other by sight. Privately she believed—and so did Vicky—that they deserved to burn in their emotional hell, but only sympathy and concern was ever voiced over the lunch table. It could wait.

She was scheduled to meet Don Rigden at two o'clock to exchange information on their research. This was of no importance. They had fixed it casually this morning when she had happened to run into Don on the library steps. He had asked if they could meet at eleven, as they had the previous week. She had been glad of the chance to tell him she would be out observing at the East Village site. She refused to be tied to a regular time. It did Don no harm at all to be reminded of her independence.

"He's ugly," said Henry Dickinson.

"What do you mean? Oh, yes"—she had seen his eyes on the spider—"I guess that's true. But you can get used to them. Actually, the males are not as ugly as the females. They're smaller and better-proportioned."

"His eyes shine."

"That's the flashlight. They wouldn't shine if I turned it off."

"Don't turn it off, lady."

Sarah shook her head. "Take a close look at him—he won't move. He's more scared of the female than he is of us."

"Why does he have so many eyes?"

"He needs them all. See how his head is attached to his body? He can't move it like you and me to look at things. So he has four eyes at the front and two on each side."

"What did you come down here for? Was it just to watch spiders?"

She nodded. "It's part of a study I'm doing."

"You're too old for school."

"College."

"They sent you down here? They have a groovy place up near Harlem. Didn't they tell you down here is dangerous?"

Don had, only this morning. The burned-out buildings on the Lower East Side were no place to be doing Ph.D. research, he had said. She had asked him if he knew someplace else where spiders could be seen adapting their life-style to colonize a habitat where an earlier ecology had been wiped out. He had made some smart-ass remark about modifications in her own life-style if a floor fell in and crippled her, but he knew how important it was to both their projects to monitor what was happening in that cellar. Sarah had a pretty good idea that he was hinting that he should come with her. If so, it was an infringement of their agreement, and she would defend her independence like a tigress.

Henry Dickinson sneezed. He was not dressed for survival in a cellar. Sarah took off her leather jacket.

He backed away, shaking his head. "I'm okay, lady."

"Not for long in this place. You'll need this. It's all right. I have two sweaters on."

Grudgingly he allowed her to drape it around his shoulders.

Just over a year had passed since Jerry Berlin, professor in the Department of Ecology, had called her into his office to give her the shattering news that Don, who had just begun graduate work, had already been granted approval for a Ph.D. study that substantially overlapped hers—the project she had sweated over for *two years*. "Isn't that great?" Jerry had blundered on like the bull elephant he could be when there was something in view. "You two can work together on this. No reason why you shouldn't set up joint experiments. The trend in research is definitely toward a team approach these days. You do know young Rigden, I suppose?"

She knew him. In each year's batch of students there is always one whose fame spreads like wildfire among the coeds. Don Rigden was the guy of arrogant good looks who of all things had danced a flamenco at the Amnesty International club disco. Devastatingly serious, he had got away with it and become a legend overnight. It seemed he was born on the West Coast, but his mother was from Córdoba. His people had five Spanish restaurants in Los Angeles, where he had learned to dance and play the guitar. So various coeds went into a Spanish phase. They put up their hair and wore calf-length skirts over white lace petticoats. No one went so far as to use castanets or to fix flowers in her hair, but the effect was sufficient. Up to a point, it worked. He dated numbers of them. As idols should, he betrayed no partiality, except toward his studies, which increasingly claimed him. He had graduated with the highest grades in his class. Sarah was unimpressed. She had put him down as an exhibitionist: she refused to believe that a blond-haired man had Spanish blood and she suspected his name was not Don at all. That was too pat by half.

After Sarah had made it blazingly clear she resented being palmed off on a student straight from graduation after she had completed two years' graduate research, Jerry had tried his peacemaker bit. He had poured Sarah a scotch and confided that this boy was by far the best brain of his year, certain, if he chose to remain an academic, of heading a department before he was far into his thirties. Jerry's plan, he told her, was to put the careers of his two most brilliant students into overdrive by inviting them to work on closely associated projects. That way, the university would stake out an area of investigative research identifiably its own, and Sarah and Don would be assured of top priority in funding and resources. Okay, if the concentration of two minds on similar problems led occasionally to a little friction, the outcome might just be some sparks of pure genius.

The heady mix of flattery and scotch had proved too strong for Sarah. She agreed to meet Don Rigden before the end of the week and work something out. But she had pressed her seniority hard. Don had fallen in with her proposal to restrict the area of cooperation to well-defined limits, leaving them free to pursue their researches independently. Maybe he had figured she would soften in time, but she was guarding her rights like a union boss.

Henry Dickinson said, "He dropped down again."

"I saw. Keep still, and we may see the female examine the web."

"Can't they hear us talk?"

"It's unlikely. They develop the senses they need most. They have a strong sense of touch, so they may pick up our voices through vibrations, but that won't bother them."

"What are you doing?"

"Making a note of the time."

"Why?"

"Routine. When you monitor animal behavior, you have to keep a record." This was a distortion of the truth. The mark she had made in her notebook was of no scientific interest. If the boy had not been there, she would not have bothered. The mating ritual of *Argiopidae* was fascinating, but familiar. The significant thing had been locating them in the cellar. But by giving the impression she was proceeding with her research, she hoped to convince Henry that she was indifferent to their predicament. In reality, she was sick with fear. She hated being trapped. She always slept with her bedroom door ajar. As a child, she had sometimes been punished by being locked in her room. It was worse than a beating.

‡ ‡ ‡

"Hey, Don, we didn't see you at lunch." Meg Kellaway's agitated voice carried across the campus lawn, causing heads to turn. Brown-haired and pretty, with a pert, pink-cheeked face that could not have altered appreciably since she was ten years old, she got to her feet and tried to look taller by standing on her toes and waving.

He stopped, turned, and nodded.

Meg ran barefoot across the lawn to him, smiling, brushing grass clippings from her white jeans. Her impulsiveness made her fun to be with, but you could get too much of it.

"Where were you? You're always there Tuesdays."

He started walking again and she went with him. "I, er, had to meet someone for lunch." He didn't want to make too much of this.

"Secrets, huh? Who was she, Don—that redhead I saw you with on Madison Avenue last week?"

"No."

"Julie Greenberg?"

He shook his head, irritated by the interrogation and its implication that sweet-smiling Meg was tolerant of his friendships with other women, as if a couple of weekends in his apartment had made her a privileged person.

"I know! That sexy grad student you do research with."

"Sarah Jordan? She has never—"

"Stupid—I know! I'm bugging you. She's a man-hater. Everyone knows that." Meg sighed. "Ninety-nine girls in a hundred would give their right arms to work with Don Rigden, and who gets him? Miss One Hundred! It's a gas, a real gas. Say, you weren't having lunch with her, were you?"

"If you want to know, Miss Jordan spent this morning somewhere in a burned-out building in the East Village observing spiders."

"Ugh." She shivered. "Nasty."

"Dangerous."

Her eyes widened. "Poisonous ones?"

"The buildings, I mean. They're unsafe. There could be an accident."

"I guess she knows she's taking a chance."

"I told her myself."

"You did? Hey, I think you really go for this chick."

"I'd have said the same to you, or anyone else. I work with the woman. A simple observation about safety isn't like making a pass, you know." He was increasingly irritated by Meg, which was sad, because she could be charming and adult. Not many equaled her in bed.

"It's all in the way it's done, honey," she told him. "Okay, case closed. I obviously caught you at a bad time. Will I see you before the weekend?"

"I'll be around."

She flushed, but she deserved no better.

He relented enough to tell her he had had lunch with Professor Berlin and the dean. "I wasn't baiting you. Imagine how it would have sounded if I had told you right off."

"You *are* moving in exalted circles. Can I inquire what it was about?"

"Sure. It's no secret. Some people from TV will be visiting our very own Henry Hudson University next week. I'll be meeting them."

"Wow! Like Barbara Walters?"

"Just some guy called Laz who makes science documentaries. I don't get to see the tube too often, but I was told he had a series running on NBC last winter. Something about human aggression."

"I heard about it. What's he coming here for?"

"Guess I'll find out Tuesday. For Jerry Berlin, it's the Department of Ecology at the top of the Nielsen ratings, no less. Mr. Laz may have other ideas."

They had reached the revolving door to the Department. He turned and glanced at the clock tower. He had less than two minutes to end this conversation. He didn't intend to keep Sarah Jordan waiting. If he were late for their meeting, it was a sure thing she would have chosen this time to be there punctually.

He raised a hand toward Meg's hair. She looked surprised, then swayed a fraction closer.

"Der fliegende Sommer," he said.

"Sounds pretty. What does it mean?"

" 'The flying summer'—the name Germans give to those minute spiders that use their threads to go kiting through space. You had one on your hair." He opened his hand and showed her.

"My God!" She jerked away and dipped her head, raking it frantically with her fingers. "I *hate* spiders. They terrify me. Kill it, Don. Please kill it!"

He brought his hands together, allowing the spider to escape covertly between his fingers. "Gone."

Meg straightened and tried to tidy her hair. "Sorry—I can't stand them." She was embarrassed now.

"There are prettier things around," Don said to help her. "You okay now?"

"Thanks, I'm fine. See you."

"Sure." He went to find Sarah.

‡ ‡ ‡

After nearly two hours there was a development on the web. From her recess in the brickwork the female put out a foreleg and tested the signal thread like a concert violinist. The grouped pinpoints of red that were her eyes glinted out of the shadow. Then, in a movement of electrifying speed, she darted to the center of the web and froze there. It vibrated from end to end.

"Why did she do that?"

"She's curious to see the thread he made in her web. Watch."

Nothing happened for over a minute. Then the female, with less agility, progressed outward to the mating bridge the male had spun. She appeared to be examining it.

"Look at the male, Henry."

"What's he doing that for? She'll see him."

"That's the chance he takes. He has to climb back onto the web to persuade her to use his thread."

When he had toiled up his escape line again, the male, with sedulous care, made a transverse movement over the taut strands to a position an inch or two below the motionless female. She was almost twice his size.

"She can see him now for sure," said Henry.

The male advanced to the gossamer bridge and tentatively jerked it. The action was repeated five or six times before the female moved. As she came to the bridge, the male drew back, allowing her to drape her legs over it and hang there.

Now there was a heart-stopping clumsiness to the male's movements, strikingly at variance with the near-balletic preliminaries. With scrambling legs he advanced on her, jabbing repeatedly at her exposed underside. The female remained immobile.

"Is he hurting her?"

"I don't think so. He's trying to mate with her. He's not too good at it."

"Shouldn't you get this in your notebook?"

"You're so right."

"If he can't do it, will he quit?"

"He's no quitter. He's gone to a lot of trouble to achieve this. Days, maybe weeks, ago he made a small pad of silk and deposited a drop of his sperm on it. He sucked that up into his pedipalps—you see the bits that look like extra legs projecting from his head? Actually, they function more like hands than legs. There, he's got it right. Now he's taking a grip on her to place the sperm in her body. When that's done, he'll retire and start over, because he has to empty each pedipalp. And when that's done, he'll run for his life, because she's hungry, and if she catches him, she'll eat him."

"Mean!"

"It's her nature, Henry."

"I should have squashed him with my sneaker."

Sarah did not argue. She was too taken up with the drama on the web. Her throat was dry with tension.

The female shifted slightly. The male altered its hold.

"What was that?"

She gestured to Henry to keep silent.

"I heard something upstairs. Didn't you?" He moved to the steps leading to the door.

Sarah looked up from the web, her concentration broken. "What is it?"

"There's someone up there. I can hear them."

"Your friends? Shout up to them, Henry. See if they're really there."

"You don't know much about kids. If they hear me holler, they'll know I'm okay. They'll just laugh and goof off for two more hours. It's better to keep quiet. Then they could figure I'm dead or something, and come to see."

"If you say so."

Footsteps crossed the floor above them, then stopped. A single set of steps, too heavy to be a child's. Sarah felt Henry's hand seek hers. She held it gently.

Upstairs, a man's voice called, "Sarah, are you there?"

Her shoulders stiffened and her hand tightened on the child's.

"Sarah?"

"Is he calling you, lady?"

She shook her head. "We'd better keep quiet," she whispered. She had recognized the voice as Don Rigden's. He must have figured something was wrong when she failed to appear for their meeting at the lab, and come down here to look for her. Wouldn't he just love this, the big rescue, after warning her the buildings were dangerous? Her seniority, so resolutely defended till now, would crumble to nothing. No, she would not give him the satisfaction of finding her. She would rot here rather than do that. "Just someone it's safest to ignore," she told Henry.

"He didn't sound like a nut."

She heard her name being called in another section of the building, then the steps receding. She was gripped momentarily by an impulse to call out, but she mastered it. When they had locked her in her room as a child, she had never once cried out to be released. Sometimes she had pressed her teeth into her lower lip until it bled, but she had waited till it occurred to them to unlock the door.

"Hey! Look here."

She turned her eyes back to the web.

"He's gone," said Henry. "The male spider isn't there. Did she eat him?"

Sarah smiled. "Not so quickly as that. He must have escaped. When he has fertilized the female, he makes a run for it. If he's quick, he gets away."

"What's your name?"

She told him, tricked into a reflex by the unexpectedness of the question.

"You knew that guy upstairs."

She nodded.

"He came looking for you. Is he your man?"

"Someone I work with, that's all."

"Why didn't you answer him?"

"I had my reasons. This way you can prove to your gang that you survived down here."

"If they turn up."

‡ ‡ ‡

They came late in the afternoon. Sarah heard the voices first, because Henry, by now accustomed to the conditions, had wandered toward the back of the cellar. She had pretended not to notice, thinking maybe he needed to relieve himself. They were into their fifth hour of imprisonment.

The floorboards creaked first. Then she heard the girls' voices, loaded with recrimination.

"He could be eaten by rats."

"Or had a fit and died."

"I said it was a dumb thing to do."

"*You* can go down there and look for him, Maxie. You locked the door."

"Let's call him."

Sarah was aware of Henry at her side.

"What should we do, lady—give them a scare?"

"No. I think you should walk calmly up the steps and show them you're not one bit scared yourself."

They heard the door unbolted. The light it admitted was dazzling.

"You still down there, Henry? You okay?"

No one was about to descend the stairs to find out.

Henry slipped Sarah's jacket from his shoulders and handed it back without a word. She put her hand on his shoulder and pressed it in a way that indicated friendship and also steered him toward the stairs.

He whispered, "Aren't you coming with me, lady?"

"They mustn't see me. I'll come up after everyone's gone."

He tucked his thumbs into his belt. "Okay, if that's how you want to play it."

"Hey! He's coming up! Jeez, Henry, are you okay?"

"Sure I am. Which one of you jerks can't count to a hundred? Do I get to be a Demon now?"

"You bet. Hell, you were down there for hours. Weren't you scared?"

"No."

"Did you see anything?"

"Just spiders."

2 One thing you could say for Jerry Berlin: he was no ivory-tower professor. He never missed a chance for publicity. A credit on one of the national TV networks was potentially more valuable than a dozen learned articles in the scientific press. So Bernice, the department secretary, had been given the morning off, and her office had been converted to a dining room. Trout with almonds, Barsac in hand-cut glasses, and a waitress from the caterer would use up most of the hospitality allowance at a sitting. This was a private luncheon not because the cuisine in the senior dining hall was unsatisfactory but because Jerry didn't want to expose his guest to the opportunism of other departments.

As a first-year research student, Don Rigden was pleased, yet still a little puzzled, to be the third in the party. "One of my newest and most promising graduate students. An original thinker," Jerry had said, introducing him, but then the professor so monopolized the conversation, chronicling the department's achievements since 1970, that Don had ventured nothing more original than a request for the vegetable dish.

Instead he studied Gregory Laz, a compact, dark-suited man with a reddish beard and deep, contemplative eyes, more the stereotype of a philosopher than a whiz kid from TV. While Jerry talked, Laz worked fastidiously at his food, separating the fish entirely from the bone before putting the fork to his mouth. He had the knack of appearing to take an intelligent interest in what was being said without contributing more than

20

a few monosyllables. His gaze rarely shifted from his plate, so when he looked into space instead, it gave the impression that deep thoughts had been provoked.

Over coffee Don was suddenly conscious that Laz had addressed a question to him, cutting clean through what Jerry was saying.

"Do you watch TV, Don?"

"Not a lot." He grinned. "There are other claims on my leisure time. Besides, I find that my research takes so much—"

"Yes. I heard about it from Professor Berlin." Laz spoke as if Jerry, who had stopped in mid-sentence, were no longer there. His words came slowly and his voice was pitched low, so that you had to lean forward to listen. "Do you know anything at all about my work?"

"Practically nothing. I was told you made a highly successful series on human aggression. I missed it. I'm sorry."

Laz made a dismissive gesture. "Okay. I'm not looking for fans. I'll tell you about it, because it has some bearing on what I want to discuss with you. I'm an independent producer. Up to last year I sold exclusively to public television. You'll appreciate that the commercial stations don't go overboard for science documentaries. I guess my work for public TV would add up to forty or fifty hours of screen time. That was a good foundation, but I'm ambitious, Don. I wanted to reach a bigger audience. Last year I put together my series on aggression, *Who's Master?*, which I figured had enough muscle to try on one of the major networks. NBC agreed to run it as a pilot. The response was positive. The series was broadcast in fringe time and made an appreciable impact."

"I'll testify to that," Jerry said. "I saw all but one of the programs myself. Boy, they were sensational. How you got your cameras in some of those places I'd give a lot to know."

"We kept fifty-three percent of our audience over the six weeks, which is better than average," said Laz to Don. "The secret is in the presentation. Program One was crucial, make-or-break night, so we planned it as the hard sell. We used all the best film sequences we had, covering the whole range of confrontation situations. It didn't matter that we used them again in the later programs. They could stand a second showing. Programs Two to Six each covered aggression in a special context—among kids, in the family, at work, in sports, and in crime. We were shooting for a big audience, so we went for action sequences. I don't use actors, Don. We showed them the real thing each time. People laying into each other is compulsive viewing. But this wasn't gratuitous violence. Through the commentary we analyzed how circumstances influence aggressive behavior, and we showed the connection between one form of violence and another. I won't pretend it was profound, but we made our points and we made them vividly."

"It must be more effective than the discussion approach," Don commented.

"A mass audience won't watch stiff people in soft chairs," said Laz, and it sounded like a slogan he had rehearsed to impress the chiefs at NBC. "My series did okay in the ratings and the advertisers liked it. The marketplace is everything in commercial TV, and this mix of real action and hard comment was just right for them. NBC liked it enough to commission another series."

"You bet they did!" said Jerry.

"What's your subject this time?" Don asked.

"Same formula," answered Laz. "I want to stay in the area of human relations and touch them on a raw nerve. That's why *Who's Master?* succeeded." He took a sip of coffee, then gave a faint smile. "Come on, Don. What's the logical follow-up?"

The question that interested Don was why all this was addressed to him, but he hazarded a response. "Maybe aggression *en masse*. I mean, organized violence, through terrorist movements and guerrilla fighting to total war."

Laz shook his head. "Good thinking, bad TV. That kind of thing has had saturation coverage. People are up to here with it. The same goes for sexual aggression, in case you thought of that. What is there left to say about sadism and rape? If you want to know, I've moved over from aggression. I'm on the other side of the coin. I mean fear."

"You're interested in the victim now?"

"Exactly."

"I like it," said Jerry.

Laz seemed not to be seeking approval, so Don gave none.

Jerry asked, "What's your approach this time?"

"I start, as before, by giving them a foretaste of the series, using all my best footage. Program Two takes up where the last series left off, showing how fear can be a response to the aggression of other people—parents, school bullies, the boss, the police. In the next program we look at fear of self, the problems of guilt and responsibility. That's difficult to film, but I have some ideas for it. Program Four is a surefire winner: fear of the unknown, the whole supernatural bit, the knock on the door at night and the creaking stairs. Then we move on to the fear of events outside our control, cataclysmic things like a plague, or nuclear war, or the Second Coming. That leaves one more, and I think you'll see what I've been leading toward, because I plan to end the series with a program on unreasonable fears."

"What do you mean—phobias?"

"You got it. Phobias." Laz looked directly at Don and studied him for several seconds. "Beginning to see where you come in?"

Don held the look and said nothing. He didn't particularly care for Laz or his ideas. There was an assumption in the question that might need to be challenged before much longer.

Laz looked away and said, "Phobias are a great subject for popular TV because they're within everyone's experience. It may be mice that have us running up the wall, or snakes, or cats. There are people who won't go near the sea. Or walk down a particular street. Those are common phobias. Since we started researching this series, I've discovered people can be scared by the weirdest things. Would you believe indoor plants? Or shampoo? I'll tell you mine. It's cats. I'm uncomfortable anywhere near one. My friends who have them have learned to lock them up when I visit. That's a minor inconvenience. In some people's lives, the phobia dictates just about everything they do."

"Like agoraphobia?" said Jerry.

"That's an example, yes. It just has to be mentioned on a phone-in, doesn't it, and the switchboard gets jammed. All those thousands across the nation serving a self-imposed prison sentence in their own homes. Incredible. It's a big subject, Don. Part of the problem with a phobia is, things get out of proportion. It's an isolating condition. You begin to think you're the only creep in the world who is terrified by moths and butterflies. But if you saw a guy on TV with a thing about cigarette smoke or shadows, it could help you come to terms with your own problem. Let's be candid: my series won't be therapy, I'm simply letting some light into a dark area of people's lives."

"Greg, we're all in the same business," said Jerry, positively evangelistic. "Tell us how we can help."

"You want to use the spiders?" said Don.

Laz nodded. "It's probably the most common of all phobias.

I *have* to include some spider sequences. You happen to have one of the best collections in New York."

"Not as good as the Bronx Zoo. Why not go there?"

"Insurance. Zoos have all kinds of restrictions. I figured if you people would cooperate, I'd have a better opportunity to get the shots I want."

Clearly Jerry had already given Laz the run of the department, but that didn't stop Don from expressing reservations.

"Most of our spiders are being used in long-term ecological experiments, Mr. Laz—"

"Greg to you, Don. Listen, I don't want to foul up your research program. I thought maybe you would have some spiders you were not working with at this time. For my purpose, the larger the better."

"What would you want to do with them?"

Laz fingered his beard and grinned amiably. "I'm glad you asked. This is just an idea of mine, but I'd like to see if we could work it out somehow. Did you see the early James Bond movies?"

The question surprised Don. "Who hasn't?"

"Exactly. Everyone and his brother has seen them sometime. Myself, I've seen them all three or four times. That's the result of too many long-haul jet flights. Don, what I'm saying is this: the shot everyone remembers is Sean Connery waking in the night to find a tarantula crawling up his arm. He has to lie dead-still while it creeps across his chest. Remember? Then he leaps up and beats it to death. I figure it would make an impact if we could re-create that scene—but with a difference. When the tarantula is nicely on its way, the guy puts out his hand for it, picks the thing up, sits up, and tells us spiders needn't scare people at all. What do you say—do you buy it?"

"I guess it's visually dramatic," Don said, trying to sound enthusiastic.

"You have tarantulas in your lab?"

"The name 'tarantula' is generic for any of the larger mygalomorph spiders from the tropics. We have some that I guess would meet your requirements."

Laz grinned. "Big and hairy. You've got the picture, Don."

"You came to the right people." Jerry beamed.

"There's another thing," said Laz. "Don, I want to ask you to appear on my show. I'd like you to do the Sean Connery bit."

Don laughed. "You're kidding. You need an actor for that."

"I've never used an actor yet," said Laz. "I happen to know you don't mind handling spiders, because I've already asked Jerry. That's why I wanted to meet you. All you need do is sit up and say something reassuring about spiders. There's a fee for this, of course."

"Sorry. Not interested."

"You're not? What's the problem, Don?"

"Look, I'm an ecologist, not a circus performer. Plenty of people don't object to handling spiders. Why don't you ask someone else?"

Jerry pushed his coffee cup aside. There was a hard edge to his voice. "Just a minute. Let's not rush this. Greg, I assume you will run the usual credits at the end of each program, listing organizations that cooperated in the making of the film?"

"Of course, Jerry."

"And you would probably list this department?"

"Emphatically."

"Thanks." Jerry turned to face Don. "Listen, I hope I don't have to spell out to you what this could do in promoting our work. We're talking about a series commissioned by one of the major networks. Millions will see it. You'll be introduced as a doctoral candidate at this university, this department."

"Yes, but you heard what he wants me to do. Christ, I hope we aren't *that* desperate for publicity."

"Are you questioning the way I run this department? Because if you are—"

"I'm simply saying that I can't see how this relates to my research."

Without raising his voice, Jerry said, "The hell with your research." He turned away and put his hand firmly on Laz's forearm. "Be assured of our full cooperation, Greg. This is a project we'll be proud to be associated with. Now, if you have time, I'd like you to look over the department, meet the inmates—the eight-legged ones, that is."

"Jerry, that's a nice offer, but not now. I'll tell you why. I have a small production team—two cameramen in particular —who will want to check everything out before we start shooting. You people are in for a bellyful of TV. I make it a rule to keep the disruption to a minimum, so, if it's okay with you, I'll do the tour later in the week with my team." He carefully refolded his napkin and placed it on the table. "Besides, I sense that you gentlemen have things to discuss."

‡ ‡ ‡

Over the weekend, Meg Kellaway had an illuminating discussion with Nancy Lim, who had the room opposite. Serene and self-composed, Nancy was her opposite in more ways than one. Before this, they had sometimes exchanged a few civil words in the corridor, no more. Nancy had been born in Hong Kong, lived most of her life in the Bronx, and was majoring in mathematics, and that was all Meg knew.

This Saturday afternoon, a time when the dormitory practically emptied as students went out shopping or to the movies, the air-conditioning was shut down for maintenance work. The noise made it impossible to study inside, so Meg took her file to the nearest lawn. She knew she would get no work done in direct sunlight, so she had joined Nancy on the one shaded bench in sight, under an elm tree. As it turned out, she did not open the file. Nancy launched into a series of penetrating questions, establishing that Meg had no date for the weekend and was at a loss to sustain a steady relationship with the guy she most liked to be with, Don Rigden.

Meg found herself confiding in Nancy some of her innermost hopes and fears. People were always saying she was transparent, but that wasn't true. Because she was an extrovert and talked easily, it didn't mean she told the world everything. Yet Nancy's questions drew confidences from her that she had scarcely admitted to herself. They were precise, direct questions and they seemed to be leading somewhere helpful, so she answered them.

Yes, she had gone bananas over Don the night she saw him dance at the Amnesty International party last year. It was physical at first, a strange taste in her mouth, a weakness in the legs, a raising of her body temperature. An urge to touch him had overpowered her. Before the end of the evening she had joined the crush at the bar and brushed past him simply to gratify the impulse.

No, she doubted if he had noticed; her purpose was to indulge, not advertise herself. But in the weeks that followed, she had externalized her feelings and joined the pack of Don Rigden's female pursuers.

Had she got to know him personally? Nancy asked. Christ, yes. And was the man equal to his dancing? Meg answered that he was proud and brilliant and articulate. And unattainable? Meg laughed lightly and said she had spent two weekends in his apartment. Then, was he disappointing as a lover? On the contrary: he was sensational. In that case, what exactly was the problem? The problem was that five weeks had gone by and Meg had taken every opportunity to signal her devotion to Don, but he had not invited her back. She was desperately afraid she would lose him. Was he making it with someone else? Meg thought not. Was there anyone else he wanted? How could she tell? Was there anyone he had denied wanting? Meg pondered the question for a moment and said there was only one who had come up in conversation, a girl he worked with, called Sarah Jordan. But she definitely wasn't Don's type.

Nancy's mathematical training showed in the dazzling clarity of her thought. As lovers, all the men in the world fall into seven categories, she told Meg. Don, whom she knew (who at the university didn't?), was in Category Four. Sally did not disclose the character of Categories One to Three or Five to Seven, but she said a lot about Four. Four was the Peacock. Superior and self-aware, the Peacock lived in the satisfying knowledge that he could, when he chose, devastate everyone in sight with a brilliant exhibition. The greatest actors, athletes, artists, and singers were unquestionably Peacocks. The world admired and envied them. Women worshiped them. Yet it was well to note that many came up against problems in everyday life. They were prone to unhappy relationships, erratic behavior, and alcoholism. For a Peacock, when he is not displaying his tail feathers, is a negligible creature.

Meg asked if Nancy was telling her, in effect, that there was no future in a relationship with Don. Nancy said this depended on Meg, and how much she was prepared to adapt.

"You mean I have to study the ways of the Peahen?" Meg asked, smiling.

"Exactly that," said Nancy, totally serious. The Peahen accepts her status as the undemonstrative half of the species, but in reality she is not pitiable. She knows she is the Peacock's turn-on. She professes only sporadic interest in his shimmering display, which spurs him to prolong the exhibition and promenade more conspicuously. Out of this, each of them derives fulfillment. No Peahen, Nancy pointedly declared, stands goggle-eyed at her mate's magnificence. Or chases him around the park.

Meg found Nancy's thesis engaging, if not totally convincing. As her relationship with Don seemed to have reached a hiatus anyway, she decided she had nothing to lose by treating him as a Peacock.

Monday, at lunch, when she generally made a point of taking her tray to his table, she went to a seat two tables down, near enough for him to see, far enough to establish that she was figuratively pecking at the ground in serene disregard.

On Tuesday it produced a result.

"Hi," he said, coming to her table after he had eaten. "Something the matter, Meg?"

"How do you mean?"

"Eating apart. This is the second day you've avoided me."

"That's putting it a shade paranoiacally, Don. Just because I happened to find another table—"

He was trying to keep calm, and the effort showed. "Hey, what is it with you, Meg? I thought we had something going between us."

"I thought people were crowding you too much. You want to talk?"

"I'll get you a coffee."

She waited in suppressed elation, blessing Nancy for pointing out that Don was Category Four. She was careful not to gaze in his direction. She just registered with satisfaction that he turned his head twice in the self-service line to check that she was still waiting. The ways of the Peahen had advantages she had never appreciated till now.

When he returned, she waited for him to pick up the conversation.

"Tell me something. Would you describe me as inhibited?"

"That sounds like a leading question."

"Jerry Berlin did last week. He called me some other things, too."

"Whatever for?"

"I told you about my lunch date last week with the TV director? He is making this series about fear." He outlined what Laz had told him. "The department is being asked to assist with the segment on phobias."

A prickly sensation began near the base of Meg's spine and sneaked upward. "If you want to talk about spiders, forget it. I told you before—I can't abide them."

"Have I mentioned the word? They asked me to appear on this program."

"That's nice—but why? You don't have a problem with a phobia, do you?"

"Not that I'm aware of. No, I'm the guy they bring on to tell people there's no reason to feel afraid. That's okay, but Laz has this stunt he wants me to do, to give it dramatic force, he says. Did you ever, by any chance, see the James Bond film *Dr. No?*"

"Did I?" She was a mass of gooseflesh. "Don't! That was the most terrifying experience I can remember at the movies. Nobody told me what to expect. When I saw that shape moving under the silk sheet, I nearly died."

"He wants to restage the scene, with me playing the part of Bond."

"Don, you couldn't! The man must be out of his head."

"Actually, Laz is no fool. He may not be an original, but he's smart enough to find a fresh twist for a winning idea. The reason I said I don't like it is that I'm a serious scientist, or I try to be. This is a showbiz stunt."

"It's grotesque!"

"Jerry Berlin doesn't think so. After Laz had gone, he really laid into me for playing hard to get. I've never seen him so mad."

He told me if I want to carry on as a research student in his department, I do the stunt. He laid it on the line, Meg."

"But why?"

"He sees the program as a commercial for his department. I told him I don't mind taking part in a serious discussion. He says you don't act the prima donna with a man as big as Laz. If I won't do the scene, they'll go someplace else, and the department will lose the nationwide publicity on account of one pain-in-the-ass graduate student."

"So, did you agree to do it?"

"You see, my objections aren't the same as yours. I don't feel any revulsion at the idea. I just feel cheapened at the prospect of doing this thing, taking part in a stunt and then being interviewed about my work sitting in bed without a shirt. People aren't going to listen to what I say. They'll be thinking this guy doesn't look one bit like Sean Connery."

Remembering Nancy's advice, Meg resisted the impulse to flatter him. "Jerry Berlin can't chuck you for this, can he? You could appeal to the student council."

"He doesn't need to chuck me. If I don't have his active support, my Ph.D. will curl up and die inside a month. He has the contacts I need; he controls the technical back-up, and he's my supervisor."

"Don, don't sacrifice your Ph.D. for this. It isn't worth it."

"That's what I keep telling myself."

"But you're not convinced?"

"I don't like being used. If I had more respect for Laz, it might be different. But I haven't seen his work, and I don't particularly like the guy."

"He's an accredited TV director, Don. His program must be responsible if it's being screened by NBC."

"That's what I keep coming back to. Laz is a professional, and he knows how to communicate. To me, this scene is crap, but I guess it makes a point. If I can't fault it on grounds of integrity, then I have to admit that what's bugging me is my own self-esteem, my image of myself as a researcher in a white coat. For that, I'm not prepared to pull the plug on my Ph.D."

"If you did," said Meg, "you'd lose your white coat anyway."

They smiled, stood, and walked to the door.

Meg studiously avoided asking when she would see him next.

It worked.

"Something I wanted to ask you," Don said as if as an afterthought. "You said you had lessons in dance when you were younger."

"Plenty of girls do."

"Did you keep them up?"

"I did three or four years."

"Ballet?"

"And modern."

"Would you care to learn flamenco? I'll tell you why. The International Club is getting up another concert at the end of this semester to aid Amnesty International. They asked me to dance. I want to perform a *seguidilla*. It's a beautiful dance— for two. I'd like you to be my partner, Meg. I'll teach you the moves. It's very simple, and the effect is riveting."

"I *couldn't.*"

"But your eyes say you will."

3 Sarah's Ford Pinto zipped along State Highway 208 toward New York City. Traffic was light at six in the morning, and she could make the forty-mile run from Bear Crossing, New Jersey, in little more than an hour, even allowing for mountain roads at the start and the toll at the George Washington Bridge as the commuter traffic into Manhattan began to build. A bonus of being a graduate student was that you could take days off when other people were at work. So this Wednesday, as usual, she had driven alone to the small town on the shores of Lake Pinecliff that was known to a select few as one of the best locations on the East Coast for hanggliding.

Gliding elated her as no other experience did. She had discovered it the previous summer on vacation at Redondo Beach, California, saved through the winter, and bought her own Rogallo in March. After days spent observing the diminutive world of spiders, the sensation of space and height was exhilarating. There were private moments high above the green slopes when she cried out in ecstasy. Essentially, she had discovered, it was a sport that inspired a sense of self-awareness without depression. There was, too, the consciousness of danger. It raised the adrenaline and triggered the senses into vivid perceptions. After a day's gliding she always stayed overnight at the town's one motel, awoke refreshed, and drove back to the city, where she breakfasted out, usually eggs and bacon, griddle cakes, and coffee, more than she ever prepared in the room where she lived.

Mentally ready for a full day in the araneology lab, she arrived so early that she had to get the keys herself, usually a technician's job.

Bernice, Jerry Berlin's secretary, cooed with pleasure at being interrupted. Her main contribution to the running of the department was keeping everyone informed of what everyone else was doing. In the course of a week it was remarkable how many staff and research students came her way on the flimsy pretext of consulting the phone book, borrowing scissors, or looking at the schedule. Bernice was forty-three and into her third marriage and claimed she could handle anything. Most of the time she sat behind her Olivetti handling plastic cups of coffee and relaying information.

"Great to see someone in this place isn't on Valium," she told Sarah. "Generally it's after ten before the first one crawls in. Coffee, honey?"

"I just came for the key to Lab Five."

"Plug that in, will you?" Bernice was busy already, separating two cups from the supply on the bookcase behind her. "To your right, honey. There should be a spoon here somewhere. Jesus, since Jerry used this office as a dining room, every damn thing has been missing. You heard about the visit from Greg Laz, the TV producer? I told Jerry straight they can have their lunch someplace else when they come back today. He says he'll take them out."

"They're coming in today?"

"The entire unit, as I understand. Camera crew, sound people, lights. You weren't by any chance planning to *work* in Lab Five? Sweetie, forget it."

Sarah controlled her anger. "Nobody told me this was scheduled for today. When was this arranged?"

"They phoned early yesterday. I thought everyone had heard. Didn't your research partner tell you? He's in it, for God's sake."

"I was off campus yesterday. I'm never here Wednesdays."
Sarah had heard that Berlin was angling to get the department
on TV. She had not attached any importance to it. So many
of Jerry's overtures to the media came to nothing. "You say
Don Rigden is involved?"

"Didn't you know? Jerry brought him in for lunch last week
with Laz. A cozy little threesome right here."

Sarah felt the blood rise to her cheeks.

Bernice was quick to follow with, "Don't ask me why Jerry
asked him. I thought you had two years' seniority. If anyone
here is qualified to go on TV and talk about spiders, it must
be you. You might not have wanted to do it, but it's nice to
be asked. I don't know how you see it, honey, but it strikes me
that equality of the sexes still has a long way to go in this
college. Do you like your coffee strong? This time of day, I do.
What is it with Don Rigden—a communication problem?
Funny, I get along okay with the guy. I guess men find it easy
to relate to me."

Sarah occupied herself with the kettle, declining the strong
invitation to unburden her thoughts about Don. All she said
—and it was enough for Bernice—was, "We have a satisfactory
understanding about research."

"Sure you have. That's obvious. Jerry regards you two as his
Super Bowl team. What beats me is why Don should go to
lunch with Laz and not mention it to you."

"It isn't important."

"I mean, it's not as if it was anything personal, like whether
he sleeps with his girl. Who is she, that dark-haired one with
the face of a fifteen-year-old who tags after him? Meg someone . . ."

"Kellaway."

"You know her, then. I believe it's cooled lately. I had it
from Della, who works in the dean's office, that there was

definitely a relationship there a month or two back. Maybe she was rushing him. I always think of Don as a guy who values his freedom. What do you say?"

"I've never thought about it. What time are the TV people expected? I'd like to get some time in the lab before they take over."

"Jerry said not before ten-thirty. They plan to shoot here this morning, with Don showing them around the lab, and in Don's apartment this afternoon."

"His apartment?"

Her eyes shining, Bernice confided to Sarah the proposal to re-create the scene from *Dr. No*. "I understand he isn't crazy about the idea. You bet he'll do it, though. Jerry was laying it on the line to him in here on Monday morning. I didn't hear exactly what was said, but you can get the drift from the tones in their voices. Don is no pushover, but Jerry has all the trump cards, doesn't he?" Without pause, Bernice switched to other developments in the department, and Sarah stopped listening. The monologue was self-fueling. Bernice's visitors were never so reckless as to give anything in return.

Sarah despised Bernice for her compulsive gossiping. It was oral incontinence, the more to be deplored because of the privileged position she held. Jerry should have fired her years ago.

Once acquired, confidences should be kept. Sarah herself gathered information, but she used it for her own purposes. She had a number of contacts—they were not really friends—female, observant, and discreet. She had cultivated them with care. They talked to her because she was a sensitive listener, appreciative of what they had to say. Compiled, compared, and intricately linked, their news provided her with a network of intelligence reaching into each area of university life her interest had penetrated. It gave her confidence and a secret sensation of power. More practically, it was a safeguard against surprise. She could face anything at all except the unexpected.

This was why the news that Jerry had invited Don Rigden to do the TV program had shaken her. By a freakish combination of circumstances, it had escaped her until this morning. She had neglected to take an interest in Jerry's wooing of the TV people because she had assumed he would grab at any interview that was offered. The choice of Don, without even the courtesy of informing her, had hit her like a whiplash. As the senior research student, she was entitled to be consulted, whatever her potential as a TV performer—and how could Jerry judge that? It just reinforced her feeling that the day Don had been launched on graduate research, her own status had dropped ten points.

She was still smarting when she left Bernice and let herself into the lab. In an effort to subdue the hurt, she picked up her clipboard and began to record developments in the glass cabinets ranged in rows along the benches. This catalogue of births, molts, deaths, and significant behavioral changes was a daily task essential to her project. It could be completed in forty minutes. This morning she was in no hurry. She was determined that she would still be engaged in it when Jerry brought the TV crew to the lab. She would leave them no doubt that there had been a serious breakdown in communication.

The humiliation continued to hurt. If Jerry had overlooked her because he was prejudiced against women, as Bernice had suggested, she would have been more angry than injured. Inwardly she knew there was another reason, a failing of her own. She had allowed Don to steal the initiative in their research. In the spirit of the proposal to cooperate closely, she had made a gift to him of her results. Two years' work. For him it had been a springboard. Already he was investigating a promising new hypothesis her preliminary results had suggested. To be just, he had several times offered to report progress on the work, but she had taken only a token interest. She had kept aloof in the belief that it would conserve her seniority. Instead, it had allowed Don—whose brilliance she could not deny—to take credit for progress she, left alone, would probably have made not long after. The impression had grown, and evidently got through to Jerry, that Don's participation had breathed life into an otherwise moribund project.

She was going to be more positive from now on.

Jerry opened the door at ten-thirty-five. He could not fail to notice Sarah taking notes at the case containing *Lycosidae*, but he said nothing to her. He said, "Gentlemen, the place is at your disposal," and the six members of the TV crew filed in, bearing a camera, cables, and lights.

Sarah turned and stared at them.

Jerry went on. "I guess you need time to set up your gear. I told Don Rigden to be here by eleven. For the present, if you need anything, Miss Jordan is here and I'm sure will be happy to assist."

Sarah said flatly, "I would if I knew what this is about."

"Hell—didn't I tell you?" Jerry was clearly embarrassed. Not, she suspected, on her account.

The bearded man she took to be Laz intervened smoothly. His voice was soft, yet there was authority in it. "Professor, it will be my pleasure to explain to Miss Jordan why her lab is being invaded."

Jerry thanked him and withdrew.

As the others started setting up the equipment, Laz crossed the lab to where Sarah was standing. He spread open his hands and grinned. "Would I be right in assuming you actually know *all* about us, but you didn't hear it from an official source, and that remark of yours was more a reprimand than an appeal for information?"

She confirmed it by smiling.

"I'm Greg Laz. Come and meet the others."

The transformation was incredible. From nonperson to VIP in seconds.

"This is Ed Cunningham. He's the narrator. The voice-over."

"And the shrink," added Cunningham, a neat, silver-haired man in an expensively cut gray suit. His eyes glittered amusedly. "In my occupation you learn to admit to it before someone else points a finger at you. I didn't catch your first name, Ms. Jordan."

She told him.

Laz completed the introductions. The last one made a point of stepping forward and formally shaking her hand. Under this guy's cheesecloth shirt was a deep-tanned torso, and he wanted it appreciated. He had a silver ingot slung from his neck. He was only average in height and nothing special in looks, but that didn't inhibit him. "Rick Saville." He squeezed her hand. "They warned us it was scary in here, but you don't scare me at all, Sarah."

She gave him a level look. "What's your function on the team?"

"What isn't? Research, continuity, catering liaison—"

"Rick is my production assistant," Laz cut in. "Sarah, I was told you keep some of the larger varieties of spider here. I don't want to interfere with your research, but if we could shoot some film, say, of a tarantula on the move, that would make a dramatic sequence."

She took them to the cases containing the tropical mygalomorph spiders. "These don't figure in our current research, so you're welcome to use them. The biggest specimen we have is the *Lasiodora klugi* in there. He's from Brazil, and we christened him Pelé."

No one came too close as she stood with her hand on the case.

"Hairy," said Saville.

"Does he bite?"

"All spiders have fangs, Mr. Laz."

"Yes, but is this one dangerous?"

"Not if you treat him with respect. Would you like me to take him out?"

"We'll get ourselves organized first. If it isn't too much trouble, I'd like you to show Ed and me around the lab. What exactly are you researching here?"

She told them about the project as they walked around, explaining how readily spiders adapted to environmental changes. She showed them how she compared specimens subjected to extremes of temperature with control groups. From their questions, they seemed genuinely interested, so she told them the story of the volcanic eruption on Krakatoa, the greatest in modern times, when two thirds of the island was destroyed and the flora and fauna were annihilated, and how nine months later not a blade of grass was visible, but a small spider was found there. "It must have traveled on a thread of gossamer, carried by the wind for ten miles, maybe twenty. A true pioneer. That was 1884, and there are now over a hundred separate species of spider on Krakatoa."

"So, no place is safe from spiders," said Cunningham, the psychiatrist.

"You can find them anyplace, from the tropics to the north coast of Greenland."

"Bad news for arachnophobiacs. Yours is a field of study most of us wouldn't contemplate, because we find spiders repellent. Obviously you don't."

"Once I did. They scared me a lot when I was a kid. I overcame the fear by studying them. If you become familiar with anything, its capacity to frighten you is lessened."

Cunningham nodded. "That's a point I intend to bring out in this program. What exactly made you face the fear?"

She smiled. "Kids go through some abominable stages growing up. I got in with a tough crowd who would have given me hell if they had found out my weakness. I knew I had to conquer it myself, so I forced myself to look at a small garden spider in our backyard. I observed it for hours, and came back the next day to see it again. Finally I was confident enough to coax it onto a piece of paper I was holding. By degrees I got to know what a spider really looked like. To a frightened person it's just an ugly dark thing with lots of legs that moves fast, but when you really get close to one and see the way it's made, how many eyes it has and how it uses those legs, you start to accept it for what it is, not what your fears have made it. In the end I think I had more affection for that spider than I had for my tough friends. Later I read some books about the behavior of spiders. I still kept a sheet of paper beside me to cover up some of the illustrations as I came to them, but in time I managed without it. Well, here I am."

Laz turned to Cunningham. "Ed, I don't know what you're thinking, but I'd like to get Sarah on film. This is too good to pass up. If we had you walking through the lab with her, discussing her attitude toward spiders as a kid and how she conquered it, we could get it on the hand-held camera. With some shots of the cabinets, it would make a beautiful sequence."

She felt a surge of excitement, but she controlled it. "Just a minute," she put in. "You're going to film my colleague, Don Rigden, not me. How will he feel if he comes in and finds the camera on me?"

"No trouble. We can film him just like we arranged. Your interview is extra."

"I'm not sure I agree to it."

"Why not, for God's sake? There's nothing to it. You simply move through the lab talking to Ed like you just did. We'll pay you the standard fee. We can make that more if you pick up a spider."

Cunningham, quick to sense that this wasn't the moment to talk money, said, "The purpose of this series is to help people overcome basic fears. Your experience is ideal for this. You can convince the viewing audience that there is a way to remove irrational fears from their lives. That's no bad thing to do, Sarah."

Laz added shrewdly, "It beats me that Professor Berlin didn't tell us about you at the outset." Before Sarah could respond, he called across the room to Saville, "Rick, we'll need a Sneaky-Peepy. Ed is going to tape a sequence with Sarah, moving through the lab."

"Terrific!" Saville called back. "The minute we came in, I knew we had to get this lady on film."

Sarah knew that if she was going to refuse, she had to make it clear now. She was under no obligation to these people. Their attempts at persuasion hadn't impressed her. They didn't give a damn about people's fears. They would come up with any reason they figured would secure her cooperation. The only honest remark had come from Rick Saville. They wanted to use her because she was a girl and it was weird to find a girl working with spiders.

So why did she keep silent and let them set up the equipment?

It was because of Jerry. He had not considered her for this. The automatic choice had been Don. Right: she would show them both that she wouldn't be bypassed so easily. She had resolved to be more positive. This was the first challenge.

The cameraman asked if they would walk the sequence

through before the take, but Laz decided that would spoil the spontaneity. He preferred to let the conversation take place unrehearsed and have the camera record it first time out, even at the sacrifice of some technical smoothness. A few imperfections in the camerawork would underscore the realism. Any serious blemishes could be edited later.

A small battery-operated mike was attached to Sarah's lab coat and a light meter was held close to her face, and minutes later she was at Ed Cunningham's shoulder, walking between the benches toward a hand-held camera. In response to his questions she described the fear she had of spiders as a small child, and how she had conquered it by steeling herself to sit and watch a garden spider. She stopped at a case of *Argiopidae* and pointed one out, showing the subtleties of the orb web, with its structural threads made of a silk different in texture from the viscid spirals on which the prey are caught. She talked animatedly of the versatility of spiders as web builders and hunters.

As they moved forward again, the cameraman backed away from them, holding the lens steady a short distance from Sarah's face. She felt no nerves. She addressed herself to Cunningham, not to the TV audience, and he skillfully fueled her enthusiasm with his comments and questions.

The film crew worked unobtrusively. Only Rick Saville, whose job it was to see that the cameraman had an uncluttered passage, intermittently caught her eye when he dipped across their path to flatten a cable to the floor.

The one difficult point to negotiate was the end of the bench at the north end of the lab, where they had to turn to come back. An arc lamp was positioned just out of camera view, but close enough to present a hazard to the cameraman's backward movement. He managed to get around it without mishap, and so did Cunningham and Sarah.

The accident was caused by Rick Saville.

He had guided the cameraman around the end of the bench by standing behind him with a hand on his shoulder. This achieved, he stepped aside to let them pass, then suddenly noticed he was going to be in the shot. He jerked away, without appreciating that the adjacent bench with its glass cabinets of spiders was immediately behind him.

His back thumped the nearest case and sent it sliding across the polished bench top. As it reached the edge and tipped, Cunningham, who was nearest, flung himself across the bench and attempted to stop it. The lid was gone, but he got a grip on one edge of the case and took the weight as it fell, certainly preventing it from smashing. But it was still too heavy to control.

It hit the ground on its side and spiders raced out of it and across the floor.

"Christ, what have I done!" said Saville in panic. His hands went to his face like a frightened child's.

Sarah moved at full speed around the bench to where the upturned case lay. The glass was cracked but unbroken. "Help me, one of you!"

Cunningham was nearest. Between them, they righted it on the floor and replaced the lid.

Saville lunged out with a foot as a spider ran under a radiator.

"Don't do that!" ordered Sarah in a spasm of fury. "Can't you understand they're terrified? If you can't help, for God's sake stand where you are and leave them to me." She snatched up one of the jars used for transferring the spiders between cases.

"These aren't poisonous, are they?" Cunningham asked.

"They won't harm you." She brought the jar down over one that had not moved far from the case. "Will you hand me another jar from the bench beside you, Mr. Laz. Everyone please keep perfectly still. The case has seven sections and there was a spider in each. One is still inside. I have just trapped another. And I don't want the others harmed."

Laz, in a subdued voice, said, "Keep shooting, Tom."

Sarah was too concerned for the spiders to care anymore about the film. So long as everyone cooperated by standing still, she stood some chance of recovering the runaways. A *Tegenaria atrica* is a fast mover. It can cover more than three hundred times its body length in ten seconds. But it is not a stayer. After its dash it is exhausted.

She coaxed the one from under the radiator with a ballpoint pen and covered it with a jar on the second try. By good luck another had run for shelter to the same place and a moment later bolted for freedom across the floor.

Without another jar available, Sarah, on her knees by the radiator, stretched the hem of her lab coat flat across the spider's path. It ran onto it and upward without hesitating. In a swift movement she covered it with her cupped right hand, drawing it up and across the palm of her left to trap it. Normally she avoided handling them, not from aversion but because their legs were so easily damaged.

She carried it to the case, and Saville backed away as she passed. Cunningham was cool enough to move the lid aside so that she could restore the spider to its compartment. It appeared unhurt.

"Neatly done," he commented.

"There are three more to catch," Sarah said.

It took almost fifteen minutes to locate them, but, once found, they were swiftly recaptured.

Rick Saville's cool returned rapidly after that. "Apologize to the spiders for me, would you? I mean, they must have figured this was some kind of amnesty until you caught them again. But Tom has some beautiful film."

Twenty minutes' tension snapped. Sarah turned on Rick and told him she didn't give two cents about the film. "Those spiders were part of an experiment it took months to prepare. Do you suppose now that we caught them it's just like setting up bowling pins again? Have you given one thought to the damage you did to their webs when you knocked down the case? What use are they now as a control group? People like you shouldn't be allowed within miles of an experimental lab."

Saville put up his hand defensively. "Easy, man. I apologize, okay? Don't let's escalate this into full-scale war. I want to be friends. If there's anything I can do—"

Laz said quietly, "There's one thing you can do, Rick. Knock it off."

When Don Rigden came in, there was nothing to indicate the emergency of ten minutes before. He glanced at the lamps and said, "You're set up already?"

Laz, for his own reasons, was saying nothing about the filming that had already taken place. "Waiting for the star, Don," he said with a bland smile.

As the film crew started to talk with Don about the way they would shoot the sequence, Sarah decided to leave. She wasn't there to watch how he performed.

On the way out, she felt someone touch her arm. It was Cunningham. He said in a low voice, "Sarah, I enjoyed our film interview and I hope you did. I'm really interested in the things you were saying. I'd like to talk some more. Would you allow a silver-haired shrink to take you to dinner Saturday evening?"

He put it so sweetly she could not refuse.

4 The silk sheet rippled and slipped over the shape of the unseen tarantula as it crept closer to Don Rigden's inert body. Don lay apparently asleep, his bare chest registering the evenness of his breathing. Inches from his left forearm, the creature emerged, dark and alien against the white material. With a squirming action it climbed onto the flesh of his arm.

When it reached his shoulder, Don moved. He lifted it off with his right hand. He sat up, holding the spider by its body, so that its legs moved freely while he spoke to the camera.

"There's really no reason to be scared of a spider, even a large one like this. They really—oh, shit!—I mean *rarely* bite, and if they do it's no worse than a bee sting. I'm sorry. The first time the damn spider gets it right, I have to blow my lines. Could we do another take?"

The screen went blank.

"That was take seven," said Greg Laz. "We tried another four after that, but I guess the spider was tired."

"Or depressed," Don murmured.

He was seated in a small screening room in a building near Forty-second and Lexington. Laz had invited him there to see the previous day's rushes. Jerry sat beside him. On Jerry's other side was Sarah. Don had no idea why she had been invited.

Already they had sat through the unedited footage of Don's interview in the lab. By any standard, it had been a letdown. He was not trained to project his personality, and it showed.

"Remember, these are only rushes," Laz tactfully pointed out. "The tarantula sequence would look better if we dubbed in some music." He said it without conviction.

"Let's face it," said Don. "There's nothing there you can use."

Beside him, Jerry Berlin was ominously silent. He had just watched his ambitions for the department sink like water through sand. If his expression was any clue to his thoughts, he suspected Don had blown it deliberately.

If so, he was mistaken. Sure, Don had expressed some reluctance when the project was first discussed, but once he had been persuaded to take part, he had wanted very much to make a success of it. In his imagination he had been through the interview many times. He had rehearsed some pretty clever things to say. When the time came, he had used several. As he spoke them, they had sounded impressive. On film, they appeared to be just what they were—pretentious. He had made the mistake of trying too hard.

Then Laz announced that he had some more film. With no further explanation, the interview between Cunningham and Sarah was screened.

Don was stunned. No one had mentioned to him that they had filmed Sarah. Jerry had not said a word about it. Don glanced his way, frowning. Jerry gave a shrug and looked away.

Don stared at the screen in blank amazement. What he saw was a revelation. It was not just that Sarah spoke fluently and with authority; it was her manner. There was warmth in her words. Her eyes shone. There was no hint of the tight-lipped intransigence he had come to believe was rooted in her character.

The contrast between the two filmed interviews was cruel. It made no difference that Sarah's had ended in confusion when a cabinet fell from a bench. On the contrary, it had strengthened the conviction that she was in control as she commanded the film crew to stand still while she collected the runaway spiders.

Jerry, so conspicuously silent about Don's performance, immediately got to his feet to register approval of Sarah's. "Can you use it?" he demanded of Laz. "What we just saw is exciting television. It's got to be used."

Laz nodded. "I agree. Sarah is terrific. A natural. She talks with conviction. She can persuade people that they can beat their phobias. What's more, as most spider haters are women, they'll really believe her when she tells them she was once as scared as they are. But just let them see her pick one up in her bare hands to save its life—terrific! There's no other word. That's not to say," he added, "that Don's isn't a first-class introduction to the subject. Maybe if we edit a little here and there . . ."

Don didn't need telling that no one would be editing his interview, or the scene with the tarantula. It wouldn't be worth it. The screening had achieved its purpose: it was clear to everyone that Sarah must speak for the department in Laz's documentary; no one could possibly object.

What angered Don was that he had been taken for a ride. He hadn't wanted to do the show. They had pressured him into it. There was no reason why he should have succeeded. He had no training in TV. Yet it went on his score sheet as a failure, made worse by Sarah's scintillating success.

He was not jealous that Sarah had eclipsed him, but he felt some resentment at the underhanded way she had done it. He remembered now that she had been in the lab early Thursday morning when the filming was done. The arc lamps had been in position when he arrived. To have got Laz to film her, she must have arrived early and convinced him she was worth it. Never underestimate the ambition of a single-minded woman.

‡‡‡

Through much of Friday Sarah considered what she would wear for her dinner date with Ed Cunningham. It was a problem. Generally she dressed casually but smartly, in pants, sweaters, and T-shirts, all good-name clothes that she replaced before the fabrics lost their crispness. They were fine for most occasions, but she had convinced herself that something more formal was called for this time. She had two evening outfits, a three-quarter-length white cotton number chosen by her mother that she had worn for her graduation party and not wanted to wear since, and a sexy red silk blouse and fitted pants that just would not do for dinner with a middle-aged guy she hardly knew.

She spent Saturday morning touring the boutiques in the East Sixties, yet finally found what she wanted in Ohrbach's, on West Thirty-fourth—a simple black dress with a high neck that was a line-for-line copy of a Paris original. The strappy high heels came from Charles Jourdan.

She had got into the dress and was trying to decide if it needed jewelry when she remembered her mother's asking the same question as she sat in front of her dressing table in a black satin gown almost twenty years ago. It must have been as far back as that because Sarah herself had been wearing the black leotard she had for her ballet, the first she had ever possessed, with a swan motif embroidered on the front. At four years old she practiced every day and had classes two afternoons a week. She hadn't told anyone that she was planning to fly to Russia to join the Bolshoi company. Anyway, this time she told her mother there was no need for jewelry, but she would look a whole lot prettier if she put her hair up. Of course her advice had been ignored.

Mother.

Christ, it was Saturday and she had not called her mother.

She had a note in her date book to call her this weekend. She had meant to do it Friday.

But why? It wasn't her birthday. Or Daddy's.

She looked at her watch. There was just enough time.

"Who is this?" the voice on the line asked. "Is it you, Sally?" Her mother never used the name she had chosen for Sarah.

"Who else? I'm sorry this is—"

"I thought you would call last evening. Where are you?"

"At college, Mother."

"At college? I didn't think this would be you. I said to Daddy last evening when you didn't call, 'I know what Sally is doing. She's coming home. She didn't call because she's coming home this weekend.' "

"I don't know what made you think such a thing. This is midway through the semester. I'm sorry I didn't call, but—"

"I said to Daddy, 'She's driving home tonight. She'll be home in two hours.' So I made a buttermilk cake, the kind you always liked—"

"You made a cake? Mother, that's absurd. Just because I missed calling you, there was no reason to expect me home."

There was a pause long enough for Sarah to know she must have said something terrible. She was steeped in guilt without knowing why.

Then her mother's voice said, "You didn't forget what day tomorrow is? You didn't forget, Sally?"

Sunday, May fourth.

May fourth.

Into Sarah's mind flashed the image of a stretch of highway east of Philadelphia near a town called Friendship. A single line scored on the tarmac surface. A crazy, twisting line that became two. Two that crossed and then stayed parallel as she had tracked them across the three lanes of the road and into the ditch beside it. There she had seen scorched grass. No one could say for certain what had caused her brother, Marty, to lose control of his new Yamaha. He had died the day before his eighteenth birthday. Two years ago. May fourth, 1978.

Sarah talked, plugging the silence with words. "I remember, of course. You can't believe I'm so insensitive. You don't think I would forget the only brother I had in the world. Only I thought maybe it would distress you more if—"

"I thought we would come together as a family this weekend. Like last year."

Last year had been like the funeral all over again, only worse, because it was unbidden. Standing by the grave. Dark clothes and prayers in church. The empty place at the table. An evening with Mother mawkishly sifting through old photos, wallowing in misery. Every topic barred except Marty, Marty, Marty.

Was this to be an annual ritual?

"It helps to share the grief, Sally. I planned for us to go to church Sunday, you and Daddy and me. I'm okay now; I promise. I won't break down this year. You know you're all we've got now."

Now that Marty was dead. Before, when Marty was trying for Yale, and astronomic fees had to be met for school and private tutoring, and parties given for teachers supposed to have influence on Yale admissions, no one had pleaded with Sarah to come home for a weekend.

"Mother, I'm sorry, but I have to tell you that I simply cannot get away right now. I can't tell you how busy I am with this research. Aside from that, I really think you shouldn't make too much of this. I mean, I *know* you can't dismiss Marty from your thoughts, but is it right to make a big occasion out of the anniversary?"

Before she finished the question, she knew it was a mistake

to have started it. There was outrage, followed by weeping, followed by her father on the line.

"Sarah, I don't altogether know what this is about"—oh, but he did, absolutely—"but your mother can do without you upsetting her at this time. Shall we see you tomorrow when Marty's name is read in church?"

She found it easier to say no to him. If there was still a residue of pity for her mother, for him there was nothing. There had been nothing for as long as she could remember. She told him coolly and firmly that she had work to do that could not be put off. Marty would be in her thoughts on Sunday and she would pay respect to his memory in her own way. She guessed Mother would understand when she gave the whole thing some thought.

And she replaced the receiver.

She almost ran downstairs and hailed a cab. She felt shaken up, but she was not having her evening ruined by *them*.

‡ ‡ ‡

At La Fondue, Ed Cunningham was waiting at the bar. Seeing him in this new setting was like meeting him for the first time. They greeted each other stiffly. He helped her out of her coat and handed it to one of the restaurant staff. He said she looked dazzling and blinked so much he could have meant it literally. The compliment pleased her, yet she was uncertain how to react to it. Last Wednesday in the lab, accepting his invitation to dinner had been a snap decision. Of the people there, only he had shown consideration for her, or given practical help when the spiders had escaped. The suggestion of dinner had seemed in keeping with his concern, as if he hadn't wanted her to leave with a totally bad impression. To have refused would have been mean, especially after he had described himself as a silver-haired shrink.

Yet now that she was here, facing an evening alone with him, apprehensions bore down, making her ultrasensitive to each inflection in his voice. What did he expect from this evening? Was this purely a public-relations exercise on behalf of the film unit? Or was Ed Cunningham here on his own account? She knew there were men of his generation who liked being seen with girls half their age. She didn't object to that. Older men had style; it would be no hardship to have the undivided attention of one. If at the end of the evening he made it obvious he wanted something besides conversation— this was strictly hypothetical—she would not necessarily turn him down. Making it with a man in his fifties would be new in her experience, and he couldn't be less of a turn-on than the guys of her own age she had slept with. It might just be a whole lot better.

She let him order her a drink; then she asked him, straight out, "Why am I here?"

He smiled, and the lines sharpened at the edges of his eyes. "That's easy. You're here, Sarah, because you were generous enough to give a positive answer to my invitation to dinner and considerate enough not to cancel when I phoned and asked you to meet me here. I really appreciate that."

"Yes, but why?"

"You want to know my intentions?"

She hoped she had not gone crimson. "Well . . . yes."

He looked steadily back at her. "You interest me. Personally and—don't be alarmed by this—professionally. I believe you are a very special person, Sarah. I'd like to know you better." He stopped and smiled again. "I know. You've heard that line before. Let me put it another way. I'm as charmed as any guy could be to have dinner with a girl as attractive as you, but I want you to relax and enjoy yourself. I promise you solemnly that you won't feel my knee pressing yours under the table. My approach begins and ends with words."

Sarah was grateful for the timing as their cocktails were placed in front of them. "To words, then."

"Plenty of them."

"Shall I call you Ed?"

"Please. Everyone does. Each day I see Edmund on my office door I get another white hair. A psychiatrist called *Edmund.* It just doesn't figure. My parents had no imagination. 'Sigmund' I could have lived with. What about your name— are you happy with it?"

"I'm reconciled to it." It was not so easy to make this sort of conversation with a psychiatrist who had just admitted to a professional interest. "Could I have a little more ice in this, do you think?"

"Sure." He made a deft switch of subjects. "Your TV manner is riveting—did you know that? Greg Laz intends to use practically all the film footage he shot of you. He claims all the credit for finding you. 'Serendipity,' he calls it."

"I ought to know what that means, but—"

"The faculty of making happy discoveries by accident. Greg doesn't underestimate himself, as you may appreciate, but he's a nice enough guy and a red-hot film director. Do you mind if I ask you something? *Was* it just an accident that you happened to be working in the lab when we arrived to set up?"

Sarah frowned slightly. "You mean was I there to try and get a part in the program? No. I was checking the spiders. It's a job we do each day."

"Too bad. I can't fault Greg's serendipity, then. You see, if you had planned it all . . ."

She didn't like what he was implying. "Of course I didn't, not the way you mean. If you really want to know, I made sure I was still there when you arrived because I wanted to embarrass Jerry." She described her injured feelings at not being informed that the lab was being used for filming. "So I was there to make a silent protest to my professor. I didn't expect to become involved in the filming."

"Subconsciously, perhaps?"

She shook her head. "Leave my subconscious out of this."

He continued smoothly. "The nice thing is, you're going to make a real impact when the series is broadcast. Tell me: that claim of yours that you used to be scared of spiders—was it on the level?"

She tilted her head reproachfully. "You *do* seem to doubt my integrity. I wouldn't have mentioned it if it wasn't true."

"Sorry." He looked truly apologetic. "I warned you I had a professional interest in you. I do a certain amount of work with phobia victims. That's how I became involved in the TV series. There are various forms of therapy you can try in these cases. Maybe you're familiar with them. Have you ever had therapy yourself?"

"Definitely not."

"That I find remarkable. You see, it's unusual for anyone to conquer a phobia without help—really beat it, I mean, to the extent of working with the things that formerly provoked such extreme reactions. That's why I regard you as a very special person."

"No other reason?" To hide a slight hurt, she burlesqued it.

He stood up. "Let's go and eat. We'll get to the other reasons."

With the relaxed manner so reassuring in men of his maturity, Ed talked Sarah through the menu. She chose the filet mignon on his recommendation. She felt from Ed a strong concern for her well-being. It was clear in the way he ordered, closely questioning the headwaiter about the vegetables and the wine and consulting her before he let him leave. She experienced the rare sensation of being simultaneously cared for and respected as an individual.

"What else do you do?" he asked when the order had been taken. "I mean, apart from research. There has to be something in your life besides spiders."

She rarely discussed it with anyone, but it was a way of keeping the conversation away from therapy. "I go hang-gliding."

"Well, that's really something! Where do you do this?"

She told him about Lake Pinecliff and her midweek trips there. He asked how she had started in the sport, so she described the four-day beginners' course she had taken the previous summer, really to relieve the tedium of a holiday alone. She recalled the exhilaration of her first solo flight and how she had promised herself while she was still airborne that she would buy her own glider. "I got it last fall, and it's *so* beautiful. A Rogallo —that's the standard delta shape, you know? It has a twenty-foot span and is white with a green inverted *V.* You should see it go!"

"I'd like to. You must be strong to control a kite that size."

"The main test of strength is carrying it up the hill. That's really hard work, but worth every step. I can't climb as fast as guys can, but I can take it in stages, and I get there."

"Are there many girls doing this?"

"Just a handful at Lake Pinecliff. There's a better male-female ratio in California, but conditions are perfect there. You get these sensational updrafts of warm air known as 'thermals' that every pilot tries to catch. With experience you can spot them. You get to know the signs."

"You've almost persuaded me to give it a try. Is there an age limit? No, I'm not serious. I find it altogether too dangerous. Does that appeal to you—the danger?"

She gave it some thought. "I guess it helps to get the adrenaline going, but really, if you fly according to the rules, it's safe."

"No one can help you if anything goes wrong," he pointed out. "The isolation would terrify many people."

"Maybe," admitted Sarah. "For me, it's freedom."

"You're self-reliant, then."

"Isn't that the only way to be?"

He looked surprised. "The *only* way? I can't agree with that. Most people draw support from others to some degree: family, friends, even psychiatrists. The loner is the exception. I'm not even sure that he exists—or could."

At this point the food arrived. While it was being served, Sarah wrestled mentally to a decision she would not have dreamed possible an hour before. She wanted to keep him interested in her. "If it won't bore you, I'll tell you why I like to be self-reliant. That's a paradox, I know. If I *were* totally self-reliant, I wouldn't be talking about it to you."

He smiled. "It doesn't disturb me. Go ahead. I'd like to hear it."

"Okay. You mentioned family. Let me give you a rapid rundown on mine. Mother and Daddy are both alive and living in a town called Cherry Hill, near Philadelphia. They have lived there all my life. Daddy is a librarian at the University of Pennsylvania. He's not crazy about the job, but who would be after thirty years at the same level? Mother has never had a job, aside from keeping the house in perfect order. She came from a good Boston family where none of the women did anything so sordid as housework." Sarah giggled a little. "She lives in constant dread that one of her brothers or sisters will come by and find her using the Hoover or washing the dishes, so she gets up at six in the morning to get the housework done by nine. The rest of the day she swans about in her best dress. But she needn't bother, because no one in her family has been near the place in years. She's pathetic."

"What sort of mother did she make?"

"I was her first, and she was totally ignorant of child care. She had been raised by a black mammy and only saw her mother on afternoons when she was not making social calls.

She didn't neglect me, exactly. She treated me like a doll, dressed me in pretty clothes and kept me clean and brushed my hair and taught me to say 'Mama,' but there was no love in it. It was just in case anyone came to call."

"And your father?"

Sarah smiled ironically. "He kept out of it. Looking back, I guess I was just a reproach to him, dressed like that, my mother's way of showing him she deserved to live like a lady. On *his* salary the best she could do was buy a pink and white dress for me once in a while. They were always pink and white with a lace frill, and I hated them all. Would she listen when I asked for jeans like the other kids wore? I don't believe she saw the other kids; mentally she had never moved out of Boston. Her own things were way out of fashion, but she had this idea they were classic clothes that would always be okay. There was this annual dinner-dance at the university, and she went each year in the same faded print dress she had persuaded my father to buy her at Bloomingdale's the year they were married. She would trim it and change the collar and try a new belt, but it had to be the same dress because it was class and it came from Bloomie's and she was going to wear it until he took her back to New York for a new one."

Perplexity had crept over Ed Cunningham's face. "Was your father really so poor? I know librarians aren't big earners, but—"

"He was playing the ponies. The Garden State Race Track was just two miles down the road. Mother didn't object, because horseracing was socially okay, and I guess there was always the chance that a long shot would improve our circumstances. It never did. But when I was four, she did manage to gouge enough out of him to pay for my ballet lessons. The doll had to be taught to dance, you see."

"Did you enjoy ballet?"

"Are you kidding? I adored it. For one thing, it got me out of the house to a place where I met other kids. For another, I was good at it. I loved the sensation of moving freely across a big, open floor. Our poky house in Cherry Hill was so cluttered you couldn't take three steps in one direction. The sense of release was indescribable."

"Like hang-gliding."

She looked at him in surprise. She had never connected the two experiences before. "That's true. Well, dancing became the main thing in my life. It fed my fantasies. I must have looked ridiculous, with the baby fat of a five-year-old, trying to execute an arabesque, but in my imagination I was Ulanova or Fonteyn and prettier than either one. Once a year the ballet teacher treated us to a trip to New York to see one of the great companies perform *The Sleeping Beauty* or *Swan Lake*. For months after that I would lie awake at night re-creating the scenes in my mind, with myself as *prima ballerina assoluta*, naturally. Okay, millions of small girls have dreamed the same dreams and outgrown them as other things came into their lives. In my case it wasn't horses or boys or the pop scene that crowded out ballet. It was a decision of my parents. I should have mentioned that when I was three my brother, Marty, was born."

"Your parents' last child?"

"Yes. They stopped at two. It didn't change things at first. He was just a baby. I don't recall any strong feelings of jealousy or rejection. It was only as Marty grew older that I noticed my father taking some interest in him—you know, playing ball and other boys' games. That didn't bother me, really. Ballet was all I wanted to play, and I couldn't expect Daddy to share in that."

"Did your mother?"

Sarah smiled and shook her head. "She was remote. Her

thoughts were all on the good life she was missing. She spent
a lot of time looking through magazines. She would read one
through from cover to cover, then start again at page one. But
I was telling you about Marty. Pretty soon it was obvious he
was a smart kid, I mean really intelligent for his age. He was
reading before he was four, actually making sense of the books
I had scarcely got through at school, and I was well up in my
class. They let him start school six months early. Even so, he
was way ahead of the other kids. He began to get frustrated
with the elementary stuff being taught."

Ed nodded. "There's masses of research now into the problems of the gifted child, but that's the outcome of the cam-
paign that parents and teachers had barely started in the sixties.
What happened? Was he moved to a special class, or put in
with older kids?"

"What happened was that in third grade the principal called
my father in and told him they couldn't offer Marty the education his intelligence warranted. Because he was bored, he was
becoming disruptive and a problem for the teachers. He wasn't
truly delinquent. If he could be educated with a select group
of kids of his intelligence, he would almost certainly have no
problems at all. But that wasn't possible within the public
school system in our area. The nearest school for kids with
exceptional IQs was New York City."

"That's right. Two or three opened in the sixties."

"Great, but you can't have an eight-year-old traveling a
hundred miles to school each day. So what else could the
principal suggest?"

"Private school?"

"You got it. With the superior facilities of a small private
school, Marty was judged to be capable of getting into a first-
rate college. So it was all fixed, and he was sent off to a fancy
private school in Philadelphia."

"How did you take this?"

"At eleven, I found it difficult to comprehend. I couldn't see why Marty had to go to a private school when there was a perfectly good public one half a mile up the road, where I went. We weren't close, but at least we shared the same house and parents. No, I don't think I was jealous. I had managed without a brother before, so I would again. But there was one thing I hadn't figured on. Marty's tuition was over three thousand dollars a year, and that meant drastic budgeting in the family. Sacrifices."

"The dancing?"

Sarah's throat ached at the recollection, but she kept her voice steady. "I had done as well as you could at eleven years old: four grades in classical ballet, two in tap and modern. I was confident that in another two years I would be good enough to join a really serious ballet school. After that, fantasy took over. Who do you think was set to be the first American *prima ballerina* to dance with the Bolshoi in Moscow? I guess I would stretch the point and make a guest appearance with the Kirov —by popular demand. And if the Queen asked, I would do a season with the British Royal Ballet." She smiled, looking down at the table. "They stopped my classes. At eleven, I was an ex–ballet dancer."

"Your dream world collapsed?"

"That was the worst day of my life. My father put it to me that Marty's education was more important than my dancing because it would affect his whole life. When I asked about *my* life, he wasn't interested. He couldn't afford the expense of my going on with ballet classes, or the price of new shoes every five weeks. As for a big-time ballet school, it had never been a possibility. He told me to grow up and find more constructive ways of passing my time. I hated him. I hated my mother for sitting in the same room leafing through *Vogue* while this was being said. I pleaded, I screamed, and ultimately I collapsed. I was physically ill for weeks."

"I'm not surprised. The way you tell it, it still hurts. Tell me, did this make you hate your brother as well?"

That was difficult. She wanted earnestly to give an accurate answer, but she could not disentangle her memory of Marty from a mass of twisted metal that had scored a crazy line across the surface of State Highway 70. "I can't say now. I guess I was deeply resentful at the injustice. But that's not the same as hatred, is it? I was mad at Marty because, to my childish way of thinking, he had pulled a trick on my parents. Instead of being punished for making trouble in school, he was being treated like he was some kind of hero. And what did I get for being a diligent pupil no teacher ever needed to reprimand? The loss of the one beautiful thing in my life." Sarah paused and sipped some wine. "Ed, I'm sorry. I don't know how I got started on this. You must hear stories like this every day. You invited me to dinner, not psychotherapy."

He pointed his fork at her in a way that compelled attention. "Little lady, I told you I'd like to know you better, and I meant it. What really gets under my skin is when my friends won't tell me one thing about their lives because I might analyze them. I'm interested in you as a person."

Sarah smiled. "It's mutual. Now tell me about yourself."

He drew back in his chair, put down the fork, and for a moment looked distinctly uneasy. "Have some more salad. You haven't eaten much."

"Come on," she urged. "I guess you're so used to listening to other people that you get out of the habit of talking about yourself. How do you relax, for instance?"

He floundered a little. "Relax? I like to think I'm relaxed most of the time. It's pretty important in my job."

Sarah insisted. "You must have *some* interest outside of your work."

His smile returned. "Like taking pretty girls to dinner? No, this is an extremely rare pleasure. I guess if I have a pastime, it's the theater. Do you like modern drama?"

She was answering his question before she realized how neatly he had sidestepped. When the coffee was put on the table, they were still deep in discussion about productions they had seen.

Suddenly she was aware of him studying her face. He was gearing up to suggest something. "Sarah, would you make my evening complete?"

She blushed and then went cold. She wasn't sure yet if she wanted to sleep with him. "How, exactly?"

He surprised her. "By saying you'll come to the theater with me next week. There's something I know you'd enjoy. Let's see if I can get tickets first."

Maybe he had read her reaction in time and changed his suggestion. Anyway, she was so relieved that she agreed at once.

‡ ‡ ‡

On Monday Don took time off to visit a theatrical costumer's on Broadway with Meg Kellaway. She needed to rent a Spanish dress for the Amnesty International concert. He had told her she would need to get it soon, even though the concert wasn't for five weeks. She could learn the steps of the *seguidilla* in jeans if she wanted, but it would never be right until she knew how to manage the dress, so she might as well get used to it from the start. She had not needed persuading.

Strictly speaking, it wasn't essential to pick up the dress at this stage. It could have waited two weeks more. But this morning Don couldn't face being in the lab with Sarah Jordan.

"What do you think?" Meg asked him. "It's a little snug across the bodice, but I guess that's the style." She swiveled her hips to show him how the skirt moved. The dress was classic in style, cut close to the body as far as the hips, then cascading in frills to the ground, dipping at the back in the conventional fan shape.

Don shook his head. "White is not the color for you." He turned to the assistant. "Do you have the same dress in red?"

"It's the only one in this style, sir."

"I like it, Don."

"Then I guess it will pass. You'll need to diet."

"Skunk!"

"Go jogging, then—or something."

With a glance, she made a sexual innuendo of his remark.

The assistant grinned, but Don let it pass. Not that he found Meg unattractive—the vibes were as strong as ever—but today his mood was too complex. He valued his independence. He knew she wanted guarantees. A steady relationship was a threat to the other things in his life. So before he made it with a girl, he liked to have an understanding that it was just a screw, with no obligation on either side. He believed in being honest. He had never been short of takers.

While Meg changed, Don paid the deposit for the rental of the dress. Afterward he let her buy him a beer in a bar on Times Square.

"So when do we practice?"

"How about Sunday morning?" Don suggested. "We could fit in an hour or two before lunch. There's a room in the gym where people used to play Ping-Pong, but the tables are gone now. A wood-block floor. Perfect for dancing."

"You wouldn't care to come to my place this evening and help me through the beginning stage in private? I could roll back my carpet. It's boarded underneath. I'll make goulash. You haven't tried my goulash." Her voice trailed away. "No? I guess I'm crowding you again."

"It's a nice idea, but I still have some stuff to write up. You know how it is when you take an afternoon off."

"Sure. Maybe there won't be too many people around on Sunday."

"You're feeling self-conscious, Meg?"

"Why shouldn't I? Didn't you when they asked you to do the stunt for TV? Hey, what happened about that? Shall I see you soon on the small screen?"

He told her why she would not. He admitted he had flopped and Sarah Jordan had totally eclipsed him.

"That's too bad," said Meg. "I didn't know you two were in competition for this."

He said he hadn't known it either. He told her how surprised he had been when Sarah's interview was screened.

"You mean it was arranged without your knowledge? Christ, that's mean! What kind of a bitch does a thing like that?"

"Let's be fair. I didn't say a word to Sarah about *my* meeting with the TV people, so why should she say anything to me?"

"Don, you're too forgiving. I think she really hates you. Watch her—she's dangerous."

Later, walking back to his apartment, he weighed Meg's remarks. Up to now he had never considered the possibility of Sarah's hating him. She was cool toward him, certainly, but that, surely, was her thing about status. Her two years' seniority mattered to Sarah. Hatred was another thing. He would probably have dismissed it as one of those bitchy things women say about each other—if he had not watched her filmed interview. That had shown him a Sarah he didn't know existed, animated, warm, and, he admitted it, a dish. Not once in their association had she let him glimpse that side of her character. Did she despise him so much? The question nagged at him all evening and into the next day.

‡ ‡ ‡

Ed Cunningham phoned Sarah on Monday after classes and calmly told her he had picked up tickets for the Wednesday-evening performance of the American Ballet Theater's production of *Don Quixote*. She was so excited that for a few seconds she was speechless, and Ed began to get anxious that he had done the wrong thing. She blurted out that this was the nicest thing that had happened to her in years, and she meant it. She knew very well that he hadn't simply "picked up" the tickets, because she had read in the paper that the spring season at the Met was a sellout. He must have gone to a lot of trouble. For her.

She was not sure how many times during the performance she reached for Ed's hand and squeezed it hard. The ballet was breathtaking, a triumph of staging, choreography, and bravura dancing. By each intermission she was emotionally drained. Ed stood with her near the grand-tier staircase and she gazed into the crystal chandeliers. It was no time for words.

When it was over, he took her for a late supper. Thoughtfully he cushioned her slow descent from cloud nine by finding a quiet table at Le Poulailler, on West Sixty-fifth, and ordering a bottle of wine before they looked at the menu.

Finally she said, "I didn't know I could still get so involved."

He smiled. "Most of the time Gelsey Kirkland was onstage, you were mentally right there with her."

"That's right. Never mind that I haven't put on a ballet shoe since I was eleven years old. I tell myself I *could* have been like her. It's monumentally conceited, but no one can prove me wrong."

Ed laughed gently. "Sure. And if only I had learned more physics in high school, the world would never have heard of Neil Armstrong."

She took the remark as it was meant—with a smile.

"Shall we order now?" he suggested. He recommended the bay scallops in white wine sauce, and Sarah said that sounded just right. Now that he had coaxed her out of her ballet fantasies, she appreciated that these, too, were moments to savor. She felt totally secure. She accepted his maturity, his silver hair and expensive dark suit, as assets, not impediments. His manner was more reserved than that of someone nearer her own age, but she valued it, because it relaxed her. She felt warmed by his confident glances and strengthened by the sculptured quality of his features. He was a very attractive guy. And his hair was quite dark at the back.

When they had talked for a while about the ballet, and their meal was served, he said, "What happened when your parents stopped your dance classes? You said you were ill for some weeks, but when you recovered—physically—what happened? Was there a change in your behavior when you went back to school?"

He knew the answer: Sarah was sure of it. She had never discussed it with anyone else, but now she talked freely, because he understood, and he wouldn't be shocked. "Yes, a pretty dramatic change. I'm not very proud of it. There's always a group of disaffected kids in a school. I took up with them. I started smoking and playing hooky. I let the air out of the tires on the teachers' cars. . . ."

"You had fun."

Ed's matter-of-fact statement brought a giggle from Sarah. "Well, yes, I had a ball. In class—when I was there—I was still quiet and amenable. I didn't go the way Marty had, giving hell to the teachers. My retaliation was more sneaky, like writing dirty things on walls. It was a long time before they got wise to me, and then they found it hard to believe. I denied everything, swore to God I was innocent. I was a coward, you see, as well as a sneak. But my delinquent friends squealed on me. After that we had the showdown. My parents were called in and it came out that I was bed-wetting and sleepwalking and generally keeping my house-proud mother in despair. So it was over to the child-guidance people. All those tests and interviews—you know the drill."

"Did it help you?"

"I guess it frightened me into conforming more. All these adults moving in on my life was pretty scary."

"How about your parents? Did it change them at all?"

"Sure. I gather it was spelled out to them that I was manifesting symptoms of neglect. My antisocial behavior was a way of seeking attention. Maybe that was right. Anyway, my mother came away from the child-guidance conference with the idea that I needed regular kissing and embracing, while it seems my father was told he should show me he cared by bringing some discipline into my life."

Ed shook his head and sighed. "It sounds only too likely, and totally disastrous in a case like yours."

Sarah gave a shrug. "I don't know. It put a brake on my bad behavior. When I got to high school, there was no trouble. I worked hard and got good grades."

"What about your home life?"

She shrugged again. "It went on. I learned to put up with my mother slobbering over me and giving me bear hugs. I knew what happened when I told her to cool it, or something stronger: my father showed me he cared by locking me in the spare room. There was no light in there."

"That's real cruelty. Did you scream to be let out?"

"I didn't give them that satisfaction. I just waited till they came back. It could be a long wait."

"What did you think about all that time?"

"What my father had said before he turned the key—that I was wicked and deserved to be punished."

Ed stopped eating and pushed his plate aside. "You really believed that?"

She was saying things she had admitted only to herself. "It's not easy to explain. I had a strong sense of guilt. Those bad things I did at school had made me feel ugly, really ugly, and that was something different in my life. It was a change from being dressed in cute little jumpers and lace petticoats and frilly white panties and living in a house where every surface was dusted and polished before breakfast. Ugliness was exciting; it was wicked and forbidden. You had to get a grip on yourself to face it, but that was worth it every time. That was how I got to overcome my thing about spiders. I was brought up to be terrified of them. If one was seen in the house, there was panic. It wasn't just the sight of the thing, or its speed across the floor. It was the knowledge that something vile and ugly had violated the cleanliness of the place."

"You really felt this antipathy yourself?"

"Ed, as a kid I wouldn't get into my bed before checking every inch of the room. Some kids say their prayers before turning in; I searched for spiders. But after all those heavy things in my life I just told you about, I got to thinking about spiders in a different way. I went out looking for them because they were ugly and I had a plan. When I found a small one on a web in our backyard, I forced myself to watch it. A few seconds the first time, then longer. I went and played for an hour and then came back to see if it was still there. I kept coming back. The next day I found I could watch it longer; I was still scared, but I was fascinated. When it moved, I nearly had heart failure the first time, but I even got used to that. I studied every movement it made. For a week I kept this up, and the spider became so familiar it ceased to be a threat. Then one evening I screwed up my courage and scooped the spider and some of its web into a glass jar I had brought with me. I screwed the lid on and smuggled my spider indoors and up to my room."

"Your bedroom—the place you checked each night?"

"You find it hard to believe? It really happened. I kept it there two or three days. They can live a long time in a jar if you put in a drop of water and punch holes in the lid. Well, I waited for the right time to put my plan into action. This is going to sound weird, Ed. One Sunday afternoon my parents went out for a drive and I was alone in the house. I collected the jar from my room and took it into theirs. Then I tipped the spider out onto my father's bed and watched it walk across the white sheet my mother had changed that morning. It really did something for me, letting that small, ugly thing take its exercise there. My mouth went dry and my skin prickled like it had when I wrote things on walls."

"Did you leave the spider there?"

"No, I didn't do that. Scaring my parents wasn't in my plan. It was enough to know the spider had been in their room. And I didn't want it killed. So after I had let it walk on both their beds I helped it back into the jar and returned it to my room."

"That was enough?"

"Sure."

"I mean, did you do it another time?"

"You bet." She laughed, and wished it sounded more natural. "Kids!"

"The same thing?"

This was starting to be embarrassing. "Well, not exactly. You don't want to know what a little monster I was as a juvenile."

"But I do." Now he laughed. "I'll rephrase that. From what you have told me, it's not at all surprising that you behaved as you did. That was no monster: it was one small girl deprived of an emotional relationship and traumatized into various retaliatory actions. There's no reason to feel guilty or ashamed."

"I don't."

The directness of Sarah's response seemed to catch Ed off guard. He frowned slightly. "You don't? Well, that's great. So, what else did you do with this spider of yours?"

"That one died soon after, but I found others. Bigger ones, and uglier. I used to let them walk over my mother's clothes. Her white bathrobe. Her precious pink underwear." Sarah gave a low laugh. "To this day she doesn't know. In time, the game got to be more sophisticated. I would hide my spider in my parents' room, someplace I was sure they wouldn't look when they went to bed, like the bottom drawer in the bedside table. Then I would think of it close to them while they slept."

"That is a little scary. How old were you by this time?"

"Thirteen, I guess. And I got more ingenious as I went on. I unscrewed the earpiece of the telephone and put one in there. It survived, too. Am I giving you the creeps? I grew out of it. Do you know how? I took a more positive interest in spiders as I got older—I mean in their behavior. I asked questions at school. I read everything I could, but there really wasn't much. Compared to other creatures, spiders have been shamefully neglected by naturalists. Yet they are so fascinating! They survive without trouble in places as varied in climate as Greenland and equatorial Africa. They were found twenty thousand feet up Mount Everest, which made them the highest permanent inhabitants in the world. If we had time, I could tell you so much, but I don't want to bore you."

"You won't do that, Sarah. Listen, I have a, uh, proposition that may appeal to you."

She was pretty sure from his tone of voice that it would not be the sexual overture she half wanted, half feared. "Go ahead."

"I told you I have some patients suffering from phobias. This has become a specialty of mine. I've had a degree of success with certain forms of therapy, and I'm writing a book. One of my contentions is that even the most extreme phobias can be treated if you win the patients' confidence. You may not remove the fear entirely, but you can definitely put it into a better perspective. If you can get them to accept that a phobia is not so much a wall in their way as a flight of steps, positive progress is possible. I have three patients right now who are at that primary stage. Getting them receptive to therapy may take just a few sessions more—or a month, or a year. What I have in mind, Sarah, is that your experience as you just described it —the way you surmounted your fear of spiders—would give tremendous encouragement to these patients if they heard it from you."

She couldn't. It was too personal. She wished now that she had not talked so openly. "I'm sorry, Ed. Talking to you is one thing, but to total strangers . . . no, it's not possible."

"Hold on, little lady. You don't understand what I'm suggesting. I wouldn't ask you to bare your life to these people. It would be no more than describing the stages in mastering your own phobia. The flight of steps. How you forced yourself to study the spider in your backyard until you were able to get it in the glass jar. You don't have to say one word about your troubles at school or at home. Believe me, this is something that could really help some pretty desperate people."

She shook her head. "I'd like to—really I would—but I guess I'm a very private person."

"Okay." He gave a shrug and a smile. "I just thought I'd see how you felt about it. You don't mind that I asked?"

Unbeknownst to Ed, the waiter had approached to see if they wanted more coffee, and must have caught the tail end of their conversation. Sarah rolled her eyes, and Ed actually colored a little, but the waiter carried on with a superb show of indifference.

When he had turned away, they exchanged smiles. "I guess I should be flattered," said Ed, "but really, I'm not into seduction."

She smiled again, but she knew as he said it that he was speaking the truth—at least for that moment, and that evening.

In the taxi she thought things over. She wanted to see him again. Talking with him this evening, she had begun to make sense of elements of her past she had understood imperfectly before. Her own frankness had surprised her. He had worked a miracle in getting her to confide so much. She felt stimulated and revitalized. She could not let it stop here.

"Ed, maybe, after all, I'd like to help with those patients of yours."

5 🕷 Don had been notified that Professor Berlin wished to see him at noon on Thursday. The last time they had talked alone was the afternoon Jerry had almost gone berserk because Don had been unwilling to go along with the James Bond stunt. Possibly that was why this summons came in the form of a typed memo delivered personally by Bernice. After all those things Jerry had said, he would find it a strain to be informal. They both would.

"Honey, I'm no wiser than you," Bernice told Don when he asked what this was about. "He told me to be damn sure you got it, that's all. I don't know what's gotten into Jerry lately. I mean, if I worked in the Kremlin, I'd have more idea what was going on. Take that TV thing the week before last. Jerry knew it was on. You did. Did anyone else, do you suppose, apart from me? Sarah Jordan sure didn't. When she came in the day they were shooting, she was ready to spend the morning in the lab. Jesus, was that young lady mad when I told her there was a TV unit coming in to film you with the spiders!"

"You told her that?"

"Sweetie, someone had to tell her. She had driven down from Lake Pinecliff that morning just to get her readings, like she always does on Thursdays. So I filled her in. I figured when she knew what was happening, she would speed up the readings to be through before the TV team arrived, but it seems when they got there, she was still working on it." Bernice switched to a more casual tone. "I heard they shot some good film of her."

"Yup."

"Lucky for Sarah. Will we see her on the tube?"

"It's possible. You mean, she definitely knew they were coming in that morning?"

"Only after I told her, darling." Bernice gave a bland smile. "I guess those readings took a little longer to get through that morning."

Don nodded. As Bernice seemed reluctant to return to her office, he asked, "Lake Pinecliff—where's that, sweetheart?"

"New Jersey. Thirty, forty miles northwest of here. It's in the mountains. Sarah goes there every Wednesday. We have a number to call in case she's wanted."

"I knew she was out Wednesdays. We have an arrangement. I figured she went home to her folks'." He said with a sly smile, "What does she do in the mountains?"

Bernice gave a throaty laugh and aimed a mock punch at his chin. "Wouldn't I love to know! I'll tell you one thing— whatever it is, she does it in a crash helmet. Once, she parked her car beside mine and I saw it sitting on the passenger seat. You can't tell me she wears a helmet just to drive a Ford Pinto."

Don's estimation of Sarah Jordan was undergoing drastic revision. Where once there had been a pathetically diligent girl so obsessive about her research that she could not even share a joke there were now glimpses of someone quite different: an ambitious, opportunistic, and—on the evidence of her TV interview—a magnetically attractive personality with a secret.

‡ ‡ ‡

Jerry had the whiskey glasses out when Don appeared, signaling reconciliation. He had found an article in a British journal about the cryptozoa, the creatures that exist in continuously dark and damp environments. It said little, if anything, new, but it served the purpose of indicating Jerry's willingness to resume active supervision of the research project.

They talked for a while about the direction Don's work was taking. Increasingly, he was finding that biotic factors such as the food chain and its influence on the density of population were leading him toward a broader consideration of the ecosystem in which spiders existed. Jerry agreed that this was a logical development. The focus of the research was still the adaptation of a single species to changes in the environment, but it would be unwise to get so close that bigger ecological considerations might be overlooked. To Don, this comment of Jerry's sounded like an oblique criticism of Sarah Jordan, until Jerry made the point that Don's was the synecological approach. By implication, then, Sarah's was autecological, concentrating on the effects on a single species of such things as temperature, humidity, light intensity, and soil composition. As a research procedure it was no less valid. You had to hand it to Jerry: he was a smart talker.

Over a second scotch, Jerry asked straight out whether the collaboration with Sarah was proving successful. Don answered warily that it was a little early to draw any conclusions, but that they had regular exchanges of information. Jerry asked how they got on on a personal level, and Don said they respected each other. He added defensively that he didn't see why it was necessary to get involved personally. Then Jerry said something strange. He asked if Don had a fear of getting trapped.

Don asked Jerry to explain what he meant.

Jerry backed down, saying that if his meaning was not clear, he did not intend to elaborate. Leaving that, he said he had to confess he had mishandled the TV people's visit. It had been a mistake to ignore Sarah when they were discussing the project with Laz. He had wrongly assumed she would want nothing to do with TV. How she had got herself in front of the camera was still a mystery, but the most incredible thing was how terrific she had been.

Don kept silent, letting Jerry do the running.

There was no way anyone could have known Sarah would be such a natural, Jerry went on. He had respect for her intellectual caliber and her determination to succeed, but she had always given the impression of being a loner, not at all a girl you would expect to project herself with confidence on TV. He had given it some thought since then, because he didn't like making an ass of himself, and he knew where he had blundered. He had mistaken Sarah's reserved manner for lack of confidence. Usually these things went hand in hand. But not in her case.

He didn't mean to suggest, he said with a hand on Don's shoulder, that there had been anything lacking in *his* TV interview. Personally, he thought it had given a more solid impression of the department's work than Sarah's had. And the James Bond stunt had looked damn good on the screen. He wanted to thank Don sincerely for consenting to do that. But they both had been around long enough, hadn't they, to know that where showbiz is concerned, you can't win out against a pretty girl.

Don kept his face blank. He had sensed where this was leading, but he was in no mood to make it easier for Jerry.

Finally Jerry came out with it. Laz had called on the phone to say he had decided not to use the sequences featuring Don. The footage they had shot of Sarah was so good that nothing else was needed.

In a way Don was relieved to have it confirmed. The whole damn thing had left him cold from the start. But he was bitter at having been used. With sarcasm he asked Jerry if he had ever thought of a career as a casting director.

Jerry gave an embarrassed grin and said he supposed he had

asked for that. He said he owed Don an apology for all that flak the other week. He didn't want this to screw up the research program. He hoped there wouldn't be friction between Don and Sarah, but in view of what had happened maybe it would be good tactics not to push the cooperation too hard for a few weeks. The synecological approach had a lot going for it.

Don did not commit himself. Nothing Jerry had said would stop him from getting a few things straight with Sarah—and very soon.

‡ ‡ ‡

Ed Cunningham's office-apartment was located at Seventy-sixth and Park, where he shared a floor with two other doctors. When Sarah saw the metal plate on the side of the building with his name and a string of letters engraved on it, she had a spasm of panic. Ever since the trouble in her teens, she had resolved to keep away from analysts. Yet here she was, preparing to step voluntarily into an elevator that would deliver her to a psychiatrist's office. How could she be certain she was not being conned into some form of psychoanalysis? She could not; she had to trust Ed. Anyway, if he *did* have ideas of analyzing her, there was nothing in it for him. No, he had told her this was a means of assisting his patients. She believed him. Recollecting the way he had put his proposition, as he had called it, made her remember her own expectation of a sexual overture —a prospect easier to face than the couch. She smiled, and it helped her relax. Maybe, after all, she would be handed a glass of champagne as she stepped from the elevator. She giggled a little, her panic overcome. She stepped in and touched the third-floor button.

"Hi, little lady. You found me, then," he said when she appeared.

There was no champagne. No couch. The room was sparsely appointed, giving the impression of spaciousness. A desk and filing cabinets on one side, against the window. Nearer, low easy chairs and a white Melamite table. Two Benjaminas in white stands. On the end wall, where it was lightest, a large David Hockney of an empty swimming pool.

Sarah said, "This is how an office should be."

Ed smiled and asked what he could get her to drink. He looked small in his apparently large apartment. He was wearing a dark-green silk shirt with a tan jacket of wool and suede and black trousers.

She said she would love a cup of coffee. "But I'll wait till your patients come and have it with them."

He shook his head. "I'm not expecting anyone this afternoon."

"But I thought that was the reason for—"

"Sure." He opened the door to a small kitchen and went on speaking from in there. "Before you meet my patients, I want to tell you how I treat them. It makes sense, doesn't it, for us both to know what we're aiming at?"

"I guess so." Sarah crossed to the window, keeping a grip on herself. Yes, it was sensible. She wanted to trust Ed, but she would have been happier with someone else there.

When the coffee was made, he brought two chairs to the window and began to talk about the treatment of phobias, describing the improvements reported in as many as ninety percent of cases in which patients were trained in deep muscular relaxation. Injections, he said, were used in some cases to induce relaxation. Patients were then asked to imagine themselves in increasingly frightening situations, yet to associate them with their relaxed state. He preferred not to use the injections, but he regarded relaxation as the best form of therapy. He liked, if possible, to trace the phobia to its origin, which was generally a childhood experience. After relaxation, he said, came knowledge. Then understanding. Then familiarization. And finally self-control.

His way of talking, the soft pitch of his voice and the absence of any overt persuasion, made the treatment sound believable, but it was difficult for Sarah to see how she could contribute anything, and she told him so. "You see, I don't fit this pattern. I got control of my fear of spiders because I wanted to get back at my parents after they stopped my dancing."

"Sure. I understand that."

"But how does that help your patients? They're adults, I presume. I was just a kid."

Ed nodded. "That's true, but what matters is that you had a strong motivation to deal with your phobia. You had no need of help from someone like me. You conquered it yourself. These people don't have your degree of motivation or strength of character or whatever it was that got you looking at spiders without panicking. They have to learn how to do it. I have to persuade them that it can be done."

"And if they meet me, they might believe it's possible?"

"Right. Most phobia sufferers have it fixed in their minds that they have some kind of kink—a flaw in the mechanism of the brain. They're wrong. They *learned* to respond the way they do in certain situations. And they can learn to respond differently. We call it behavior therapy."

"You mean I learned to be scared of spiders?"

"That's my reading of it—without having a detailed account of your childhood. You told me your mother was fanatical about cleaning the house. You said the worst thing about a spider was that it violated the cleanliness of the house."

His recollection of her words surprised and impressed her. "So I did."

"Your mother's strong reaction was imprinted on you from an early age. You learned to react with terror at the sight of a spider. But when your mother failed you totally by arresting the main thing in your life, you rebelled against her. You rejected her standards and the things she had taught you. For a time you kicked back by behaving antisocially. That was a cry for help, and the help it got you wasn't to your liking. You didn't want displays of affection from your mother. You wanted revenge. So you took it—secretly. You taught yourself to overcome the fears you had learned from her. And what started out as—you won't mind if I say it?—a pretty adolescent and negative gesture ultimately became a thing of positive value in your life. Here you are earning a Ph.D. out of your knowledge of spiders. Even going on TV. So the story has a happy ending."

Sarah mouthed a smile, but inside she was reeling as if he had struck her. Nothing in his rapid analysis of her life so far was inaccurate, but put together like this in terms of cause and effect, making more sense than she had ever perceived for herself, it pained her. She felt like a case history, a card in a file.

He was talking now about the way he investigated the origins of phobias, tracing them to the conditioning given by parents and others.

Sarah heard without listening. She was torn in two. She could manufacture some excuse to leave this place and never see Ed Cunningham again. Or she could make him understand that she demanded to be treated as a unique individual, not one more client for the couch.

"Hey"—he cut into his monologue—"suddenly you look like the sun went out. What is it, Sarah? Did I say something terrible?"

His concern was real. It showed in his eyes.

Sarah said, "Why do you talk to me like I'm one of your patients?"

He frowned and rubbed the back of his neck. "Is that what

I was doing? Christ, I hope not! That's ridiculous. I mean, I didn't bring you here—"

"Why did you bring me here? I'd like to get it straight. Is it just because I'm a self-cured arachnophobiac?"

He stretched out his hand and rested it on hers. "Little lady, understand this. I happen to like you enough to want to know you better. Okay? If you don't want to participate in my work, just say so. That needn't stop us from talking some more—if you want to, that is."

"And have you dissect the rest of my life? No thanks, Ed."

He was silent for several seconds. "That's what this is about, then." He shook his head slowly. "Oh, boy, am I getting old! I can't even talk to someone as sweet as you without the shrink taking over. . . . I'm really sorry. Would you let us start over?"

The earnestness of his apology made her uncomfortable. "I'd like to think about that. Tell me some more about your work."

He described two of his patients, a woman who was terrified of birds and a man who constantly wore gloves because he could not endure anything touching his bare hands.

When he had finished, Sarah said, "Would it really help these people to hear about me?"

"I'm positive it would, or I wouldn't have mentioned it."

"Okay—but there's one thing."

"Name it."

She got up and crossed the room to a framed certificate recording his membership in the American Psychiatric Association. "You belong to a profession that sets its standards high."

He frowned slightly. "Of course."

"The way you behave toward your patients has to be above reproach, isn't that right?"

He nodded.

"I mean, if, for example, you were to kiss one of them, that would be regarded as unprofessional, wouldn't it?"

"Absolutely."

"And if the APA got word of it, you could lose your license to practice."

"Aren't we getting too hypothetical? It wouldn't happen. All of us in the profession know that you have to keep personal attachments out of it."

"Okay. So now that we both have it clear that I don't seek your professional advice and you won't feel obliged to give it, I want you to kiss me."

He laughed in a way that showed he had seen this coming. "Then if I'm ever tempted to suggest psychoanalysis, you have a gun at my head. I'll say one thing about your mind, Sarah: its defenses are in very good shape. Tell you what—I'll give you a kiss. Not to put my career on the line, but because I'd like us to be friends. Do we have a deal?"

She smiled back. "I can't see any objections."

He came over to her and put his hands on her shoulders.

Sarah made sure that the kiss was mouth to mouth, but it was as light as his touch.

"Okay, then," she said. "When do I come again?"

‡ ‡ ‡

Around five on Friday afternoon, as Sarah was leaving the library, Don was close behind her, and caught up before she had reached the foot of the steps. This was not chance; he had been waiting twenty minutes in the catalogue hall for her to come by. Getting to talk with her away from the department required strategy, because she organized her life in a way that left little time for unscheduled contacts.

"Hi. Mind if I walk with you?"

In the sunlight of late afternoon her hair—she was wearing it loose and long—was almost pure red. She shook some off her shoulder and, without turning to look at him, said, "Why not, if we're going the same way. I'm only going back to my room."

"How about an ice cream first?"

"That sounds like a nice idea, but—"

"There's a place at Ninetieth and Columbus."

When they had been served, he said, "Sometimes it's nice to talk without Bernice knowing about it."

She smiled.

Don went on. "I mean, I hope I'm not totally paranoid, but it amazes me how much Jerry seems to know about what goes on in that place."

Sarah nodded. "Did he, by any chance, have words with you this week about our research projects?"

"Why, yes. You, too?"

They exchanged smiles with some reserve in them.

"He seems to think you and I need a cooling-off period," said Don. "Is that the impression you got?"

"Something like that." She looked down at her ice cream. "This isn't what he meant."

Don grinned.

Sarah continued. "He figures you have hurt feelings about what happened over the TV program."

"Is that so?"

"Well, do you?"

They had come to the point sooner than Don expected. "If you want it straight—yes, I do."

"Would you like to kick my butt?"

"I bought you an ice cream, didn't I? No, I'm not mad at you. If I'm mad at anyone, it's myself. I didn't want to do the thing. Not their way, anyhow. I let Jerry stampede me into it. My sequences were crap."

"I'd like you to know that I didn't cold-bloodedly plan to cut you out. The way it happened, I knew something was going on with TV, but I didn't know the crew was coming in that morning. I got in early from Lake Pinecliff as usual, and Bernice told me. Naturally, I wasn't wild about it. Okay, I admit I did a double-take when Bernice told me they were going to film *you*. But it was Jerry I was mad at. He hadn't even mentioned it. I mean, he didn't even let me know the lab was being used that day. I could have stayed at Lake Pinecliff. That was why I made sure I was working in the lab when they arrived —to get back at Jerry. Oh, you bet it backfired. He wasn't one bit put out. Just asked me to show them around. And that was how I got involved."

"Sure." Don believed her. This was the first time in a year she had volunteered anything outside their area of research. "No hard feelings, I promise you. And none on your side? For both our sakes, I wish Jerry had asked you first. That guy has a few things to answer for. What's his game now, do you think?"

"According to what he told me, it's called autecology—"

"And synecology," chimed in Don.

They laughed together, and it was a new step in their association.

"Do you have family at Lake Pinecliff?" Don asked.

"No, it's just a place where I go hang-gliding."

That explained the crash helmet. "Hang-gliding? Hey, that's terrific. You know, I figured there had to be something in your life besides spiders. But don't you get scared launching off into nothing but air?"

"That's the attraction." She talked about the exhilaration of flying, and for a minute or so he was treated to the vitality he had previously glimpsed in the film interview. "You ought to try it," she said.

"After a recommendation like that, how could I refuse?"

At this she looked startled, evidently realizing she had said

more than she intended. She gave a quick, forced smile and
said it was time she got home.

Don remembered something he had brought with him as a
pretext for approaching her, and took it from his pocket. "Jerry
lent me this to read. It's a paper on the cryptozoa by some
British professor. He seemed to think it might be useful.
Would you care to have it for a few days? I couldn't see too
much in it that bears on my research or yours, but who knows?"

"Did Jerry ask you to hand it on to me?"

"As a matter of fact, he didn't."

She smiled. "Then I'll certainly take it."

Without any more being said, the paper became a token of
their collaboration in the face of Jerry's advice to the contrary.

Before they got up to leave, Sarah said, "Do you suppose by
any chance that Jerry could have a tail on us?"

He smiled. "Anything's possible."

"As we go out, take a look at the girl on the stool at the lunch
counter. Since we came in, I don't think her eyes have left us.
I'm sure I've seen her around campus."

The girl was Oriental. He had an idea he had seen her once
with Meg Kellaway. He didn't want his dance partner getting
upset about nothing.

That evening he called Meg and fixed a lunchtime rehearsal
with her for the following Wednesday. She sounded no different from usual.

6 On Monday Sarah returned to Ed Cunningham's and witnessed a therapy session. The patient was a twenty-four-year-old six-foot-three black. His name was Frank, and he was terrified of dogs. At one point in his early childhood a Dalmatian had put its front paws against his chest and tried to lick his face. The force of it had knocked Frank off balance, and he had cut his head on a stone step. For the twenty-two years since then he had taken elaborate precautions to avoid dogs. He went out only when circumstances demanded, and then his mind was so full of the possible dangers that he sometimes forgot his reason for being on the street. He had lived in New York all his life and never once been in Central Park.

After Sarah was introduced, and Frank agreed that she could sit in, he described his problem for her benefit. Then Ed attached a metal disk to each of Frank's hands. Wires led from them to an apparatus that Ed explained was devised to measure the electrical conductivity of the skin. A pulsating sound would increase in frequency in response to electrical activity generated by anxiety. Frank had used the apparatus before and understood that it was an aid to controlling his reactions. He was asked to relax as much as he could. Then Ed asked him to listen to a tape that described a number of encounters with dogs. The situations were graded to increase the level of stress each time. In the half hour of therapy they went through the tape three times, and Frank showed a small but discernible improvement.

When he had gone, Ed explained that over a number of weeks the force of the stimulus would be increased, using pictures of dogs, then sound recording and film. Eventually, when the machine—which was only a learning aid—had served its purpose, he would go out on the streets with Frank and they would walk past dogs. It had to be taken in easy stages, but Frank was already responding well. Next time, Ed said, he would like to spend some of the session letting Sarah describe the change in her feelings about spiders. He was confident that Frank would be encouraged by her experience.

Another patient was expected in a few minutes, so Sarah prepared to leave.

"Thanks, Sarah. I really appreciate this."

"It's no trouble. I hope I can be useful next time." Without thinking too much about it, she stepped forward to kiss him, but he had turned away to return Frank's file to the cabinet. She could not be sure if the move was just to evade the kiss. On an impulse she added, "Friendship is important to me."

"Really?" He turned and studied her face. "I had the impression you managed very well on your own. Who are your close friends?"

"I'd like to think of you as one."

"Why not? As we said, a friend and not a patient. But you have other friends?"

"Naturally."

"I mean, people in college?"

He really meant people her own age. He meant that girls in their twenties didn't usually make it with men in their fifties. She was afraid he was about to spoil things between them by saying something negative. She told him in a rush, "I went out with Don Rigden last week. I'm not the lonely person you seem to be hinting at."

"Don—the guy you do research with? That's good."

"Next Monday, then?"

She got into the elevator and smiled back at him. She was glad no more had been said.

‡ ‡ ‡

The following Wednesday morning Don was making his rounds in the araneology lab when Bernice looked in. "Hi! Am I glad to find you! When Jerry told me to look for you, I thought you would be off campus. People are always off campus when I go looking."

"Jerry wants to see me?"

"Not you, sweetheart. He has to chair a seminar at Hunter College this evening, and all the big guns are going to be there. He was in here at eight-thirty this morning—I repeat, eight-thirty—tearing my filing system apart to find some research paper he needs to quote from. Then he remembered he gave it to you to read. 'Crypto'-something. Does that figure? Anyway, he's out all day and he wants to pick it up when he gets back at six. Dig it out, would you, baby?"

"Christ, I lent it to someone else to read, and she's off campus all day."

"Oh, no! Jerry will blow his stack. Who is this—Sarah Jordan?"

"Yes. She definitely isn't here. I always take the readings on Wednesday mornings so she can have the day clear. She'll be at Lake Pinecliff. Now, where could she have left the damn thing?"

"You could call her. I have her number at Lake Pinecliff."

He used the phone in Bernice's office and got the Bear Crossing Motel. The desk clerk said Miss Jordan was out in the hills, but someone was going that way, and he would get a message to her to call back.

He waited nearly an hour with Bernice and heard the dirt on almost everyone in the department. The call came at eleven-twenty. He apologized to Sarah for taking her away from her gliding. She said she guessed it must be important. He told her his problem.

"That *is* a problem," she said. "You see, I have the paper right here in my car. I haven't even read it yet. Look, why don't you come out and get it? You can drive here in an hour."

"You really don't mind?"

"Why should I? Come on, I'll show you what a great flier I am."

He asked Bernice if he could borrow her car for the afternoon, and she tossed him the key. Leaving her questions unanswered, he said he would be back with Jerry's paper by five, and went straight to the parking lot.

‡ ‡ ‡

Three men assembling a glider on a ridge of Bearfort Mountain confirmed that Sarah had just got airborne, so the solitary green and white kite moving across a cloudless sky had to be hers. Don stared up at the small black figure riding the wind. She'd known how long it would take him to get here. Perhaps this display was laid on for him. But why? After a year of frost, what had started the thaw?

Whatever it was, he welcomed it. Anything was an improvement over her remoteness in recent months. She had not been uncooperative; she had scrupulously observed their agreement about research, and reported regularly on progress. But she made every contact between them so formal that it became a tedious ritual.

He had sometimes asked himself if she was acting from insecurity. She got precious little support from Jerry, whose job it was to supply it. Her work was competent but not innovative, and she was intelligent enough to know it. It was not impossible that she felt threatened by a newcomer with Jerry's obvious backing and some original ideas.

If that was the problem, maybe she believed she could fight it for the first time. Getting chosen for the TV series had given her a victory over Jerry and Don as well. She had discovered something at which she was a winner. And in Don she had now identified an ally. They were conspirators against Jerry.

Bearfort Mountain was extensively forested, but the hang-gliding enthusiasts had located a stretch of clear terrain at least a thousand yards square on either side of the ridge. The green and white Rogallo made a ninety-degree turn into the wind and started to descend. Its manta shape increased in size as it crossed the face of the forested slopes to the west and approached the landing area. The figure in crash helmet and leather suit was definitely female. She was pressing the control bar forward to nose the sail up and get it in full flare for the landing.

Don set off down the slope in pursuit. As he ran, he lost sight of Sarah under the steep-angled kite. The touchdown was smooth. The dacron fabric lost its tautness and rippled gently over her.

When he reached her, she had her gloves off and was unhitching the harness from the glider.

"Hi," she said.

"Can I help?"

She put her hand on the buckle that secured the body harness below her chest. "You could unfasten this."

It meant standing face to face. He moved close and she unstrapped her crash helmet and shook her hair loose. Her face was flushed from the wind and she was short of breath.

He was sexually aroused and he did not believe it.

He could not do much about it with Sarah holding a twenty-foot-wide sail that threatened at the next gust of wind to knock them both off their feet. When he had unfastened the chest strap, she asked him to hold the sail while she attended to the thigh straps that secured the padded seat to her own. Freed from the harness, she told him she was sorry but she would have to dismantle the glider before doing anything else.

He held the king post while she folded each sail and rolled it to the center. She worked briskly and surely, keeping the fabric stretched to eliminate creases.

"It looks like a lot of hard work for a few minutes' flying," he commented.

"No, it's fun," she told him. "I really enjoy this part of it."

When the glider was reduced to a column of fabric and a triangle of aluminum tubing, he carried it for her to the motel, and they had a drink and a sandwich there. Sarah talked excitedly about her experiences while gliding. She showed none of the reserve that made their discussions about research such a pain. "You really should come out here and learn," she told him. "You take it in stages, and it's amazing how soon you get through the ground-handling and start to fly. Then the big thing is how high you can go, but in no time at all you're thinking about time and distance, and after that you're into maneuvers. Why not give it a try? You could learn on my kite if you like."

She really meant it.

"You're on. When do I start?"

"How about a week from today?"

"You're forgetting something. There are the readings to do in the lab."

"They don't take long. Come out here for the afternoon."

That was the plan they made.

When Don drove away from Bear Crossing with the paper

on the cryptozoa next to him on the seat, he felt positively grateful to Jerry Berlin. Sarah away from the department was another person, relaxed, lively, and attractive. It was as if she had broken out of the personality he had known—or not known—for a year. Almost—he smiled to himself—like the molt of a spider.

For an instant there came into his mind Sarah in her black leather, toiling at the wires of the glider, winding them into a coil. *I really enjoy this part of it.*

Then more human considerations took over as he considered his first lesson in hang-gliding next Wednesday, and whether the invitation might be taken to mean anything more.

It was five o'clock and he was back in New York before he remembered the lunchtime dance rehearsal with Meg.

‡ ‡ ‡

Thursday started routinely for Sarah with the drive down Highway 208 to New York City. Her mind was on Ed and how she could let him know, without being too obvious, that she was seeing more of Don Rigden. She needed to assure him that she had men friends her own age. He wanted to know that she was not alone in the world and looking for a father figure. If she could satisfy him on this point, he might be less guarded in his meetings with her. It mattered profoundly to her that Ed should let her get close. She didn't care how much older he was. She wanted him.

She wanted, simply, to belong to him—not necessarily in a physical sense. If he desired her, she was his, but she would not insist on sex. In her experience it was no big deal. She had tried it enough times to know that it left her cold. The only truly stimulating experiences she could recall were when she was a kid of twelve or thirteen making her rebellion against her parents. The gang she had joined—the kids notorious for playing hooky and for vandalism—made bodily candor into a proof of loyalty. As a lapsed teacher's pet, she had aroused exceptional interest. Her initiation in the back of an abandoned van —the sense of self-importance as they had taken turns to glimpse her new and gingery pubic hair, and the giggling indelicacy of having a penis rest in the palm of her hand—had been an intoxicating experience: pure sin laced with childish curiosity.

Full sex when it came at fifteen denied and destroyed the fantasies her adolescence had created. She met the soldier at a party given by a school friend, Jane Melford, in Cherry Hill. He told her it was his last night on American soil before being flown to Vietnam. She listened and felt sorry for him. When the party broke up, he said he wanted to drive her home. She figured he might try something, but he was sweet and a little scared and he might easily be killed by the VC, and—what the hell—she couldn't keep it forever. If the rest of her class could be believed, she was the last but two, and they were *creeps*. He drove half a mile and pulled off the main road onto a golf course and switched off the engine. He didn't force her, he pleaded with her. The one thing she had not expected was words. He didn't lay a finger on her. Just begged. And she couldn't get him to understand that she was not unwilling. In desperation she took off her panties and lay ready on the backseat. He had no erection. He was in tears. He lit a cigarette. She didn't know whether to put her underclothes back on, so she just covered herself with her dress and sat up. When he had smoked two, he suggested they go for a walk. They got out of the car and walked along the fairway for maybe five minutes. Suddenly he said he was ready and pushed her down into a bunker. Wet sand chilled her buttocks. He penetrated her and she clenched her teeth to stop from crying out. He was finished in less than half a minute. Two weeks later she hap-

pened to see him on Walnut Street in Philadelphia. The uniform he was wearing was that of a mailman.

It took her three years to get over the humiliation. Then she
had three guys in a month to find out if it could be better than
the last time. There was less pain but no pleasure. One kept
going so long she had to fake it to get him off her. Since then
she had given most would-be seducers the brush. As for the few
she had given it a try with, she could have had as much fun
on an exercycle.

Yet she clung to the expectation that someday the right guy
would know how to turn her on. It was possible it could be Ed.
He had style. He treated her with understanding. He was
positive but not insensitive. And he was beginning to turn up
in her dreams.

The morning followed its usual pattern until just before
noon, when Jerry Berlin walked into the lab and asked what she
was doing Friday. He wore an unctuous smile that made her
dislike him more than usual.

"Why—do you need me for something?"

"Not I, my dear," he said with a significance she was meant
to note but not understand. "This is extracurricular."

She said ironically, "Like they need me on the football
team?"

"Have you ever had lunch in the Rose Room at the Algonquin?"

"Is this some survey you're doing, Jerry?"

"I'm serious. You really made an impact with the TV people. I got a call from Greg Laz last night. He just finished
putting together the segment he was filming here. He screened
it for some of the top people at NBC. They like it a lot. In
particular they like what they saw of you. You're invited to
lunch with Laz and"—Jerry walked to the window and took a
look into the far distance—"Havelock Sloane."

"Should I have heard of him?"

Jerry turned to face her and said in a throwaway tone, "He just happens to have won the Emmy Award for the best documentary two years in a row."

"Fantastic for him," said Sarah, "but where do I come in?"

"Isn't it obvious? You're telegenic, Sarah. You have the qualities a big man like Sloane can use in a major documentary. It's all in front of you!"

"But, Jerry, I'm deep into my research project. I'm not looking for work on TV."

"Don't worry about that. We'll meet that when it comes. The big question now is, what are you going to wear?"

‡ ‡ ‡

She went, she told herself, because her life up to now had not been overstocked with rewarding experiences. She was entitled to hear some nice things for a change. At the end she would thank them for their generosity and explain that her academic career had to come first.

Jerry had handed her a check for two hundred dollars, saying it was her share of the department's fee for the Greg Laz series; Don, he assured her, was getting the same. She spent most of it on a skirt and jacket, bottle green with a pale leaf design overprinted in a broad band on the skirt. The color brought out the gold tones in her hair; she hated being labeled simply a redhead. She justified the new outfit by telling herself she would wear it the next time Ed invited her out.

Her hosts were already sitting in the main lobby of the Algonquin. Laz guided her hand deferentially to Havelock Sloane's. The great man held it a moment, studying her in a way she found flattering. He was about sixty, solemn, thoughtful, slow in speech. He was obviously used to good living, but by the shape of his physique she could tell he practiced some form of conditioning. Sarah found herself speculating whether his hair was his own; something about it was wrong, though it was uniform in shape and color.

They took their drinks to the table reserved in the Rose Room. The headwaiter greeted Sloane by name and motioned his staff to the table.

When they had ordered, Sloane sat back in his chair and looked around to see who else was lunching there, while Laz brought Sarah up to date. *"Never Fear,* the series, is scheduled for its first airing four weeks from Saturday. Program One will be shown at ten-thirty in the evening. We should both be pleased, because that's prime time." He gave a broad smile. "Sarah, you couldn't have guessed when you agreed to talk to Ed Cunningham in your lab that morning we were there that it would turn out to be the high point of the series. I liked it so much that I used some of it twice—in Program One, which introduces the series, and Six, which deals with phobias in detail. To get your sequence in full I even cut out a couple of interviews with phobia sufferers I originally planned to use. All told, you get nearly nine minutes of viewing time, which is a lot, believe me."

"I'm sure it is," said Sarah. "It's terrifying."

"Not at all. It's damn good film, or I wouldn't use it. You may not be aware of this, young lady, but in TV terms you have very exciting qualities. You photograph well, you're cool and very watchable, and you talk as if the camera isn't there. More than that, you put things in a way people understand. You don't wrap it up in egghead jargon. NBC screened the series for some of their top people two weeks back, and after it they weren't talking about schedules. They were talking about you, and how they could use you in something bigger."

She smiled and shook her head, but before she said a word, Havelock Sloane broke into the discussion. He was not the sort

of man you interrupted. "Tell me what you think of this, Ms.
Jordan. A fifty-minute documentary feature, directed by me in
association with Mr. Laz. The subject: spiders. Christ, you say,
Havelock Sloane is out of his mind. A mass TV audience won't
watch spiders. They'll switch channels by the millions. So how
do I keep my audience? This way: I tell them in advance they
won't see a single spider on the program. Crazy?"

Sarah was not sure how to react. She gave a noncommittal
shrug.

"You got to admit it sounds crazy," Sloane insisted with a
trace of petulance.

"Okay, I admit it," said Sarah, laughing. "What's the
catch?"

"No catch," said Sloane benignly. "Just an idea of mine.
Spiders are too ugly to feature on a prime-time program,
right? But they can be really interesting; you convinced me of
that in Greg's documentary, and I did some research of my
own. The whole ritual of the web—terrific. I don't have to
tell you. So how can I show this beautiful thing to America
without creating mass panic? Miss Jordan, instead of spiders,
I use people. I scale up the spiders' world to man size. Get
this: I'm not putting anyone in fancy costumes. Give the
viewing audience a convention—in this case, people playing
spiders—and they accept it for what it represents. You may
find that hard to believe, but I tell you from long experience
in television that it's true." He paused to let the point sink
in. "But the rest is totally authentic in appearance. And action. We show a web being built and used to catch prey. We
see how the victim is bound up in silk. We see the mating
ritual. It's a tremendous technical challenge, but we have the
skill and resources to do it. I see it almost as a ballet; I want
to use electronic music to create an atmosphere." He stopped
talking and sat back in his chair for a moment as if he were

hearing the music. Then he turned to Sarah and said, "It needs a narrator—someone to take the audience through the more complex sequences and tell them what's going on. I decided to ask you. I think you could do this job better than anyone in the business."

Before Sarah could respond, Laz said, "How about that, Sarah? Havelock wants you as his presenter!"

To be asked was better than a compliment. It was proof positive that the nice things Laz had said were backed by an offer from one of the top men in TV. If she weren't so dedicated to completing her research, she might have agreed to take part. But that project was the main thing in her life. She wanted it to be so good that no one could doubt her ability again. And she wanted to deliver it on schedule, long before Don's was ready.

"I want you to know that I'm thrilled to be asked," she told Sloane. "I really do appreciate the offer, but I'm afraid I have to turn it down. I don't know too much about TV, but I do know enough to be sure that this isn't the kind of thing I could do in a couple of days. It would be weeks out of my research, and I'm already behind on my schedule. Please, will you understand that my studies have to take priority."

Without a word, Havelock Sloane put up his hand for the headwaiter. Sarah's stomach lurched and she went white, certain that she had just caused the abrupt termination of the lunch.

Sloane spoke some words into the headwaiter's ear, then told Sarah, "He will bring a phone to the table so you can square it with your professor." As if that settled the matter, he turned to Laz and said, "With hair like this, she should look sensational in black."

"I don't think I made myself clear," said Sarah. "I can't take part in your program. My research is too important."

Laz said, "People take years over a Ph.D. You're not scared of Jerry Berlin? He won't make waves."

How could she explain the intricacies of university politics? "My position in the department isn't too secure. If Professor Berlin got the idea I was putting other things first—"

"I told you, Jerry won't make waves. This isn't a back-door operation. He knows we're seeing you. You know we arranged this lunch through Jerry himself. Did he give you one word of discouragement?"

"Well, no, but—"

"It has his backing, that's why. He'll be mad if you *don't* take it." Laz turned to Sloane. "Havelock, will I be breaking a confidence if I tell Sarah—"

"Go ahead."

"Sarah, we plan to spend up to fifty thousand dollars on the sets alone for this production. Havelock just told you about the giant webs. We'll build examples of each of the best-known structures—the orb, the sheet, the tube, the triangle, and so on —six or seven nylon webs big enough to fill a room. There will also be scale models of the stages in building the things. Jerry has been told that in return for the technical help his department is giving, we intend to present the sets to the university. They'll make a nice exhibit. Good publicity all around."

"The department is helping with this?"

"You're kidding. Our designers will be in your spider lab all next week taking pictures and making sketches. It's all arranged. So you see"—he spread his hands—"it's a cooperative venture. No one's going to blow the whistle on your research if you take part."

A waiter had arrived with the phone.

"You still want to call Professor Berlin?" asked Sloane.

She shook her head.

Without looking at the waiter Sloane said, "Thanks—the lady changed her mind."

"Okay," said Laz, "let's talk schedule."

So Sarah gave in. After what had been said, the other escape hatch she had in reserve—that she was an ecologist and not a trained biologist—was not going to cut any ice either. She decided she had better accept her new role as TV performer with good grace. That settled, she began seriously to think about herself as a new face on NBC-TV. It was a little frightening, but she believed she could handle it. Deep inside, she was churning with excitement.

‡ ‡ ‡

Don had called Meg on Wednesday night to apologize for missing their dance rehearsal. He admitted it had gone clean out of his mind when the red alert for Jerry's research paper came up. He told her about the drive to Lake Pinecliff to collect it from Sarah. He mentioned he had watched her hang-gliding.

Meg let him know she had waited over an hour in the flamenco dress, but she was not as angry about being forgotten as she had the right to be. It seemed she was impressed by his explanation. She repeated her opinion that Sarah was dangerous to get involved with, and left it at that. They arranged to meet for a rehearsal Friday evening, and Don said he would take her afterward for a Mexican meal at Fonda Los Milagros, on Fifty-fifth Street.

He was generous about her dancing. She had mastered the steps and she moved with the music, but really she had plenty to learn about flamenco. From somewhere she had picked up the idea that it was all about hip mobility. The effect from the rear was absurd—buttocks jiggling like maracas. He even said so, though less crudely. By stages he helped her correct the fault. She never discovered how totally inelegant she had looked.

For dinner they had *pollo tapatio,* seasoned chicken with onions. Meg wanted to dance to the mariachi music, but Don managed to distract her by talking about his parents' restaurants on the Pacific Coast. After coffee he walked her back to her dormitory. He could see she was disappointed not to be invited back to his place. She must have counted on this becoming a repeat of the weekends they had spent together earlier in the year, and without doubt the screwing would have been sensational, but Don didn't want the complications. Meg was his dance partner now. For more intimate coupling he had another partner in prospect.

She asked him in for a coffee, but he pleaded work and kissed her in a way that signaled the end of the evening. She held him and pressed her thighs against his and made a remark about the strains put on people by the absence of body contact in Spanish dancing. He asked when she could meet him next week for another rehearsal, and she suggested Wednesday at lunchtime. He agreed, then remembered he had a date to go hang-gliding with Sarah. He asked if Meg could manage Thursday instead. She said she couldn't, and what was the matter with Wednesday?

For the first time, he lied to Meg. He said Jerry had arranged a tutorial for Wednesday.

She swallowed it. They agreed to rehearse Friday evening.

7   When Sarah walked in, her mother was serving
Sunday lunch. She had on that old shirt of
Daddy's she wore over her respectable clothes when she was
cooking. A period of chaos followed as the steaming saucepans
were abandoned so that the place settings could be removed
from the kitchen to the oak table in the front room.

Sarah protested that she wanted to be treated like one of the
family. Her father, in the vest and trousers of his Sunday suit,
complained that the meal was getting cold. He was in the chair
by the window. He did not look up from the portable TV.

The air was thick with recrimination when they finally were
seated around the table. Was it too much to have picked up
a phone and said she was coming? If she had called, there
would have been a roast instead of hamburger from the freezer.
Sarah made apologetic noises. It was no use explaining yet that
she had news for them. Before they were ready to listen to one
word she said, she was required to make reparation for failing
to come home on the anniversary of Marty's death. She had
to listen to an account of the service at which prayers were
offered for his immortal soul. Her mother, despite the distress
she had felt at the remembrance of her son and the inexcusable
absence of her daughter, had a precise recollection of who was
in the congregation and which of them had made remarks,
after the service, implying that Sarah should have been there.

While they served up more rebukes with the cold apple pie,
Sarah asked herself why she was here. She could have been at

Lake Pinecliff, where the conditions would have been ideal, the sun warm enough to create thermals oceans wide. Her parents assumed that her conscience had brought her home, but they were wrong. She had come home to tell them she was going to appear on TV. She didn't want them to hear about it before she told them herself. She wanted to get their reaction firsthand.

Her achievements at school and college had not made much impression at home. At the stage when she started getting good grades in high school, her brother was officially categorized as a child with an exceptional IQ, and there were meetings with teachers and educational psychologists to see that he was given an intellectually demanding program of study. When Sarah announced that she was majoring in ecology, her father commented that it was a pity she had to get involved with a subject no one in Cherry Hill knew anything about, but presumably professors kept thinking of newfangled subjects to keep up the enrollment. The year she graduated, Marty was accepted at Yale. She got her graduate fellowship while everyone was in shock at the news of his fatal accident.

TV had taken over her parents' lives. They watched it all day long. The commercials fortified her mother's belief that there was still the superior style of life that her brothers and sisters in Boston were enjoying and that she was denied. Her father watched anything at all. He didn't need to go out anymore to escape.

Sarah knew them too well to expect them to express any pride in her success. She was not seeking approval. She simply wanted to face them with the fact that their dumb, disappointing daughter had broken into TV without really trying and would shortly become as real in their lives as Barbara Walters or Johnny Carson. All she wanted was to see them chew on that.

It came up in a casual way after coffee, when they were

stacking the dishes. Her father already had a golf match going on the portable. "He's going to buy me a dishwasher," said her mother. "A Whirlpool."

"Does he know yet?"

"He sees it on TV most nights. You must have seen it, too."

"I don't watch much, but you could be seeing me soon on the tube."

Her mother put down the plates she was holding. "Sally, what do you mean?"

"Just what I said. I'm going on TV. Look out for a series called *Never Fear* starting on NBC three weeks from Saturday. I'm in it."

"I don't believe it. *You?*" Her mother eyed her as if she had just got back from Mars. Her lips moved as if she were talking to herself. She crossed the room to where her husband was watching Jack Nicklaus on the long fourteenth. "George, did you hear that? Sally has just told me she is going on television."

It was like watching a silent film. Their reactions were so histrionic, as disbelief turned to mystified acceptance, that Sarah could hardly keep herself from laughing.

Her father turned down the volume and stared at her.

She described the details of Greg Laz's program.

"Why should they pick you for a thing like this?" her father asked in a tone suggesting she must have done unspeakable things to be considered for it.

"It isn't as if you're anyone special," said her mother, with-out malice.

"Maybe you're not the best judge of that."

"If Marty had lived, I would have expected to see *him* on TV."

"Marty was going places," said her father.

"I can't understand how this could have happened," said her mother, as if the house had caught fire.

They could not accept the fact that the daughter whose

existence they had consistently ignored was recognized by the communications medium they revered.

"They're full of promises, these smart guys who make these programs," said her father. "When you get there, you'll find they don't need you."

"The program is done. It's in the can."

"What did they have you *do*, for heaven's sake?" asked her mother.

She told them she had been interviewed by one of New York's top psychiatrists.

"Psychiatrist?" said her mother. "What do they think you are—some kind of loony? Is that why they put you on TV?"

"If they did, I'll get it stopped," said her father. "I'm not having one of my family displayed to America as a crazy."

"I appreciate your concern," Sarah said ironically, "but you've got it all wrong. This is a program about irrational fears. They talked to me because I don't have any."

"I don't understand you," said her mother.

"Did you ever really try?"

"What is that supposed to mean?"

"Skip it, Mother, and relax. There isn't a single thing in the program to upset your fine relatives in Boston or anyone here in Cherry Hill. I keep my clothes on and my language is irreproachable. Okay?" She turned up the volume on the golf commentary. "It's time I hit the road."

Driving back, she felt revitalized.

‡ ‡ ‡

At the therapy session on Monday, Frank, the man with the dog phobia, listened to Sarah's account of the way she had mastered her childhood fear of spiders. It seemed to help him. His frequency count on the conductivity test showed a distinct improvement by the end of the session. Now he was gone, and the next patient had canceled, so there was time to tell Ed the news.

If he had heard about Havelock Sloane's offer, he was tactful enough not to mention it. His face lit up as he listened. When Sarah had finished, he put his hand over hers and said, "Terrific! I'm so pleased for you. We must drink to it."

He poured her a cognac.

She basked in his approval. He told her he was proud to have been the first to interview her on TV. There would be a lot of media interest in her from now on.

"I can't think why," she said, wanting to hear more. "It's only a documentary—nothing glamorous, like a song spot on a talk show."

"Little lady, you're so wrong. Pretty girl and ugly spider— it has a polarity that can't fail to attract. Don't let anyone kid you that this is just another wildlife documentary. With Havelock Sloane involved, it's going to be big. You'd better get yourself an agent, but soon."

She laughed.

"I'm serious."

"I'm not proposing a career in show business."

"That's immaterial. When this breaks, you're going to be a celebrity, and the sharks will move in. You need protection. Have you told anyone else about this?"

"Only my parents. Jerry Berlin knows, of course."

"Would you like me to find out about agents?"

She was unconvinced, but it was great that he cared. "If you really think it's important."

"It is." He made a note on his pad. "Well, how did your parents take the news?"

She gave him an account of her visit home. She admitted getting satisfaction from their inability to come to terms with her success. "Deep inside, I'm not a nice person to know."

"Were they ever nice to you? I don't think you should feel guilty about this. Obviously it did you good. You needed to get things straight at home, assert yourself. I'd say it was a significant step in the maturing process."

"Ed, you'd make it sound right if I blew their brains out with a shotgun!"

He smiled. "I could. They gave you justification." His hand went to the cognac bottle, but she covered her glass. "Sarah, tell me some more about your brother."

She weighed that. It was a shade too clinical for comfort. She knew what interested psychiatrists. She didn't want to be analyzed. She wanted Ed to forget he was a shrink. On the other hand, how could she get near him if she didn't confide in him? "Marty? I thought I told you everything. There was an accident. He came off his bike on Highway Seventy, twenty miles from home. No one could tell why it happened. I drove out to see the place myself. By then they'd removed the— But I found the marks on the road."

"Why did you go?"

"Conscience, I guess. It didn't seem real when they told me. I felt nothing. No, if I'm completely honest, I was secretly pleased that my parents' hopes had crashed with him. I didn't like myself for that, so going to look at the scene of the crash was a kind of penance."

"Did it shock you?"

"It made it real."

He nodded. "Retribution is a powerful force in your life, and this time you turned it inward. You're a fascinating person, Sarah."

She liked hearing him say that. She wanted to tell him it was mutual, but it was too soon. She had to disarm him by degrees.

"I'd better be off. I have some reading to catch up on. I'm going out to Lake Pinecliff Wednesday. I promised Don Rigden some lessons in hang-gliding."

He took the bait. "That's great! I thought you two didn't get along too well."

"He's okay. He's had some disappointments lately, but we're working on it."

She was practically certain his skin color deepened a shade. "Sure."

When she got to the elevator, she turned as if she had just had a thought. "That agent—will there be a chance to discuss it with you first?"

"Why, of course! But we shouldn't lose any time. I'll make some inquiries. Maybe we could have lunch on Friday."

"I'd like that."

"Fine. I'll pick you up at the lab—if Don won't take offense."

"It won't hurt him to see that I have some other friends."

She hummed a tune as she walked up Park Avenue. At last some good things were coming into her life. And she was in charge.

‡ ‡ ‡

They started running down the hillside stride for stride, locked together by the harness, hands gripping the control bar. The sail above them was level with the line of trees blue-green on the horizon. "Come on!" urged Sarah. "Hammer the ground!"

She held the nose angle steady as Don responded. The harness straps tightened. Takeoff.

It was smooth. They kept the running action going until their legs were treading air.

Now Sarah pulled in the bar a fraction to level the sail, and
they were gliding freely on a fresh breeze, the land shooting
under them.

"Scared?" She had to shout. The helmets were not sound-
proof, but they made the wind sound like a force-nine gale.

"Not with you in charge. It's sensational!"

She knew what he was feeling. Floating on air is as superior
to powered flight as running is to using a wheelchair. It is
intensely exhilarating. Fears you felt before takeoff are subdued
by the buoyancy of the sail. The wind frisks your clothes, sings
in your helmet, dries your mouth. Above you it beats against
the sail fabric, and your heart beats in time. It is new and yet
familiar. You are flying as you do in dreams.

The slope slipped away and so did the sense of speed. They
appeared suspended over an almost-still terrain.

"Hey, how about that?"

She looked where he was pointing, and saw thirty or forty
deer racing for cover. Ahead was Lake Pinecliff, fringed by
trees.

She had not told Don this was the first time she had taken
control of a two-seat Rogallo. The principles were no different
from those of solo gliding. The kite was riding high. You could
wait weeks for conditions as good as these. She would take him
over the lake and turn downwind to make the landing, see how
his nerves held up.

She, too, was savoring a new sensation. Without her to
control the glider, Don Rigden would be helpless. He had to
trust her. This heartthrob, mooned over and pursued by num-
berless coeds, had put himself in her charge. Jerry's protégé,
the white hope of the Ecology Department, the researcher
slotted to outshine everyone, herself included, was beside her,
trussed in his harness.

She was aware of his helplessness, but was he?

He would be.

Things were clearer from up here. This was stimulating, playing spider and fly for a few minutes above the New Jersey landscape, but it was just a foretaste.

She was going to fly high at the university. If Jerry or Don wanted to come, he would do it with her consent. And at his peril.

Her breakthrough in television was power. She had seen it work on her parents without fully appreciating its possibilities. Their stupid vanities were nothing beside Jerry Berlin's ambitions. He thought he was smart, doing a deal with Laz and Havelock Sloane, trading Sarah for the sets and for the good publicity. A foot in the door at NBC.

Jesus Christ, she would take him for a ride and make him pay.

The Rogallo was losing height by degrees and they were on course to hit the lake.

"Can you swim?" she called to Don.

He smiled, but it was not an easy smile.

Don was safe this time, but he was in for some shocks. The days when he could pave his future over a drink with Jerry were finished. He would find there were other priorities.

As they lost altitude, the sensation of movement returned. The lake started racing toward them.

They were over the water, maybe seventy feet up.

"Okay," shouted Sarah, "we're turning. Push the bar to your right."

The counteraction caused their bodies to swing left. The wing tip dipped and the glider banked. They made a full turn and were on course with the wind. The sounds almost stopped.

"Better be ready to run. Here comes touchdown."

The glider swooped back over the rough turf beside the lake. Birds scattered on either side.

"Push!"

The forward movement of the control bar raised the nose

into the flare position for landing. Their feet hit the ground and they ran with the kite for at least a dozen strides before stopping and toppling gently to the turf.

"Fantastic!" said Don. "Terrific, Sarah!" He turned, gripped her shoulder, pulled her toward him, and kissed her.

She did not respond. She waited a moment and then pushed him off. "Basic ground drill, Mr. Rigden. After landing, attend to the glider."

That night she slept alone in the motel as usual, just as she had planned.

She had enjoyed drinking with him until the bar closed, studying his low-key but well-tested style of seduction, the subdued voice and steady gaze. It came easily to him—as the girls did. He was well above average in looks. The mouth was finely shaped and wide, the smile generous, eyes deep blue, nose even, brow wide; but the hair was the unforgettable feature: fine, dead straight, and white gold.

She didn't want him.

When the blinking of the lights signaled "last call," he said coolly, "How about bed?"

She said, "I know where mine is."

"Is that an invitation?"

"Not this trip."

His face changed. It had to be his first turn-down in years. "Did I say something wrong?"

She shook her head.

"I mean, I'm not sure how to read you, Sarah."

"I thought I made it clear. Thanks for a nice evening."

He recovered enough to say with a smirk, "Thanks for the ride—up there."

She let that pass. She didn't want a fight. She wanted Don to stay around. The good things to come in her life would taste so much sweeter if he was there to watch.

She walked to the door leading to the rooms and then looked back and said, "Good night, Marty."

She wasn't aware of her slip of the tongue until she noticed Don's totally baffled expression.

‡ ‡ ‡

"You'll like Harry Shakespeare," Ed had promised over lunch. "He's young and dynamic and nobody's fool. Would you believe he's also English?"

In his Sixth Avenue office, Harry had pictures of Diane Keaton, Meryl Streep, and Cheryl Tiegs. "Don't get the wrong idea," he explained with a faint smile. "That's my wanted list. Miss Jordan, how are you? Undecided, I'm sure, until we both know how I can help you." Harry Shakespeare's hand was cool, his grip confident. He had a glass eye and a mouth that drooped.

She liked him.

"So you haven't talked money yet with NBC," he said when she and Ed had outlined their reasons for coming. "Dear old Havelock is a charming fellow and a most inventive director, but he does have this tiresome tendency to forget that fees are involved."

"There *is* the agreement to donate all the sets to the university," said Sarah.

"Splendid, but that's public relations, not remuneration. If you anchor a major documentary with his name on it, you stand to collect five thousand dollars minimum, my dear."

The figure staggered her. "Nobody has heard of me."

"Let me surprise you, then. Ed, when you phoned yesterday and said this talented and pretty young graduate student you knew was going to narrate Sloane's next documentary, didn't

I ask right away whether that was Sarah Jordan you were talking about?"

Ed confirmed it.

"Not much happens in this town without interested parties getting to know about it," Harry went on. "I've no reason for thinking my spies at NBC are reporting exclusively to me. You can take my word for it that anyone with a stake in television will have made a note of your name this week. That's nothing. I think you'll find that Havelock has plans to get you known from coast to coast before his program is aired."

"Which is why you need Harry's help," put in Ed.

"Point taken," said Sarah. "Do we talk fees, or percentages?"

Harry Shakespeare laughed. "Who said you needed an agent?"

‡ ‡ ‡

Havelock Sloane's production team assembled for the first time on Tuesday, June 3, 1980, in the RCA Building in Rockefeller Plaza, where NBC has its headquarters. Sarah arrived in the lobby at nine-fifty A.M. and reported to the reception desk. They put through a call and told her to wait, as someone was coming down for her. She took a seat where she could watch the elevators. It would be exciting if she could spot one of the *Today* show performers coming off duty.

There *was* a familiar face that she could not place for a moment. For sure it wasn't Tom Brokaw.

He walked right up to her and said, "Hi, Spider Girl. Isn't this terrific?"

He wore tight-cut black denims and a pink shirt unbuttoned to the waist. From his neck were suspended a stop watch and a silver ingot.

She got up. "Hi. For a moment I wasn't sure—"

"—if this is the jackass who upset your spiders? Tough luck, Sarah—it is." Rick Saville put his arm firmly around her and guided her to the elevator. "You want to know what I'm doing on Havelock's team? When I heard they'd signed you up, I zeroed in. Greg squared it with Havelock. So I get my chance to make amends."

They entered an elevator with five other people. He kept his arm around her.

"So, *do* I?"

She didn't want to talk in front of these people. She shrugged.

"Get to make amends, I mean."

"If you like."

They got out of the elevator, and she gently but firmly removed his hand from her shoulder. "Thanks, but I can stay upright without your aid. I'm generally sober at this time of day."

The rehearsal studio was full of people in groups drinking coffee and snatching looks at other groups. Rick took her straight to Havelock Sloane, conspicuous in a white cashmere sweater, holding court with several senior-looking people with clipboards, including Greg Laz. Sloane stopped in mid-sentence and said, "Ah, Sarah is here. Friends, I want you to meet Spider Girl."

It was not a flattering introduction. It could have thrown her completely if Rick had not already greeted her in the same way. But it was pleasing to see the way these people looked at her. She knew how it felt to be *somebody*.

"Her name is Sarah Jordan, and she has an agent named Shakespeare who might just be a descendant of the guy who wrote *The Merchant of Venice*. This morning he zapped NBC for more ducats than they knew they had." He made the introductions. "And now that my leading lady is here, I'm going to get started."

A general movement began toward the end of the room where some chairs were arranged. Sarah was between Rick, who had brought coffee, and Greg Laz.

Havelock fired a question at his audience that got down to basics. "Anyone here react badly to spiders?"

A tense silence.

"Liars! There ain't a guy in this room hasn't been scared shitless by a big one sitting in an empty bathtub. They are shit-ugly creeping bastards that show up when you least expect them. Anyone disagree? Okay, we're straight on that. Now some facts. Archaeologists tell us that man may have inhabited the world for a million years. Spiders have been around at least three hundred million, so maybe they have more right to that tub than we do. The human population of the world is a little over four billion; you could find that number of spiders in a few fields one quarter the size of Manhattan. For each man, woman, and child in the world there are approximately seventy thousand spiders. Would you like to look under your chairs?"

There was some nervous laughter.

"We're going to shoot a fifty-minute feature on spiders without showing one of the goddamned things. We scale up their world to man size and use people. No costumes. Just people in plain clothes. That way we break through the aversion barrier. Then we can show America some sensational things which not even most scientists have realized. Did you know that the infant spider is the greatest hang-glider pilot in the world? Or that the way a spider grows is by striptease? Or that their mating has more ritual than high mass in St. Peter's? I want to simulate all this. I want to film an orb web being built with nylon rope against the New York skyline; we're working on the idea of slinging it between those spikes on the Statue of Liberty's headgear, but there are certain technical problems."

More stirrings of amusement in the audience.

"I'm serious, for Christ's sake," said Havelock. "Sure, it's a terrific stunt, but so is every orb web ever built. Spiders are brilliant climbers. It wouldn't surprise me at all if we find webs up there on the Statue already. This is just a way of showing people spectacular things that happen in their own backyards. If we can't get a public building, we'll use a tower crane. The climber is already hired. We also have some beautiful sets being built in Studio Eight in this building. Giant webs where we can show how the spider catches and binds its prey. And the mating. We start rehearsals in there tomorrow. That's all on the production schedule you'll get in a few minutes. Before we look at details, I want to make one thing clear. This is going to be difficult and demanding. We're breaking new ground in documentary TV and the problems are manifold. That's why I picked you guys: look around you and you'll see more talent than you ever met on one production before. I'm not just confident; I'm one hundred percent certain you can perform the miracles I demand. One thing I guarantee—no spiders."

Havelock had won total support. They laughed and then they applauded and kept applauding.

"This has got to be the one that wins Havelock his third Emmy," Rick told Sarah.

"Name-dropping time," Havelock announced. "My associate director, Gregory Laz, who made that highly praised series *Who's Master?* and has just completed a sequel that is better than that. On your feet, Greg."

Laz turned and gave a wave.

"Greg will supervise the location work. Pete Shapiro, designer, whose sets you must see . . ."

As the introductions proceeded, Sarah only vaguely recognized most of the names. But it was nonetheless a thrill to be working among such talent and experience. She had a shock when Havelock said, "Finally, the young lady who will narrate the show. I predict that she will do for spiders what Roone Arledge did for ABC Sports—our Spider Girl, Sarah Jordan."

She stood up and said, "Hi," and someone said, "Hi, Spider Girl," and there was some laughter and then the meeting broke up.

A small, white-haired woman touched her arm and said, "I'm Billie Shulman, Costume, and I know everyone is crazy to meet you, so I'm going to grab you right now and take you off for fitting."

"But I don't think I need a costume. Isn't it plain clothes?"

"Correct, honey, but Sarah Jordan plain isn't Spider Girl plain." She turned to Rick. "If she's needed, you know where to find her, okay?"

In a very short time Sarah was standing in bra and panties in the fitting room, having her measurements taken. "You're easy," Billie Shulman told her, "but you have to be right. Havelock wants everyone in black—and that sounds simple, doesn't it? But, honey, it's a disaster if the fabrics aren't right. The cameras are sensitive to the smallest differences in shade. And black's a godawful color to work with. So it's no use telling me you have a beautiful black leotard at home that you'd like to wear. You have to settle for the NBC garments. The only things we let you provide for yourself are these"—she tapped Sarah's panties—"and they must be black bikini-style without trim. You won't be wearing a bra."

Sarah couldn't follow what this was about. "No?"

"You should worry! Your figure's a dream. Would you take off the bra now, please?"

"Pardon me, but there must be a mistake. I don't need a leotard to talk about spiders. I'm only narrating the program."

"And I'm only providing the costumes, sweetheart. Better talk to HS when we finish."

Sloane was still in the rehearsal room with a group of technicians around him. Sarah waited ten minutes and several people introduced themselves and shook her hand. She was getting a taste for life as a celebrity, but she had to get things straight with Havelock Sloane.

"Sarah, my dear, you've been waiting!"

"I wanted to talk to you about my costume." She told him the problem.

He took her arm. "Don't let it bother you, my dear. I have something to show you." He guided her into the corridor and toward the elevator. His entourage of six or seven followed close behind. It was like royalty on a visit.

They all got out of the elevator and entered a control room lined with an electronic console and monitors. Sloane opened another door and they were at the top of a staircase looking into a TV studio two floors high and as big as a concert hall. In the foreground was a scaffold web of gleaming white nylon cord, at least thirty feet in height. So accurate was it in construction that Sarah wouldn't have been surprised to see a giant *Theridion sisyphium* dart down from the cluster of lights overhead.

"Come on!" urged Havelock. "It rates at least an 'Oh, my God!' "

"I'm speechless."

"I'll show you something better than this." He started down the stairs. Sarah followed with the others.

From ground level the place looked cavernous, with unlit areas extending way back into the recesses. Ahead in the dimness were more webs. Cables like creepers lay across their path.

"Someone give us some light here," Havelock ordered.

Immediately there appeared ahead a mass of dead leaves the

size of hearth rugs, and among them, skillfully camouflaged, the gaping, silk-fringed nest of a tube builder.

"Look inside if you want," said Havelock, "but include me out." He led them around a flat to the next set.

It was an orb web, still under construction, a beautiful, shimmering thing stretched between scaffolding artfully disguised as a window frame. The two technicians high on the rigging took nothing away from its realism. There was no question anymore in Sarah's mind that Havelock's idea of using people would work brilliantly.

"Like it?"

"Love it."

"It's a gift to the university when we finish shooting."

"I wish it was mine."

"I think you really mean that, Spider Girl. Where do you live—Grand Central Station? Listen, while we're in production, it *is* yours. All the sets are yours. I want you to climb over the things, get the feel of them, tell us if anything's wrong. Which brings us to costumes. The way I see it, we don't want to film you parading through the studio pointing out sets like some lousy PBS documentary. That would be death. We have to integrate you with the sets, put you on the webs, not on the studio floor in front of them. You with me?"

Sarah nodded.

"So you need a web-climbing costume."

"Wouldn't a T-shirt and jeans be okay?"

"My dear, you'd be a knockout in anything, but this is a big-budget production. The viewing audience isn't crazy about casual clothes. Remember, we also have to dress the rest of the cast."

"There are others?"

"It's not a one-girl show, Sarah. You can't play every part. We need guys and gals to play male and female spiders. Some moths, a housefly. I'm putting them all in black tights. Didn't I tell you I see it as ballet?"

"You did, but—"

"What's the problem, my dear?"

"I thought I was the narrator."

"You bet."

"It sounds like you want me to play a spider."

"Does that bother you?" Havelock took one of her hands and sandwiched it gently between his. "Are you worried about your image? Look, nothing we do in this production will make you less attractive to people. I already told makeup I want you Number One in the poster sweepstakes before this program is screened. The publicity boys upstairs are working on your schedule right now. They've already arranged for a two-page feature in *TV Guide*. Greg's series is the lift-off, and then we have maybe two months to get you into orbit. Have I scared you?"

She was more stunned than scared. She shook her head and tried to catch up.

"To come back to what you were saying," Havelock went on, "we're billing you as the narrator, okay? But this show can't look like amateur night. I want you at the center of the action. I want the public to identify with you, to *feel* what it's like at the center of a web as well as have you explain it. I want them to see that web vibrate when a male arrives, and I want them pissing in their pants with tension when he approaches you. Yes, if you want it straight, you're presenting the show *and* you're playing Spider Girl—it's the same thing." He let go of her hand and started to walk away. "So do we have a deal, or would you like to call Shakespeare and tell him you want out?"

She let her eyes travel over the strands of the web to where the technicians were finishing a spiral. She answered, "You have a deal."

8 On the first Monday in June, when exams were finished and people were waiting for their grades, talking nervously and loudly in groups over lunch, Meg spotted Nancy Lim alone at a table and took her tray over. It was weeks since they had talked.

"I'm so glad I found you," Meg said. "I've been meaning to thank you every day, but I just haven't seen you."

"What for?"

"Your advice—about studying the ways of the Peahen."

"Oh!" Nancy put her hand to her mouth and giggled a little. "I almost forgot. Did it do any good?"

Meg was so infected by the giggles that her eyes began to water. "It did!"

When their giggling had subsided enough, Nancy said, "Well, what do you know? Do you mean you have something going again with, uh, what was his name?"

"I sure do!" Meg described how her newly cultivated reserve had spurred Don into asking her to partner him in the *seguidilla* at the Amnesty International concert. "We've been rehearsing regularly ever since, and the concert is Saturday. Jesus, I was so scared! He's unbelievably good at flamenco and he rented this sensational white dress for me. It's years since I did any dancing. We worked on it, and he was so *kind,* and I tried my best, but, Nancy, flamenco is murder to learn. After I had got the steps and knew the music, I thought it would come right. How wrong could I be? I was proficient to a degree, but both of us knew it was nothing like it should be, and it wasn't getting any better. I practically convinced myself I had a block about flamenco."

"What did he say?"

"He's a super guy. He kept his cool and went on with the rehearsals. Once when I was really down, he took me out to dinner."

"He wasn't dating you otherwise?"

Meg shook her head. "It's kind of hard to explain. I think I told you before that I shacked up with him two weekends last semester. It meant a lot to me at the time, and I'm positive Don liked me—my body, I mean. Only I was so far gone about falling into bed with this fabulous guy everyone was crazy about that I totally failed to understand his needs as a person. Christ, that sounds corny! What I mean is, Don has a horror of being suffocated by a woman. He needs room to breathe. I got too close. It was lucky for me that I took your advice; otherwise our relationship would have been dead and buried. The dancing is Don's way of keeping it alive. It's another chance, and I can't afford to flunk this one."

"You make it sound like exams."

"It's the most important one I'll ever take in this place."

"How do you pass?"

"By showing I care enough to try. And by not making demands. I worked at the dancing so hard I had complaints from the girl in the room under mine. One rehearsal Don didn't show up, and I was *suicidal.* It turned out he had to go on an errand for his professor, but he forgot to let me know. I was in real danger of losing him. He made it up by taking me out to dinner, and that was nice, and I almost blew it by throwing myself at him, the strain was so awful. I kept repeating over and over to myself what you had told me."

"What was that?"

"You don't remember? The Peahen doesn't chase the Peacock around the park."

They both laughed.

"Well, I cooled it, and kept hoping my *seguidilla* would come right. Last Friday it did. We had a rehearsal as usual in the old Ping-Pong room, and I don't know why, but suddenly I got it all together—the steps, the arm movements, the poise, the rhythm—all in perfect harmony. I wasn't even thinking about the problem of managing the dress. I just let it happen and I *knew* I had it—even before Don kissed me. He switched off the tape and held me and our mouths met and the *1812 Overture* was playing in my head. I asked if he wanted to try the dance once more to be sure, but he said he couldn't be more sure. You know, the way he said it, he wasn't talking about the dance at all." Meg smiled contentedly.

"Did you—?"

"The same night. Nancy, words can't express it. It sounds crazy, but all that waiting and uncertainty paid off. It wouldn't have been so sensational without it."

"I'm so happy for you. What happens now?"

"Well, the party's on Saturday and I just *know* the dance will go right. We're not rehearsing again, because we reached the peak and we don't want to go over. We made no promises, but if I read it right, I'll be cooking breakfast in Don's apartment Sunday morning."

"And after?"

"We'll see how he wants to play it. Put it this way: the girl in the room under mine won't get disturbed anymore by dancing."

‡ ‡ ‡

Ed Cunningham was not really a fitness freak, but he believed in keeping in shape. Twice a week he worked out at a handsomely equipped health spa four blocks from his Park

Avenue office. There, beside the pool, a few months previously, he had first met Harry Shakespeare.

They met again in the sauna the week after Shakespeare became Sarah's agent. Through the steam he sounded more British than a costume movie. "Decent of you to bring me a new client, old man. I do appreciate it. We came to a useful agreement with NBC and I'm confident there are more goodies to come."

"I knew she could use your help," said Ed.

"A sweet girl," said Shakespeare, "and most unusual. The proverbial nerves of steel. You met her working on the Laz documentary series, didn't you?"

Ed nodded. "I was interested in the way she mastered her fear of spiders."

"Are you psychoanalyzing her?"

"Christ, no. She wouldn't want that; nor would I. She has a horror of psychiatry. I simply got her to tell me her story, and then repeat it to some of my patients. I'm writing a book on the treatment of phobias."

"I see. I only asked because I notice you loom rather large in her thoughts. I've talked to her on the phone several times and she seems to base all her decisions on whether you would approve or disapprove."

Ed was silent for a moment.

"If you had been treating her, old boy, I would have said she had an old-fashioned crush on her shrink."

"I'm aware of this," said Ed, "and I want to discourage it. If she'll take advice from you—"

"Just a minute. You can't back off now. This girl is going to need all the support she can get when the media move in on her."

"No, I simply want to cool it a little. There's a young guy she works with—Don Rigden—who has dated her a couple of times. He's a responsible guy who I'm sure would like to help if she'll let him. That's why I'm backing off, as you put it. But I aim to be there in the background."

"Just so long as she doesn't transfer her affection to me, old boy," said Harry Shakespeare, wiping the sweat from his forehead. "Between my girl friend's divorce and my own, my life is complicated enough."

‡ ‡ ‡

"What's the world like from a cobweb?"

Sarah looked down from the center of the orb web to where Havelock Sloane was standing on the studio floor, hands on hips. This morning he was in a pale-green denim suit and white turtleneck sweater. Very snappy, but from this angle there was no question that he was wearing a hairpiece.

She raised her hand and returned the greeting, thinking he would then move on. But he remained, and so did his semicircle of disciples.

"How does it feel up there?"

This was her third day of getting acquainted with the web. Havelock had told her to use any free time between rehearsals learning to move on it.

"I have sore feet. The rope kind of catches them sideways."

"We'll have Costume fix you some thicker sneakers. Are your hands holding up?"

She showed him two red palms.

"That's the kind of dedication I'm looking for," Havelock called up, and she could not be sure if he was serious. "Let's see how you move now."

She gripped the strand above her with both hands and tucked her legs in to ease back through the space. The way the web was strung, it tilted away from Havelock, and Sarah was now on the underside. Keeping legs and arms bent, she scaled the rungs formed by the spirals in a rapid movement that took her to the scaffolding under the arc lamps.

"Not bad. Now would you come down to the center again on this side."

There was only one way to do as he asked, and that was backward. She straightened the sides of her leotard, turned, and put her weight on the outermost spiral. She made a smooth descent without looking down, and although the spacing was uneven, her feet met the rope cleanly each time. At the center, she turned neatly, tucked her backside into the hub of the web, and reclined as if on a hammock, easing the weight off her sore feet.

"Sarah, my dear, that move is a knockout from here, and it's too bad we can't let America see it. They'd forget all about spiders. It's not possible you could come down face first? That's the way the spider moves, but I figure you'd be in danger of breaking your neck. Am I right?"

"I wouldn't care to try it. You need an acrobat for that."

"I'll get the tech boys to look at it. Maybe we can string the web horizontally and get a high camera angle on you. Take a break now, sweetheart. Get some extra-thick sneakers. I want you back here by eleven-forty-five to try something different."

It transpired that Sloane wanted to work out a routine on the web to simulate the courtship ritual. "This is where we need your expert knowledge, Sarah. Take us through the stages leading up to coition, would you, and we'll see how we can stage it."

So she pointed to the crevice where the female would lie in wait, out of sight of suitors or prey but linked by the signal thread to the center of her web. And she described the strategy of the male, first anchoring a thread of its own, high and clear of the web, as a safety thread to swing back on in emergencies.

One of the technicians pointed out a rope already in position above their heads. Havelock asked for it to be uncoiled.

"Let's run through it, see how it looks," he said. "First we need a stand-in for a horny male. Where's Rick?" This earned an easy laugh and brought Rick down from the control room. "Do we have some harness?" asked Havelock. "The safety thread should be attached to his back—is that right, Sarah?"

They spent the next half hour fixing rope, pulleys, and harness, to give Rick enough mobility. With two men off the set handling the line, the essential movements of the drop, swing, and climb were tried until they were passable.

"Okay, it's not world class, but it'll do for now," said Havelock. "Sarah, my Spider Girl, would you please go up to your lair now and wait for vibrations on that signal thread? Let's play it like the spiders would, so far as conditions allow. Scare him a couple of times with dashes to the center, then let him spin the mating thread—we'll have to imagine it at this stage—and see if he turns you on by jerking the web. If he can't, I guess you eat him." This got another laugh, and Havelock added, "He's not the main course—just standing in till your mate arrives for rehearsals. A beautiful boy straight out of drama school."

"I like them on toast," said Sarah, and they all laughed again. But as she climbed the web, she was uneasy about the hyped-up mood of hilarity. People laughed like that when they were nervous. She would have been happier with everyone relaxed.

The crevice where she was required to lie in wait was a small platform set on scaffolding among the lights, screened by wood and canvas. There really was a signal thread of nylon rope connecting it tautly with the center of the web. There was also a cushion Sarah had brought in the previous day. She made herself as comfortable as she could in the cramped space, her chin resting on her knees. Below was a side view of the web, spirals foreshortened into a single bar of gleaming white.

"Okay, let's go," called Havelock. "Action!"

She had no view of what was going on, but she heard the squeak of pulleys as Rick was lowered toward the web. The moment he made contact, she felt the signal thread twitch against her thigh. That was followed by a series of jerks as he transferred his weight to the web, and then he was in view, smaller than she expected, cautiously moving up the lower section.

She waited a few seconds, as the spider would, judging the moment to strike. The tension excited her like the make-believe games she had adored as a child.

She moved.

It was a rapid descent down the signal thread, and Rick reacted just as quickly, thrusting himself away from the web and into space. He dropped maybe six or seven feet and then reached the limit of the safety line. It gave his body a strong jerk and set it swinging. He rode it out for a couple of swings and then started climbing upward. The technicians helped by hoisting him up.

"Not bad!" declared Havelock. "It could work. Let's go straight into the mating sequence. You both okay?"

Sarah nodded and Rick took off his shirt and let it fall. Climbing the rope had made him sweat.

"Can we keep you out on the web for this one, Sarah?" asked Havelock. "Does the female go back to base each time, or can we assume she is alerted to the possibility?"

"It's okay to meet him halfway."

"Good girl. So what happens when he hits the web?"

"He gets settled and begins plucking one of the lines to indicate his intentions. It's a tentative signal at first; then it gets more confident. When he's ready, he spins the mating bridge between two of the radial lines. His object then is to entice the female there by repeatedly jerking and tweaking the lines. If he succeeds, she'll indicate submission by hanging upside down from his bridge. Then he moves in fast—"

"And that's where the damn commercial break comes," said Havelock. "But it should make good television. Did you get it all, Rick? Listen, we don't have a mating bridge as of now, so until we can fix that, let's use any place on the web that feels comfortable."

So the mating sequence started with Sarah holding the signal thread two spirals above the hub of the web. She watched Rick on his line, lowered to a point way below her, almost on the perimeter, and she felt the tremor as he touched down. She pressed her torso against the web. She was in contact with the signal thread with her instep, inner thigh, abdomen, and face. It began to pulsate rhythmically. She was not sure if she liked the feeling. She moved her leg and hitched herself higher. From there she could watch Rick's movements without straining. He was creeping higher, plucking the line as he came. His face was pale and he was not smiling. He looked small. Vulnerable.

If this was sex as spiders made it, at least it was a change from being humped on a lumpy mattress. It intrigued her that Havelock should have picked Rick for this role; maybe he had noticed Rick giving her the eye.

She eased her body closer to the signal thread and sampled the rhythm again. It was unsubtle. Just a repetitive beat, about as seductive as a jackhammer. And that was a pity, because Sarah could imagine ways in which love on a web might be made attractive.

She went through the motions, pretending to be enticed by the performance, descending by degrees. When she got the scent of his body, she leaned lower and put one hand on the bridge he had selected. His eyes met hers; and she looked into them and knew he was physically aroused by the ritual. She might have mocked him, but she returned a brief, sensuous look before swinging down and tucking her legs over the line to hang in the mating position.

"Thanks—it has possibilities," said Havelock. "It needs a lot of work, obviously, and there are some major technical problems, but I'm encouraged. Okay, kids, we'll pick it up again at two. Sarah, sweetheart, you and I have some talking to do."

She lowered herself from the web. "Right now?"

"As soon as you're ready. Why not get your coat and we'll grab a sandwich someplace nearby where we can talk alone."

He took her to a deli in the next block, a come-down from the Algonquin, but this time he wasn't pitching for a contract. They ordered sandwiches and coffee, and Sloane waded in. "Sarah, my dear, you were lousy this morning. If you had been a trained actress, I'd have told you right there in the studio, but you're not, so I spared your feelings. It was crap. If you can't do better than that, I might as well tell all those people to go home. Do I make myself clear?"

It was such a savage put-down, she reacted like a dumb teenager—went pink, got to her feet, and started to walk out. As she passed Havelock's side of the table, she felt him grab her wrist. She was swung around and her backside hit the padded banquette beside him.

"I hadn't finished," he told her in his slow way, without letting go. "I happen to believe you can carry this show for me. First we have to understand each other a little better. Will you give me credit for knowing how things work in this business and listen to my advice?"

She nodded, and he released her wrist. She looked ahead at a blank wall, shaking from the shock. Until this moment her life had seemed so well defended it could hold no unpleasant surprises. At home and at the university she knew just where she stood. She had lines out to each conceivable source of danger or attack. If Jerry had said her research was crap, she would have had an answer ready, because Jerry was on her list of two-faces. But Havelock had caught her off guard. All the ballyhoo over her TV potential had drawn her out of her safe limits. She faced the hideous prospect of a letdown as devastating as the day her parents had stopped her ballet classes.

"Try and understand what we're doing, Sarah. People playing spiders is a stunt, right? It's kinky and controversial. The natural-history crowd will want to lynch me. It doesn't bother me; controversy is news and news is publicity. I'm going to play that one for all it's worth. I want the whole country watching my show. But after they switch it on, I'm not playing games anymore. I mean to give them an insight into spiders they didn't know was possible. So how do we work this miracle? Any ideas?"

She had not given it much thought, but she had to recoup some dignity. "I guess by using people, you eliminate the revulsion commonly felt for spiders."

"Right. Only it goes deeper. Show a TV audience a spider, and half of them switch channels. The other half might watch, but they don't identify with the thing. It's too damned ugly. Show them a man building a web against the New York skyline, and they're mentally up there with him."

Sarah saw the point Havelock was making, but as a scientist she saw the flaw in it. "Isn't that because he's a man doing a dangerous stunt? The point about web-building is that it has no dangers—for a spider."

"Right," said Havelock. "We have to persuade the audience to look at the man and believe he is a spider. Then they appreciate the technical problems in building a web."

"It's asking too much."

"Not if they've already made the mental jump of seeing people as spiders."

"How is that supposed to happen?"

"It's your job, sweetheart. We start with you in the studio. You convince them that you really are a spider."

She turned to face him. "That's crazy!"

He kept his eyes on her and said nothing.

"How can I, dressed in a leotard?"

"Sarah, take my word for it, a costume with eight legs would strain credulity much more. You're a very attractive girl, so you're watchable. If we made you ugly, put hairs on your limbs and fangs in your mouth, they wouldn't take you seriously. We're operating on another level of persuasion. We let them see you're pretty. We say here's this dream of a girl standing on a giant spiderweb: now, watch. And by the way you act, you convince them that you're not a girl. You do it with such conviction that they reject the idea that what they see has a human intelligence. So, what else are they looking at but a spider?"

It was fantastic, but it sounded possible, even plausible, put that way. Except that Sarah couldn't see herself doing it. "If I were a trained actress—"

"You'd fuck it up completely," said Havelock. "Sarah, you *know* spiders. You know what makes them act the way they do. You can do this, but you have to make the mental jump yourself. While you're on that web, you have to become a spider. When it happens, you'll know. I'll know. More important, the audience will know. I told you this morning was crap. You know why?"

"I was too self-conscious?"

"Right. It was in your movements, your face, your eyes. You were thinking, How can I do this and keep my dignity? So you held your chest out and your ass in and your knees together and each time you stopped, it was like a picture in the family album."

She gave an embarrassed smile.

"Do you believe me when I say it looked ridiculous? If I wanted to remake a Busby Berkeley movie, I wouldn't be hiring *you*, sweetheart. You're Spider Girl. Can we agree on that?"

"I'm not sure."

"I mean, if it offends your scruples, let's tear up the contract. I have scruples, too. I don't force people into doing things they hate. The reason I hired you is that I got the impression you understood spiders like no one else I know. That you had a respect for them."

"I have."

Havelock took a bite of his sandwich. "They get a lousy press, don't they?"

She laughed and said, "Sure, but they're not all bad."

"Prove it, then. No one ever had a better chance."

"I'll need a lot of help."

"Sweetheart, that's guaranteed. We can give you special lighting, shadows, music. But what it comes down to is, do you believe in yourself as Spider Girl?"

"I can try."

"Okay. This afternoon, I'll leave you out of rehearsals. Get on the web and forget who you are and what you are. Don't move around. Just sit up there and find out what being a spider is like. It's a matter of self-conviction. When you believe it, you'll do it right. And then we have a show."

‡ ‡ ‡

On the afternoon of the concert, Meg ran her steam iron over the Spanish dress, and it took nearly an hour, there were so many flounces. She polished the block-heeled shoes that she would use for the dance. She took a long shower and washed her hair. She was excited, but not too nervous. She knew she was ready. She would not let him down.

He was to call for her at seven-thirty. At seven she wrapped the shoes in tissue paper and put them in her overnight case. She added a brush and some combs, her makeup bag, her gold chain and cross and pendant earrings, the fan she would hold, and the red carnation for her hair. She closed the case and got the dress out of the closet, put a clothes bag over it, and hung it on the door.

Someone had slipped an envelope under the door, a ridiculously long white one. Some kind of joke? She picked it up. In one corner was written in very small letters BREAK A LEG TO-NIGHT. She looked inside. It contained a peacock's feather. She smiled. Nancy.

At seven-twenty-five she opened the case and tucked an extra pair of panties and her toothbrush under the other things.

Don was right on time. As her lips were already made up, he kissed her forehead, and said she looked fantastic. He had brought her a present, a new fan, a beautiful antique carved from ivory. He said she had better try it a few times to be sure it would open easily. For some reason it was difficult. She fumbled it two times out of three. He suggested they leave it behind, but she said she would get it right while they were waiting to go on. So she put it in her case. She took out the bottle of Spanish sherry she had bought the day before and poured two glasses. It was Amontillado, too dry for her taste, but she figured Don would not care for sweet sherry, so she pretended to enjoy it. After the first sips, it warmed her throat and flowed through her body. The rest was easy to take.

The performances were to be staged in the open air on the East Lawn of the campus, a fifteen-minute walk from Meg's dormitory. The scheduling was a little uncertain, so they were asked to be ready by eight-fifty. The guitar accompaniment would be provided by José-Maria, a part-time musician Don had heard at a Greenwich Village café and persuaded to make the tape they had used for rehearsals.

The heat of the day still hung in the air as they left the building, Don carrying Meg's case and his own, she with her dress folded over her arm. She was wearing her black satin skirt and a green top with a reckless plunge. She had found it in Gimbels the previous Saturday, for when the performances were over, there would be refreshments and dancing.

Taped music carried across the campus to them as they started along Busch Boulevard, beside the Physics building. Her body gave a shiver of anticipation. It was strange to hear heavy rock among these stately buildings and see girls in skirts and guys smarter than they ever looked by day, all converging on the source of the sound.

The organizers of the event had erected a large platform in the center of the East Lawn. Meg learned later that it was the university boxing ring, but it was well disguised with banks of flowers and a canopy overhead, decked with lanterns and loudspeakers. Scores of people were already seated on the grass around the stage, and farther back, rows of chairs were ranged. At one edge of the lawn was a barbecue, with guys in tall chef's hats cooking hamburgers and chipolatas.

"All those people!" Meg said.

"Don't worry. By the time we go on, it will be dark. You won't see past the front two rows."

Two rooms in the Social Science building had been reserved for the performers. It seemed the other acts were dressed to go on already, mostly in casual clothes. But there was a screen at one end, and Meg went behind it to get into the Spanish dress.

The girl who offered to zip her up said she looked fit to ravish, and Meg laughed and said she should be so lucky.

Out on the lawn the program got under way with a soul group. People were still arriving, only to find there was standing room only. Meg preferred not to stand by the window with the other girls, watching the scene. She busied herself putting up her hair and fixing the combs and the flower. After that, she worked on her eyes; under the lights out there she would need heavy shadow and a strong color.

Two guys and a girl from the School of Dental and Oral Surgery did a slick and popular comedy act featuring a bizarre dental operation, and then a girl sang protest songs and a law student did impressions of world-famous politicians. The first half ended with a reggae group. Meg had mastered the new fan, and decided to use it.

Then one of the committee asked if she was ready, as they were on second after the intermission. Don appeared, now in the classic black flamenco suit and hat. With it he wore a proud, imperious look, certain to inflame his numerous adorers and make them grind their teeth in envy of Meg. He said she looked sensational. Then he introduced José-Maria, who was thin and old and Andalusian. His guitar, José-Maria told her, had played for all the greatest dancers at the *feria* in Sevilla. Meg shivered a little; now she felt nervous.

The singer onstage was into her last number. They were waiting in the shadows.

"Okay?" said Don. "Just give yourself to the music."

The vocalist took her bows and left the stage. The emcee said his part, recalling Don's brilliant flamenco dancing at the party the previous year. This time, he said, Don was joined by a partner no less sensational, the lovely Meg Kellaway.

Don held her arm as they climbed up to the platform, José-Maria leading. There was applause and some muted screams and a few irreverent shouts of *"Olé,"* and then they had mounted the steps and it was dead quiet and everyone was waiting.

Meg stood in one corner of the platform, close to the scaffolding post that supported the canopy. She had her left hand on her hip, her face angled to present the profile. The program was to open with a solo *sevillana* from Don. He was statuesque in the opposite corner.

José-Maria played the first chords, and the sound worked like the sherry, for after its first arid taste, it drove deep to the belly and warmed the blood. It was the urgent, grinding note of the real Spain. The old Andalusian smiled at the fingers of his left hand as they pressed and released the strings.

And now Don came alive by stages, like a reptile, head, back, and thighs rigid, feet matching the rhythm with tiny, hard steps that took him slowly to the center, fingers snapping loud as castanets.

Meg watched the dance in gathering excitement. She felt her body respond, tensing so that she was conscious of every stretch and fold of its surface. It was answering the sexual invitation, demanding to be touched. The conventions of the dance prohibited contact, and that, perversely, quickened the instinct. Arousal and restraint—the polarity of sex and the tyranny of flamenco.

When the rhythm changed to the more languorous tempo of the *seguidilla,* Meg allowed her head to turn and her arms to move with the reluctance the dance demanded. Slowly she advanced on Don, and he responded with hand claps and the drumming of heels on the boards. She was exquisitely torn between the discipline of the dance and the fire of the music. She was conscious of the hundreds surrounding the stage, yet oblivious of them. It was simultaneously public and private, this celebration of passion.

Their eyes met and held the look without a glimmer of affection, for although the swaying body and the sinuous arms are the hallmark of the classic *seguidilla*, the face remains masklike, scornful of the body's animality. But they swayed in unison and Meg knew it was magic.

Then it stopped, and the audience were standing to applaud. They were cheering. They were screaming. They wanted more, but it had been agreed there would be no encore.

They were mobbed as they left the stage. People were surging forward. It was frightening, because although the nearest appeared to want only to touch and congratulate them, others were pressing from the back. A student with glasses was pushed face to face with Meg. Their bodies crunched. Probably from embarrassment, he kissed her. In jerking her face away, she knocked the glasses off one ear and they dangled from the other. There was nothing he or she could do; their arms were pinned. She felt a heavy foot on the train of her dress and the tearing of stitches, and she called out angrily, "Get off my dress, you punk!"

It was Don.

Someone appealed over the public address for people to take it easy and give them room. The carnation was snatched from Meg's hair by a girl she had never seen before. Some of her hair came loose. The dress slipped off one shoulder.

Then her arm was grabbed by someone who turned out to be a campus cop, and she was hauled sideways through the press of people. It bruised her arm, but it got her clear and to the Social Science building. She thanked him and ran inside and shut the door and burst into tears.

The girl who had been in the dentist sketch came over and put an arm around her and tried to calm her. She offered Meg some coffee from a Thermos and Meg drank a little of it.

She recovered enough to examine the dress. Two of the frills had been torn away from the skirt, but the fabric, amazingly, was undamaged—unlike Meg herself. When she took off the dress, her arms and legs were speckled with red marks that would become bruises.

She got into the skirt and top and unfastened her hair and repaired her makeup. Outside they were dancing on the lawn, and she was not going to let this ruin her evening. No one would see her bruises in the dark.

She waited three quarters of an hour for Don to appear from the other dressing room. He did not come.

She went to the room the men had used for changing. Don was not there. One of the concert committee said he had left an hour before with José-Maria. He thought they were going to Jax, the bar up the street.

She couldn't understand his leaving like this without telling her. Had he taken offense at her remark made in a moment of panic and not meant personally? She went back to collect her things, and she could not keep back the tears. The girl who had comforted her before asked what was wrong this time. Meg explained. The girl said why didn't they go looking for Don? She got her coat and Meg picked up her gear, and they walked off the campus and up the street.

"Jax Bar, they said?" the girl inquired. "I think I must have seen it. It's kind of familiar. What did you say his name is— Don?"

Meg nodded. She was too upset for much conversation.

"That's Spanish, isn't it—like Don Juan?"

"No, just Donald."

"Like Duck?" The girl giggled. "Sorry! My juvenile sense of humor. Don Juan wasn't much anyway, I was told. He had this horny reputation and he was forever chasing the chicks, but my English Lit professor says he was probably impotent. What a drag!"

"Don isn't impotent."

"Hey, don't get me wrong. I'm just trying to help you relax."

"Thanks. I appreciate it."

Jax Bar was situated in the basement under a secondhand bookstore. They couldn't see much for the cigarette and pot smoke, but they approached the bar and Meg spotted him alone at a table under a flickering TV. His back was turned to them.

"That's him."

"Great! I'll leave you two."

"Will you be okay alone on the street?"

"It's only a block."

"Thanks."

"You're welcome. Don't lay into him. Make up, huh?"

Meg had her overnight case in one hand and the dress draped over her other arm. It must have looked odd, but she didn't care. She had found Don.

Softly she said, "Hi."

"Meg?" He looked up in surprise. "What happened?"

She put down her things and sat opposite him. "That's what I'd like to know, Don. I was waiting there an hour. You didn't come."

"I had to get José-Maria a cab. He's an old man. It shook him up, all that hassle."

"It didn't do much for me."

"I guess not. You didn't get hurt?"

"Some bruises. If you want to know, Don, I *am* hurt. Hurt that you went off like that without so much as mentioning it. Did I do something wrong? Was it the dancing?"

"The dancing was fine. Can I get you a drink?"

"Not here. How come I find you sitting alone in a bar?"

"I bought the old man a drink."

She kept her voice reasonable, but it took an effort. "Don, he isn't here anymore."

"I told you, Meg. I put him in a cab."

"Then you came back here?"

"Uh-huh."

"But you knew I was still at the concert."

"Sure. I was coming back. It goes on till twelve-thirty."

"Swell. What was I supposed to do all that time—read the bulletin board in the Social Science building?"

His eyes were on the TV screen. "You could have joined in the dancing. I don't claim exclusive rights."

So that was it. His independence bit. "If you think I would dance with other guys after you escorted me there, you don't know much about me. Listen, I got the message a long while back that you want to play it cool, at least in public. I haven't pressured you lately, have I? I just don't like being abandoned after . . . after . . ."

He turned and took hold of her hand. "You're right. It was a dumb thing to do. I guess I fouled up your whole evening. I'm sorry, Meg. I want to tell you that you were just incredible in the dance. Perfection. You know what the old man said? It was like being back at the *feria.* That's the highest compliment he could give. There were tears in his eyes, Meg."

"He was great on the guitar. It helped. Can we go back now? I'd like to dance?"

He glanced at his watch. "Give me a little longer. There's plenty of time. You sure you won't have that drink?"

She couldn't imagine why this sleazy bar attracted him. "I feel uncomfortable here—dressed like this."

"Go on back if you want to. I won't be long. Leave your things. I'll bring them along."

He sounded so casual, as if he didn't know how much the words hurt.

"I don't want to go out in the street alone."

"Then stay. I'm not forcing you, am I?"

They sat in silence for a while. She tried to account for his inflexibility. It didn't seem like a power thing—he wasn't enjoying her helplessness. Maybe the jostling after the dance had shaken him more than he cared to admit. Maybe he didn't want to go back among all those people. She wouldn't think any less of him if he told her. In fact, it would make him seem more approachable.

"I was thinking . . ." she began, but he put up his hand to silence her.

"Just a minute."

He was watching the TV screen again. The announcer said, "Next on NBC, the first of a new series on the subject of human fear from Gregory Laz, who brought you the highly praised series *Who's Master?* Stay tuned to Channel Four for *Never Fear.*" The commercials rolled.

"Don, is this the program you were—?"

"Yeah."

"Is *that* why you've come here—to watch it? But you're not in it, are you?"

"No."

"You told me they decided to use Sarah Jor— Oh . . ." Her body gave a twitch and she couldn't go on.

"What's the matter?" he asked. "Okay. Sarah's in it—just a minute or two of film. This program is the appetizer for the series. They show you clips from all the others. I'm interested to see how she comes over. I work with the girl. I have a right to be interested."

"You told me you saw the rushes."

"That's not the same thing at all."

She could feel her eyes fill with tears. This was the reason he had walked out on her. He didn't want to miss Sarah Jordan.

She got to her feet and reached for her case.

"Sit down!" he said, and it sounded to Meg like a snarl. "Don't act so dumb."

"Don, you know I can't watch. I can't bear to look at a spider."

"Nuts. This show is supposed to help people like you."

"I can't."

"You're jealous, aren't you? You think I have something going with Sarah? For Christ's sake!"

"I've had enough!" She opened the case, took out the fan he had given her, and flung it on the table. "You can take your ivory fan, and the damned dress you rented. It's torn in two places, but since it was your clumsy feet that did it, I'm not worried about it. Thanks, I don't need you to walk me home. I'd rather take my chances on the streets."

She slammed the case shut, turned, and ran up the stairs. She waved for a cab and got one immediately.

She didn't even look around to see if he had followed her.

9 Sarah's life was almost totally taken up with TV. There was so much expertise and talent around at rehearsals that she could not escape the pressure to make herself worthy of it. Naïvely she had started out thinking she might keep her research ticking along with an hour or two in the lab each day, but after a week she was in Jerry's office to say it was impossible. He could not have been kinder. He told her to forget about the project for the rest of the summer. He arranged for another student to take over the daily lab check. Any small anxieties Sarah might have had regarding her replacement's encounters with Don Rigden were allayed when she met the girl; she was six feet tall and a disciple of the Maharaj Ji.

Sarah spent hours on the web trying to think herself into the role of a spider. The mental jump Havelock had demanded was a leap in the dark. Paradoxically, it would have been easier if she had known less about spiders. If she had been prepared to explain their behavior in human terms, as people generally did, she might have convinced herself and Havelock and the viewers of America. But she could not accept that spiders were calculating or malevolent. Nothing in her studies suggested that their behavior was anything but instinctive. The intricate construction of the orb web was programmed into the behavior of the garden spider by evolution. It was not learned; the young spider separated from its mother would build a perfect web without example or instruction. If difficulties were introduced,

147

it made no intelligent response. Spiders were incapable of choice because they were driven by instinct. They could not "think."

So the jump was from intelligent to instinctive behavior. She could not make it.

She tried explaining the difficulty to Havelock. He said maybe she was trying too hard. He told her to take the afternoon off, get away from the studio for a while.

It was a Monday. She decided to call on Ed. She had missed the last two therapy sessions with the phobia patients.

She could not have picked a better afternoon to visit. Frank was about to brave the city streets and any dogs that might happen to be on them. His face lit up when Sarah walked in. He was really pleased to see her. So with Sarah on his right and Ed on his left, he stepped out along Park Avenue. They walked three blocks, turned left on East Seventy-ninth, and finished the adventure at the Metropolitan Museum, having passed without mishap two Afghans, a poodle, and a Pomeranian. They congratulated Frank and saw him onto a Madison Avenue bus.

Ed suggested they take a walk in Central Park to ease the tension they both had felt on Frank's behalf. Sarah put her arm through Ed's and told him how busy she had been at NBC.

"Is that bad?" he asked.

"I guess not. When it's over, I'll get back to normal living."

"You'll have lost nothing?"

"Some afternoons with you."

He smiled. "We can catch up. How about the more important things, like your research?"

"That's okay. Jerry's being very sweet."

"He has a stake in this, of course. How about the gliding? Last I heard, you were giving lessons to Don Rigden."

"He had to take a raincheck."

"You're not seeing him at all?" Ed looked concerned.

"We'll pick up again." She added, because Ed obviously was angling to know if the friendship had died, "He's not a quitter."

"But there's still a note of reservation in your voice."

"About Don?"

"Maybe about the whole project."

"You can read me, can't you?" She held his arm tighter. "I wish you were part of it."

"I wouldn't be much help with this one. It's not my field at all. Have you been watching Greg's series?"

"I saw the first two. It's a lot better than I expected."

"You saw the clip of our interview in the first program?"

She smiled. "That's the second time I've seen it and I'm still embarrassed by it. I tried so hard to make an impression on you."

"It didn't show. You were as cool as any professional, yet totally natural. Haven't you noticed how people act up when a TV camera is turned on them? I know that I do. And so do the giants of the industry. Carson, Frost—they all have their TV manner. You don't. You're totally unaffected, and that's so rare it could even be unique."

"It was the circumstances. It all happened so fast, I didn't have time to gear up for a performance."

"Whatever it was, it was hypnotic."

She laughed. "Ed, that's exaggerating it. Me in my lab coat talking about spiders wouldn't have that effect on anyone."

"No? How about Havelock Sloane?"

"Him?" Sarah shrugged. "He's crazy."

"Really? Why?"

They turned off the path and down a slope through trees to the lake, where it was quiet, and they sat on a rock and looked at the colors in the water. She told Ed about Havelock's production. She described the sets and the costumes and the plan to present people as spiders.

"It's exciting and original and I'm sure it has popular appeal," she said, "but, Ed, it isn't working. And the reason is me. I'm no good at playing a spider. I can't do it."

"He wants you to act—is that it?"

"He says it isn't acting. It's a matter of learning to identify, and I have an advantage over any actress because I know what motivates spiders and I've studied their behavior."

"So?"

"So I go up on the web each day and try to imagine I'm a spider. They say I'm getting better at it, but I know I'm not. The whole thing is crazy to me. I can't think myself into the character of a spider, because spiders don't think. There's no scientific evidence that they have the power to reason. If a fly hits the web, the spider doesn't think, 'Good, that's my lunch. I'll wind some silk around it to stop it from escaping and then sink my fangs into it.' It simply responds to the vibrations on the web. Its behavior is automatic. My problem is that I don't have that automatic reaction, and never will. But anything else is phony. Does it make sense, or am *I* crazy?"

"It makes sense," said Ed. He picked up a stone and tossed it gently into the water. They watched the rings multiply. "Like I said, you're a totally natural person, Sarah. That was a bonus in Greg's kind of program. Here, it's a handicap. Sloane is asking you to do something that conflicts with nature. It's a problem."

"It's impossible."

"Hold on—I wouldn't say that. Just for the record, let's get this clear: you don't object to playing a spider because it's a creature people despise?"

"No, that doesn't bother me."

"You want to do this program if you can?"

"Only if I can do it convincingly."

"Okay. See if this helps. Have you considered whether you have anything in common with a spider?"

Sarah frowned. "How do you mean?"

"Seems to me we have to find a starting point. Up to now you've gotten nowhere because each time you hit this problem that spiders are motivated by instinct. Let's forget that and approach it another way. Will you try?"

She could not see how this would help, but she wanted to cooperate. "I guess we have certain instincts in common with them—survival, the sex drive, protection of the young. Is this what you have in mind?"

"No. I wasn't thinking in general terms. I was thinking of you in particular."

"You mean *I* have something in common with spiders? They interest me, yes, but as for what you're saying . . ." Her voice trailed away as she tried to imagine what he meant. "Like my hang-gliding?"

Now he looked mystified.

"When spiders are young, they spin threads long enough to catch the breeze, which lifts them in the air," she explained. "They travel miles that way. Very high, too. That's how they migrate. As a form of flight, it's unique to spiders. Sloane is using some hang-gliding sequences in his film to illustrate how it works. So I guess that's one experience I share with spiders."

"It hadn't occurred to me, but you're right. My thoughts don't fit as neatly as that." He threw another stone in the water. "I'm no authority on spiders, but would you say they're self-sufficient, for the most part? They make their own way in the world without relying too much on help from their own kind?"

"I see." Sarah smiled. "You figure I'm a loner?"

"Circumstances made you one, little lady. Am I wrong—or do you keep most people at a distance?"

"Not wrong. It's a fair parallel. Anything else?"

"Well, there's the web."

She laughed out loud. "Come off it, Ed. That's too much! I live in one room in a brownstone on West Eighty-eighth."

"Sure. Don't be so literal. Your web isn't like the ones in Sloane's studio. It's invisible, but it works better than his."

Still smiling, she took off her shoes and walked to the water to dip her feet in. "Okay, I'm interested. Tell me about my web."

"As I see it, it's like this. There's an area around you—I'm speaking figuratively—that you make damn sure you cover pretty thoroughly. Anything happens, you want to know about it, right? You told me there are girls you meet for lunch, not friends but people who update you on what's happening around the university. Those are your lines out. You have this network of information. It cross-checks, so you get strong signals if anything comes your way."

"Like men?" said Sarah, enjoying the game. "All girls make it their business to check out the local talent."

"Right, but not with your thoroughness. Yours is as tidy as an orb web. Your meetings are regular."

"They were till I got caught up in TV," said Sarah.

"So maybe you're a little unhappy because you feel disoriented. You're getting out of touch."

That was exactly how she felt. She had not spoken to Vicky, her Tuesday lunch companion, or Stella (Friday) for three weeks. "Ed, I'm beginning to think there's something in this. Is there more?"

"I'm not sure. Only *you* know if this makes sense, but the female spider doesn't go in for steady relationships with the opposite sex, does she?"

"We *are* down to basics." But it was true. The men in her life had been studs. They had come for sex and taken it and gone. And she felt nothing for them. She hadn't wanted a relationship with any man until Ed came into her life. Broke in, clean through the web. If it had functioned properly, he would never have got near. "Maybe there's something in what you say. I guess there are parallels I hadn't thought about till now. But how can this help me?"

He got up and came to the water's edge. "If you really want to make a success of this program, give up trying to act the spider. You've tried and it doesn't work. Be yourself."

She approached him and studied his face. "I don't follow."

"These things we just talked about are central to your life style, right?"

"I guess so, now that you point them out."

"You act that way without really thinking about it. You guard your territory, check developments all around you—"

"And give no encouragement to guys," said Sarah with a grin. "You're saying I don't need to try because I already have the behavior pattern of a spider."

"Enough to work on, anyway," said Ed. "If you look at it positively."

"Ed, you're so right! Here I am, trying to fathom what motivates a spider, and I'm running my life on the same principles! This is what I need. It gives me something to build on." She put one arm around his neck and kissed him lightly. "You know me so well!"

He looked at his watch. "Time I was going."

Sarah stepped into her shoes and took his arm again. "Havelock should pay you a fee for this. You just solved his biggest problem. Things were getting pretty hairy in that studio."

He laughed at the aptness of the expression.

"Well, you know what I mean."

"Sure."

They crossed a small bridge and picked up the footpath again.

She said, "Havelock calls me Spider Girl."

"Does that bother you?"

"Not anymore. It did at first. I think I could even get to like it."

"The media will—I guarantee. You could be stuck with it."

"There are worse names."

"Don't I know it! Mine, for example."

" 'Edmund.' Yes, you mentioned that before. It's almost the only thing you've told me about yourself. Why don't you ever talk about your life?"

He looked away at the crowd around Bethesda Fountain. "It's my training, I guess. It could complicate things." His step quickened.

"Only with patients. You can talk freely with friends."

"Sure—if it comes up." From his tone, he didn't expect it would.

Sarah said, "Generally I'm pretty reluctant to say much about myself. Talking to you is different. Exceptional. By nature I'm a very private person. I keep in the shadows, like the spider."

"That won't be possible anymore," said Ed. "You're out on the web now."

"True." She sounded, and felt, dubious. "But I'm still kind of anxious."

"That's to be expected. Anyone in public life will tell you—"

"No, it's not stage fright. I know I can project myself okay. I'm apprehensive. I had control of my private world. I don't have control of this one."

He stopped walking and turned toward her. "Sarah, you have to let Spider Girl take over."

"I don't understand you."

"As I see it, we have just identified an area of your personality that makes some sense of what you're being asked to do. You must capitalize on that. Make it work for you. Maybe there are other things latent in your character that you can use. Find out what Spider Girl is like and what she can do for you."

"I'll need help."

"There isn't any more I can do. It has to come from you. What it comes down to, Sarah, is asserting parts of your personality that you may have suppressed in private life. You're coming out into the open, so you have to equip yourself. I'm sure you can do it."

"It's a challenge. There *is* one thing you can do." She took his hand. "It would help my confidence if you were there in the studio the day we start shooting for real."

"When is that?"

"It should be Friday. But I guess you have patients to see."

"I do, but"—he started walking again, keeping hold of her hand—"I'd like to help. I'll see if I can reschedule my appointments. Besides, I want to meet Spider Girl myself."

‡ ‡ ‡

She began by treating it as a game. She had always enjoyed this kind of thing. She regularly read her horoscope in magazines (she was a Scorpio), and whenever she saw one of those personality tests—"How Tolerant Are You?" or "Are You Superstitious?"—she went through it in high anticipation of self-enlightenment. In the same spirit she wanted to see how she measured up as Spider Girl.

The web amused her most. She could believe in herself as the female controlling her territory, which the male invaded only at her pleasure or his peril. She thought of Don Rigden's laborious attempts to get near, and it made her smile to picture him left dangling on the end of a thread.

Because it was amusing, she was attracted. And because it was based on real observation of her character, she found it stimulating. She was flattered. No one before Ed had troubled to analyze her so closely.

She slept well that night. The next morning, in the studio, she went on the web and rehearsed a sequence with a drama-school boy who was supposed to be playing the part of a housefly that gets caught in the web. Instead of trying to project herself into the character of a spider reacting to the capture of its prey, Sarah decided to do as Ed had suggested: act on her own impulses.

The web had been strung in a different position. It was now almost horizontal, which made it possible to move across it more naturally, instead of coming down feet first. An overhead camera would create the illusion of verticality. Sarah crossed to her crevice and waited out of sight while Havelock explained what he wanted. It took longer than necessary because the boy kept interrupting with questions. He had a plump, well-cared-for look, and he wanted it known that he had studied the Method.

Sarah had not spoken to him. She crouched in her hideout, massaging a leg that was threatening to cramp.

A long time was spent in working out the way the boy would get onto the web. Finally it was agreed he would jump from a hoist and they would film the drop in slow motion to simulate flight. He tried it a couple of times before he got the idea of diving into the web. Then he thought he could do it better if he tried it a few more times.

Each time he hit the web its trampoline effect gave Sarah a series of violent jerks and rasped the signal thread against her thigh. She could feel it burn through her tights.

Sloane finally came to the limit of his patience. He said if the boy wanted one more try at the dive, he was welcome to go to his office on the fifteenth floor and try it out the window. Or else they would rehearse the full sequence.

So the boy was hoisted up again and performed his dive and hit the web. Then he revealed the second of his acting skills —wriggling, to try to get free.

Sarah let him have the stage a few seconds more. Then she attacked. She crossed the web in a rapid crawling motion and was on him. Her hands did not touch him. She used her teeth. The spider poisons its prey first.

The back of his neck below his hairline was pale, and it folded as she bit.

He yelped and his body twitched. One of his hands clawed the air under the web. He was not acting anymore.

Sarah grasped the hooked end of a thin nylon line fixed to a reel on her belt. She hitched it to the cotton of his T-shirt and started winding it tightly and rapidly around his shoulders, then down the body and around his legs. When the end of the line came loose from the reel, she brought it under his thighs and pulled it so hard that he rolled over on his back. He was wide-eyed and gasping. She hauled on the line again and he rolled over toward the hub of the web. She glimpsed the oval mark of her teeth starting to pink on the back of his neck, and she was pleased. She wound the cord under his hips, watching it tighten around his buttocks. He was wearing black jeans, but the line cut through the flesh like a wire through cheese. She held it tight a couple of seconds, then secured the loose end. She made sure he was incapable of getting free. Then she returned more slowly to her crevice.

"Christ!" said Havelock. "That really works. Someone untie the guy. Sarah, sweetheart, I thought you were going to make a meal of him right there, and so did he. It was totally convincing. I don't know what it was, but believe me, this is the breakthrough."

"It hurt," complained the drama student.

"That's show business, son," said Havelock. "No sweat—take a break till Friday, when we have the cameras rolling. Do it like you just did, and we should only need one take. Spider Girl, are you coming down? I have news for you."

He took her to the cafeteria and bought her coffee. The news was that NBC had fixed a spot on the *Today* show for August 11, the Monday morning after the airing of her main appearance in Greg Laz's phobia series. "They figure they have something hot on their hands, and they're right, only they don't know how hot. It's time to light the fuse, Sarah."

She nodded. Ed had seen this coming.

"There's a guy I'd like you to meet this afternoon. A journalist, name of Harry Dohn. He's free-lance, and the best feature writer in New York. Harry's work is syndicated worldwide. Now, I've told him a little about you, and he's interested. Basically the angle is 'pretty girl meets ugly spider and doesn't panic,' okay? But Harry will want to dig a little, give it some human interest, understand?"

"I guess so."

"Don't let him scare you. Tell him whatever you want. Simple things. What you think is trivial may be just what Harry needs. He'll want to show that you're like every other girl in America, with one difference: you can pick up spiders. So if he asks dumb questions, like what breakfast cereal you like best or what time you go to bed, humor the guy. It could be important. Would you do that for me?"

Sarah smiled. "Relax, Havelock. I won't bite his neck. Not if he keeps off my web, anyway." It seemed as good a time as any to ask if Ed could come and watch her filming on Friday, so she did.

"You have a shrink?" said Havelock guardedly.

"A friend. He's the guy who interviewed me about phobias."

"Him." He looked relieved. "Sure. Tell him to come along. He's welcome."

‡ ‡ ‡

Harry Dohn had a loud suit and a quiet voice. He was short, a little overweight, and about forty. His eyes were his most expressive feature. They were apprehensive and concerned, and they registered surprise at most things that were said. The rest of the face was forgettable except for its excess of color, the result, she guessed by his breath, of a liquid lunch.

Sloane introduced them and then left Sarah to show Harry Dohn the sets. His questions, as Havelock had predicted, were dumb.

"These are giant spiderwebs?"

"Right."

"And you're going to anchor a program about spiders for Havelock?"

"That's the plan."

"But you already did one program on spiders."

"That's right. For Gregory Laz. Only it was about fear. Spiders came into it indirectly."

"You handled them, I understand."

"That's correct. Would you like to see the sheet web next? It's a beautiful thing."

"Ms.—uh—Jordan, I think I've seen enough. Could we sit down somewhere, do you suppose? My feet don't cooperate too good in the afternoons. TV studios never have chairs—have you noticed? But I saw some beautiful armchairs in Reception. Shall we, uh—?"

So they took the elevator down and parked themselves on a leather couch behind a palm in a tub. Harry put on a pair of tinted glasses and took out a rumpled envelope for his notes. The tone of the questions changed.

"It's different things, acting a spider and talking about the things. Does that disturb you at all, Ms., uh—?"

"Sarah. Not in the least. I have a lot of respect for spiders, Mr. Dohn."

"Harry. Respect—for cannibals and killers?"

"It's a mistake to judge them by human ethics. They don't have the choices we do. They respond to certain signals, and that's it."

"Like the military obeying orders?"

"No. More like a computer following a program. They don't have the option of doing any different."

"And you admire that?"

"I respect it."

"What do you admire about them? Anything at all?"

She tried to think. "I like their construction skills. Their efficiency as hunters—"

"And killers?"

"That, too—only let's get this straight. I'm talking in spider terms."

"Sure, Sarah. You obviously have no problem identifying with spiders."

"I've studied them for years, Mr. Dohn."

"They should be so lucky!" he said unexpectedly. "Did anyone ever suggest you could find something more, uh, responsive to study?"

"Like men? I think the spiders have it right, Mr. Dohn. Theirs is a female-dominated world, as you know."

"That's something else you admire, then?"

She laughed. "It has certain attractions, but this isn't getting us very far, is it? You can't really compare our world with theirs."

"No?"

"Well, there's a basic discrepancy. We have the gift of reason. They don't."

"Okay. Now, tell me something else. When people call you Spider Girl—as you can bet they will—what will they mean by it?"

"That I'm not scared of handling spiders."

"No, Sarah. It's more than that. You get a label like that and you've got an image. That's what Havelock Sloane is counting on. How are you going to shape up when people figure you're half girl, half spider?"

Her answer to this was crucial. She must not start out by denying the image. She had to be positive. "I'd welcome it. It's a fascinating prospect. I mean, anyone can see how many arms and legs I have, so if there's anything in this, it's not physical, it's in my life-style. Actually, I have a lot in common with spiders."

"Go on. I'm interested."

"You just made my point for me," said Sarah, smiling. "You find it interesting that I admit to being Spider Girl. Every woman wants to be interesting, right?"

"Point taken." He made a note of it. "These things you have in common with spiders . . ."

"Plenty of things. If you really want to hear about it, I'm one of those people who don't go for bright lights and sunshine. I like the dark places, where I can merge with the background. I can keep dead still for a long time, watching things. But when I move, I go fast. I'm pretty aggressive."

He lifted an eyebrow. "I can't see that. I had you down as friendly."

"Try crossing me, Mr. Dohn. I bite."

"Yeah." He took off his glasses and peered at her. "I heard about that. Some guy on the web this morning got his neck chewed."

"That was in the script," Sarah said smoothly. "He was

playing the fly. I wasn't speaking literally. What I mean is, I have a kind of web which is territory I regard as mine. I built it and I guard it. Anyone comes near, he's in for a shock." Just then Don Rigden surfaced in her thoughts, and the concept of the web grew a little more firm.

"You built this web yourself?"

"It's the lines I put out to the world," she explained. "I started as a kid, with my relationship to my parents and family. Then I had to build a second line for school, and another for high school, and then one for college. I have a line for my graduate studies, another for leisure activities, and I just started one for TV. Some get broken and need repairing, but they're all interconnected and they make this structure that is my life." She looked at him and smiled. "Can you buy it?"

"Fascinating. So you see yourself guarding all this?"

"I keep it under control, yes. When something new touches it, I get signals. I study the vibrations, so to speak, and I know what I have to deal with."

"Like the next meal?" suggested Dohn with a grin.

"A spider doesn't actually eat its victims," said Sarah seriously. "It sucks them dry."

"Christ," said Dohn, "I like that, but I don't think I can use it. We don't want you to sound too sinister. You don't really think of people like that?"

"If you want to survive in the world, you have to know who can help you and what you want from them," answered Sarah, and she meant it. "Let's take you as an example. You landed in my web this morning. From the signals I get, you're not here to begin the courtship ritual. Right?"

"That wasn't in my plans, no. I'd be a little uneasy about getting away afterward."

"So I take a look at you," said Sarah. "Spiders are very discriminating. There are many insects they won't touch, like beetles, mites, woodlice, ants. If one gets caught in the web,

they jettison it. But I can see you have something I want, so
I approach you."

"What's that? What is it you want?"

She laughed. "A good write-up, Mr. Dohn. Guarantee that
and you might get away."

‡ ‡ ‡

That afternoon she left the NBC building early and called
in at the department to see how her stand-in was coping. It
turned out that she had gone home early, but Bernice informed
Sarah that the girl was doing a terrific job. "She's here early
each morning to check the spiders, and she stood in for Don
Rigden a couple of times when he was busy with that Amnesty
International thing. You heard about that? He did some Spanish dance with that brown-haired coed who used to follow him
around a lot. Meg-somebody. Anyway, she had no track record
as a dancer, but Don must have rehearsed her pretty good,
because their dance was a show stopper. Pretty little thing.
Nice body. You must have seen her around."

"Meg Kellaway," said Sarah.

"That's her. There's a lot of talk that she and Don broke up
after the concert. Isn't that sad? I mean, just when they should
have been on a high. He *is* a moody guy. Since you took off,
we've had hardly a civil word out of him. I thought the new
girl might turn him on, only she's a little too religious. She talks
a lot about joy and inner peace and she has this saintly smile
all day long. I figure she isn't his type."

"Is Jerry around?"

"Golf afternoon, sweetie. Listen, Jerry's got a great idea.
He's going to throw a party for the start of the new semester.
Saturday, September sixth. I know it's a long time off, but get
it in your diary."

"What's it in honor of?"

"Our link-up with TV. He plans to open the academic year with an exhibition of the sets from Havelock Sloane's spider special. You know Jerry—he doesn't miss a trick! He's inviting Mr. Sloane and Gregory Laz and all the big guns from NBC. It's sure to get a lot of coverage. He told me to make sure you keep the date free. You're our VIP these days. Now tell me all about the filming you've been doing."

When she finally got away, Sarah went to the araneology lab and let herself in. It was quiet there. She sat on a stool in front of the case containing the *Lasiodora klugi* they had named Pelé. But her mind was full of the news she had got from Bernice. Jerry's party was the perfect answer to a problem she had worried at fruitlessly for too long: how to persuade Ed to take her out again. It was ideal, an occasion they each had a strong reason to attend. And there was time to work on it, meticulously plan the way she would disarm him and show him she was his, and he need never again treat her like some patient with a crush on her analyst.

She already had a few ideas. His last words to her that afternoon in Central Park had been "I want to meet Spider Girl myself." Okay, so he was interested. Maybe even a little excited. She would not make the mistake of rushing into this. She would keep him in suspense. Aside from that, she wanted to size up the possibilities for herself. She could already see that if she handled this badly, she would lose all credibility. The interview with Harry Dohn had been a useful experience, but half the time she had not known what she would say next. She had to decide exactly who Spider Girl was, how she behaved, dressed, and talked. Soon there would be more interviews, including the *Today* show, when each word she said was definitive, like carving a statue out of stone.

She watched Pelé retreat into the cavernous hole at the bottom of the cage. She had always felt a certain sympathy for this particular spider. It was a single specimen that had already outlived all the others in the lab. It had been there when she first saw the place as an undergraduate, back in 1976. She had observed two of its molts, and it was probably fully mature now, but there was no mate for it. How and why it had been acquired by the department she had never discovered, because it had never been used in the research program. It was just a mascot, the one resident of the lab with a name of its own.

Without any clear purpose in mind, she lifted the lid off Pelé's case and picked up a stalk of grass with a budded end that the spider could get its fangs into. Jean Henri Fabre, a French entomologist revered among araneologists for his pioneering work with spiders, had once described the way to coax the black-bellied European tarantula from its lair by using a spikelet with a fleshy end. She speculated idly whether the method would work with a Brazilian mygalomorph, and inserted the stalk into the shaft, twisting it to resemble prey, a curious bee, possibly. It seemed Pelé was not fooled. She kept it there, trying various stabbing movements, but she could not feel the slight resistance that would have indicated success. The old spider was not to be drawn.

Maybe only a young female would tempt him out when he was not hungry. Maybe he was past caring.

She heard a door open at the end of the lab, and she withdrew her hand and closed the lid of the case. Don Rigden had come in. He was in a warmup suit. There was a tennis racket under his arm.

"Sarah, it's great to see you. I had some typing to pick up from Bernice and she told me you were in. How's the world of TV?"

"Hard work. So much rehearsing. I hope to be through in another week. I'll be glad to get back to normal living."

"Like appearing on the *Today* show?"

She shrugged. "News travels fast in this place. I don't have to ask who told you about that. I heard from the same source that you had a big success at the Amnesty International thing. I wish I had known about that. I like dancing."

"Really? Have you done any yourself?"

"Only as a kid. It stopped when I was so high."

"I wish I'd known. I might have conned you into being my partner."

"I don't know the first thing about flamenco."

"If I can learn hang-gliding . . ."

"Don, you're making me feel guilty. We must get together again soon." She watched the pupils of his eyes dilate, and she knew she had him on that thread. She smiled but noted mentally that she ought not to think in spider terms. It could narrow her scope of action.

"Are you free this evening? How about taking in a movie?"

She smiled across the cases. "Thanks, but I need the evening to catch up on myself. This sounds corny, but I really do have to wash my hair."

"Tomorrow? How about a disco? You like dancing."

"Don, please understand when I say that I'm really beat after a day at the studio. Raincheck?"

"Sure. Just so long as I'm not cut out by one of those whiz kids from TV."

She laughed. "Relax. They only chase guys."

10

"How about that, Doc? Pretty impressive, huh?" said Havelock Sloane.

"Extraordinary," said Ed Cunningham.

He had just watched the taping of the fly-killing sequence. He had seen it first from the studio floor where Sarah had asked him to stand. Then, at Havelock's invitation, he had gone into the control room to see how it looked from the camera positioned above the web.

They had tucked Sarah's hair into a black beret and given her black gloves. From above, under the powerful TV lights, the web was shimmering white and she was a black thing that moved with a speed and ferocity that was startling, frightening, and feral. The biting and binding of the victim was accomplished with horrific conviction.

"Shall we run it through again?"

"Thanks, but no. It made its impact the first time."

On the monitors now was the reassuring image of Sarah with the beret removed and her hair loose on her shoulders, talking to Rick Saville on the set. They were watching a production assistant untie the drama student who had played the fly. As soon as his arms were free, he touched the back of his neck and then examined his hand. Someone gave him a cigarette. He climbed off the web without assistance. He did not join Sarah and Saville.

"Okay, you guys," said Havelock through the intercom, "we can use that. We'll break till eleven-fifteen." He switched off

167

and swiveled in his chair. "First take. This kid is a professional. I like her commitment. She told me you get the credit for that."

Ed gave a shrug. "Not really. She's self-motivated."

"She was pretty anxious to have you here."

"So I gathered."

"You want to join her for coffee? Don't let me stop you. Judy, my gofer, brings mine back here."

"Thanks, I'll stay. I think Sarah has someone to buy her coffee."

"I'll get yours sent up, too." He arranged it with Judy. They were left alone in the control room. Havelock said, "It's good that she has you as a backup. The pressures are going to be pretty terrifying."

"I'm not her shrink."

"She's not your patient, you mean, but I figure you have an interest in the way that brain ticks over."

"Sure, I'm interested, but I don't have the influence you seem to imply. Any advice I give is strictly nonprofessional. She says categorically that she doesn't want an analyst."

"Hm. Maybe there was something in her past," Havelock speculated. "It's pretty obvious she needs support, even if she won't accept it on a formal basis. Must be hard for you."

"It is. This way I get the full emotional dependence you sometimes have to accept from female patients, but I don't have the structured doctor-patient relationship to help control it."

"She has a crush on you?"

"You could put it that way."

"What will you do, Doc?"

"The obvious thing is to back off fast, but I can't do that while she's under so much pressure."

"No. For Christ's sake, don't do that!"

"Besides, she interests me. You saw the TV interview she

gave me? I've no reason to doubt her account of her childhood terror of spiders; in fact I discussed it more fully with her later. Whether we class it as a phobia or a taboo doesn't matter. She overcame it without outside help, licked it to the extent that she actually chooses to work with spiders and is capable of identifying with them."

"That really is weird."

"Yes, but it's a reaction not unusual in phobia sufferers. We call it 'counterphobic behavior.' The patient becomes so attracted to the phobic object that she seeks it out repeatedly. This is often the case when they master the phobia without help."

"The girl has guts, that's for sure."

"She's quite ferociously determined," Ed went on. "I can understand the way it happened. The thing that intrigues me is whether there were any side effects on the personality. From my observation of phobia sufferers, I've noticed that conquering the fear isn't always the end of the story. There can be a secondary reaction. You see, the phobia sometimes serves a purpose of its own in keeping the personality in a state of equilibrium. Remove it and you set up a problem elsewhere."

"You're losing me, Doc."

"Phobias, fears, taboos, often represent deep conflicts in the unconscious. The guy who won't go on the street because he's terrified of dogs may unconsciously be punishing his wife, forcing her to be the breadwinner and the fetcher and carrier. If you cure the guy, his hostility to his wife may become more overt. The personality gains in one area, deteriorates in another."

"That figures," agreed Havelock.

"It's an effect that bothers me a lot in my practice. I don't want to solve one problem by setting up another."

"You think Sarah may have a personality problem?"

"I'd like to be sure that she hasn't, Mr. Sloane."

Havelock released a long breath. "Doc, I want you to know that you're welcome here anytime. Frankly, there's a lot of money staked on Spider Girl, not to mention my reputation. She's going to be terrific. You saw. Only—"

"You don't want her freaking out on you."

"You just said it. If the girl wants a shrink, I'll pay, no trouble. Okay, it isn't like that. You're not operating professionally. But it's still lost time for you, so if I can underwrite your expenses—"

"No way," said Ed Cunningham. "I appreciate the thought, but it's out of the question."

‡ ‡ ‡

Sarah didn't mind that Rick Saville called her Spider Girl when he offered to buy her coffee. The last time he had said it, the day she had first appeared in the studio, she had resented it. Now she took it as a compliment.

She was happier at this very moment than at any time she could remember. She heard Rick's small talk as they made their way to the cafeteria, and she made intelligible responses, but it was as if she were on a drug trip. She was high on success, the strongest dope. She knew for the first time in her life that she had done something superlatively well. And she could keep it going for take after take.

They found an empty table and Rick sat opposite her and leaned forward, his silver ingot suspended over the coffee, fixing her eyes with a steady, smoldering gaze no doubt tested and proved on the clipboard-carrying female section of the production team. His talk matched his look; it was an incantation of praise of her performance for the camera. But she didn't need to listen. She *knew* it had been superb.

"The look on your face as you attacked the guy—petrifying," said Rick. "The camera couldn't catch it from overhead, but we did on the studio floor. And, Jesus, so did that poor slob playing the fly!"

It had been superb because she had let it come from herself, as Ed had suggested. She didn't need to agonize anymore over the futile exercise of thinking herself into the brain of a spider. This was so simple. And she could keep on doing it.

"We go straight into the mating sequence next," Rick went on. "I can't wait to see how you handle that. It's been shaping up beautifully in rehearsals."

Spider Girl was no longer a part she had to act. It was a part of herself. And locating it, liberating it, was the most thrilling experience of her life.

"I must say that I'm kind of proud that Havelock chose me as the first to try out the mating ritual with you. I know it was a little rocky here and there, and you honed it up into a very smooth performance with that Hispanic guy from the drama school, but I won't forget you made your debut on the web with me."

It wasn't going to end with this program. There was the *Today* show. There would be press interviews. Radio. More television. Her agent would keep her fame flowing right through the long summer months.

"I watched your rehearsals closely. The ritual really generates some tension now. You know why? I wouldn't say this to Havelock, but it's pretty obvious to me that you directed that scene. Havelock didn't tell the guy the right way to vibrate the web, you did. You're in control, and it shows."

Spider Girl was dangerous and exciting. Women would envy her. Men would be attracted, but respectful.

"I don't mind admitting I envy the guy. I mean, it really looks like he knows how to turn you on when he drums that web with his fist. He has a good set of muscles, I can see."

"His muscles have nothing to do with it," said Sarah, switching on to the conversation. "Any guy would do who can make the right signals. The ritual is the turn-on, not the individual."

"So if I learned the routine . . ."

"You'd know how to have your way with a female spider," said Sarah with a ghost of a smile. "Isn't it time we got back?"

‡ ‡ ‡

Harry Shakespeare called her when she got home.

"Have you seen this afternoon's *Post*?"

"No."

"Go out and buy a copy, my dear. Buy a dozen copies and give them to your friends. You'll see why. Now, tell me how the filming is going."

"We're pretty busy. Today we shot six sequences in the studio. Havelock says he's happy so far."

"Are you happy?"

"Sure."

"I think we can add a little to your happiness. There's a lot of interest building up, Sarah. I'm getting regular calls from the press, but I want to hold them off until you finish filming with Sloane."

"NBC has had some inquiries, too."

"I'm sure. Now, listen. I don't suppose you thought when you started out that there would be merchandising possibilities in this. I got a call an hour ago from a young dress designer called April May—yes, it's a trade name. She's pretty big in the fashion world just now. She was featured in *Vogue* and *Harper's Bazaar* last month. April has seen your picture in the *Post* and she'd like to design some clothes for you to model as Spider Girl. Her idea is to get a spread in one of the big fashion mags featuring you dressed by April May, in sets designed by Ted Gorey if he'll do it. She's offering two thousand dollars and

ten percent of her fee from the magazine. And you get an April
May outfit of your own to wear on the *Today* show. Would you
like me to clinch it?"

"Please." Sarah was thinking already of her mother turning
the pages of *Vogue.* "How lucky can you get?"

"There are other offers coming in. Big offers from men's
magazines. But I'm not even going to ask you how you feel
about that kind of work, because any offer they make now will
be ten times bigger when you've made it to the top. You can
turn it down then if you like. If you agree, we might let Pro
Arts make a poster of you. It's time the blondes had some
competition. You'd have your clothes on for that one—a bikini
at least."

"I'm not sure yet if I want to do that."

"Fair enough, Sarah. Think it over. But the April May
suggestion needed a quick decision. She may call you tonight
to arrange to fit you. Now go out and get the *Post* and enjoy
page eight. I'll be in touch. Cheers."

THE SPIDER INSIDE HER
Henry Dohn

Take a long look at this girl. She has just set a fuse to 1980s
glamour. When the big bang comes—and it will be soon—you will
see the beauty world blasted sky high. As the smoke clears you will
see heaped everywhere the ruins of charm schools and model
agencies. Once-cool blondes will limp away, whimpering with
shock. Beauticians and manicurists, cosmeticians and dress designers will hobble among the ruins, fingers burned, eyes popping.

Sarah Jordan is 23 and she has natural flame-red hair. She has
gray-green eyes and finely shaped lips. She never uses makeup. Her
figure is curvy, her legs long. Is that so different, you ask?

What's different is that Sarah will show us something so obvious
yet so momentous that it will change forever the way we look at
women. Beauty with ugliness.

Sarah is beautiful. Sarah has a passion for spiders. Switch to a TV series called *Never Fear* on the NBC network on Saturday, August 2nd, and you'll see Sarah let a large black spider run up her clothes. You'll see her catch it in her bare hands and transfer it to a case where she keeps six others, in a university laboratory that houses hundreds, from hairy tarantulas to minuscule money spiders. She works with spiders.

Sarah knows spiders like Ms. Fawcett or Ms. Tiegs knows the lens of a Pentax.

I have news for Farrah and Cheryl and models the world over. Sarah is coming in.

And Sarah has done something no publicist or adman ever dreamed up. She has become a spider. Beauty in ugliness: an idea that will hit America like electrons hit the atom.

Spider Girl.

In September NBC will screen a $500,000 documentary that will star Sarah as Spider Girl. Dressed simply in black leotard, she will initiate America into the mysteries of the spider world by transforming herself into one of those creepy, hairy things you would not watch for five seconds, let alone an hour. But you will watch Sarah. You will see her build a vast orb web, move about it with extraordinary agility, catch a man-sized fly and enact the sensuous and sensational mating ritual with a male who risks death to perform it.

The concept of using people to play spiders is the inspiration of Havelock Sloane, winner of two Emmy Awards *(Action of the Tiger* and *Fire-Raiser)*. Sloane is convinced that Sarah is a spinner of success. "I couldn't make a program as daring as this without a girl of extraordinary quality. She's totally convincing as Spider Girl because it comes from inside. She *knows* spiders. She isn't repelled by their ugliness." Having watched Sarah rehearse on the giant nylon webs in NBC studio 8 last week, I believe every claim Havelock makes for her. She is beautiful and she has no mercy. She attracts and destroys. She is perfection and poison.

This quiet-speaking ecology graduate student from Cherry Hill, New Jersey, has a lot of respect for spiders. "Actually, I have a lot in common with them. I like the dark places, where I can merge with the background. I can keep dead still for a long time, watching things. But when I move, I go fast." She believes the female-dominated world of the spider is worth emulating. "Anyone comes near, he's in for a shock." After meeting Sarah, I'm prepared to believe that.

Spider Girl isn't just a TV gimmick. She has what Havelock Sloane calls "the genuine ability to immerse herself in something the rest of us are conditioned to think of as ugly, scary and creepy." The result is irresistibly exciting.

Girls, if you want to stay attractive through the 1980s you'd better throw out those expensive perfumes and beauty aids. Invest in a crocodile or a rattlesnake. Study the behavior of your ugly pet. Imitate its detestable habits. When a guy comes too close, bite. And don't be surprised when he likes it.

For Sarah, the future is full of promise. Already the communications industry is zeroing in. She is to be featured in *TV Guide* and she has a spot on the *Today* show. She has a confident, engaging manner that will make her a surefire television personality. And I can tell you that she will shock you and scare you, but she will never bore you. "I really do have the ways of a spider," she told me. "I'm pretty aggressive." I believe her. So does the guy who plays the part of the fly caught in Spider Girl's web. He has her teethmarks on his neck to prove it.

The videotaping was finished in another four days, and Havelock Sloane celebrated by taking Sarah and Greg Laz for another lunch at the Algonquin. Greg had shot some spectacular film of a stuntman building an orb web slung across a tower crane, with the Manhattan skyline as background. They had worked through the afternoon and into the evening and finished with the web in silhouette. There was also footage of hang-gliding over the Pacific, featuring a boy of sixteen who had competed internationally in the America Cup championships in Tennessee.

Havelock was bubbling with excitement at the prospect of editing the tape and film into a coherent program. He had decided to use Sarah as a voice-over, providing a commentary interspersed with electronic music. It would be two or three weeks before she was required to make the recording. "They'll be crazy weeks for you, Spider Girl," he warned her. "If you decide to go into hiding, we won't blame you. Only give us a number to call, okay?"

He was right. When she had started the project, she had assumed it would end on the last day of filming, and she would get back to her research. She intended to work through July, when most of the university was on vacation, and then to take a two-week break, possibly in California, sometime in August. It didn't work out that way.

Filming ended on a Thursday. On Friday morning she went to April May's, on West Thirtieth Street, to be measured. From there she was driven to Michel Kazan's for a shampoo and blow-dry, facial, manicure, and pedicure, all courtesy of Havelock's budget. At four P.M. she checked in at Abe Seltzer's photography studio on West Twenty-second, and enough shots were taken to feed the press until her April May creations were ready. At five-thirty she was in the Peacock Alley at the Waldorf-Astoria being interviewed by *Woman's Day,* and at seven-fifteen she met her escort for dinner at the Hilton, a free-lance writer named James Zlotowitz. She hoped for his sake that he was a big earner, because by then she was ready for a five-course meal.

It went on like that for two weeks. She didn't even have Sundays to herself. Harry Shakespeare would call on the phone at nine-forty-five sharp each day and give her the schedule. There were dailies, weeklies, women's magazines, teenage magazines, foreign magazines, and even, on one occasion, an ecology magazine. Yet it all seemed strangely unreal, because apart from the Harry Dohn feature, there was nothing to see for all the interviews she gave out. The magazines generally were due for publication at least a month later, and the newspapers preferred to hold the story until the week of the *Today* show, when the final program in Greg's series was due to be aired.

She soon got to a point where she could fit her interviewers into categories. Those she liked best treated her with high seriousness, putting out intelligent questions about the research she did and encouraging her to tell them some of the more remarkable facts about spiders. She made a point of giving them quotes they could use about the way spiders had influenced her personally. She particularly disliked the smart-ass journalists who were convinced the whole thing was a publicity stunt and tried to buy her enough martinis to pry a confession out of her. And she found that most female interviewers were predisposed to treat her as a head case; they made it clear that they had been pressured into the assignment. The "woman's angle" didn't take in spiders. As Sarah was not interested in discussing sexual equality or clothes, there was not much to talk about.

It was a strange time. Being treated as a celebrity was fun to a degree, but after a few days she began to see that these people didn't really envy or admire her at all. Some of them put on an act that she recognized as a routine right down to the wineglass stopped a couple of inches from the mouth to indicate amazement. A few didn't try. They treated her as what she was: another job to be got through. And that was how she began to think of it. Being lunched and dined in smart restaurants was pleasant, but it bored her. The questions, compliments, and promises bored her. She would have liked to provoke one genuine reaction, but that wasn't the purpose of the exercise.

She told Harry Shakespeare how she felt. He said he understood. "Work at it, my dear. Think of the good times to come."

There was precious little time in the day to think of anything. In bed at night her brain became hyperactive, and sleep was difficult. Maybe it was the food or the wine or simply the pace of her daily schedule, but her thoughts refused to go to sleep. What was the point of it all? Fame? She didn't particularly want fame. But she had no choice now. The features were written and ready for the press. Publicity fed publicity. The good times to come promised only more interviews, more nights without sleep.

The good time was over. It had ended the day they filmed the last sequence on the nylon web in the studio. Till then she had *been* Spider Girl. Now she could only talk about it. The searing intensity of those hours on the web was only a memory. Yet it had been a more real, more profound experience than anything in her life. She wanted nothing else.

At two A.M. one night she felt so unhappy that she picked up the phone and called Ed.

"I was asleep," he told her. "Is there something wrong?" He sounded more concerned than angry, and she was relieved.

"Would you talk to me? I'm feeling so low." She told him about the interviews and the publicity. "Ed, I've had enough, but I know I can't stop it. I have my schedule for tomorrow and the next day and Harry Shakespeare says there are plenty more in the pipeline."

"You want a break from it?"

"I want it to stop."

"It will. When it happens, it will be quite sudden. Then you can pick up the checks and get what you want—a new car, clothes, a vacation."

"What I want is unattainable."

There was a pause.

"What's that?"

"I want to keep on being Spider Girl. I really came alive on that web. It was a revelation to me. It gave me a sense of identity I never had before."

"It was an act, Sarah."

"No!" She was stung by the comment, so casually spoken. "I wasn't acting. I told you I couldn't get into the role of a spider. You must remember that."

"Okay. So we found another way to do it. And you were sensational. Only it's finished now. You have to accept that. It was a one-shot. It will never happen again."

"How can I make you understand? I was incomplete before this. There was a gap in my life. When I became Spider Girl, I was a whole person. I was fulfilled."

"Sarah, it's understandable that you should feel this way. It's a terrific experience to star on a TV show, and there's no question that you were brilliant in the part. Real life is bound to seem unexciting for a while after that."

"Life was never real for me before this."

" 'Real?' " His voice had a harder quality. "Nothing about this was real. People in tights playing spiders. Cobwebs made of nylon. Arc lamps and cameras and sound equipment all around you."

"What happened inside me was real."

"Listen, what you're suggesting is not just a delusion. It's dangerous, Sarah. You may think reality is dull or depressing, but you can't abandon it."

"Ed, I'm not losing my mind, for Christ's sake. I just want to raise my life to a higher level."

"So do millions of people. They try religion, philosophy, meditation, drugs. TV documentaries are something new, I admit."

"Are you putting me on now?"

"I'm trying to make you understand that this is crazy, Sarah. You were Spider Girl for a couple of weeks while the program was being made. It was exciting and exhilarating. But it's over. The media will still call you Spider Girl, and that's okay so long as you treat it as what it is—just a name. You're Sarah Jordan and I am Ed Cunningham and I'm telling you now to take something to help you sleep. In the morning I'll call Harry and ask him to ease up on the interview schedule. Then we'll fix a time to talk this over. I know I have to bear some responsibility for this, and I'm going to help you all I can. Will you do as I ask, now?"

"Okay. You will fix a time for us to meet?"

"Very soon."

"You're not angry that I woke you up?"

"No. I'm glad you thought of me. Sweet dreams."

"God bless."

She took a Seconal right away. She felt calmer for talking to him, but she was not convinced that he was right.

As she drifted toward sleep, she drew her knees to her chest, and in a short time she was in the cavity above the web, waiting for the signal thread to vibrate.

‡ ‡ ‡

Harry Shakespeare's call woke her at nine-forty-five. He told her he had heard from Ed Cunningham and he understood perfectly that she wanted a break from the press. He had canceled the two appointments set for that morning. There was a fitting at April May's at two-thirty, and he assumed that was still on (she confirmed that it was), and there was a change of plans anyway for tomorrow because Havelock was ready to mix the sound and he wanted her at NBC. The next engagement after that was the big one. The *Today* show on Monday morning.

‡‡‡

The outfit was totally unexpected. A white silk pantsuit, fitted as close around the hips as anything she had ever worn. A choker, also white, attached to the bodice by eight white silk strands that fanned over the plunge front to give the effect of a cobweb. Silver sequins sewn irregularly on the strands represented dewdrops. The master touch was the cluster of black sequins arranged on the left side of the bodice to give the clear impression of forelegs and palps and a head emerging from under the silk.

She adored it.

April produced sketches of other designs on the spider theme. There were two evening gowns, a night dress and companion negligée and pajamas. They would be made in black and white silk for her to model in the fashion-magazine feature. The pantsuit had been made first, for the *Today* show. It was agreed she could wear white pop socks and the black slingbacks she had bought for her dinner with Ed. After much consideration it was decided she would not wear a bra under the silk. She waited half an hour while they made some small adjustments, and then she left the salon with the suit wrapped in tissue in a bag. There was a cool breeze when she stepped onto West Thirty-fourth Street. She decided to walk as far as Fifth Avenue, looking in store windows, savoring her freedom.

‡‡‡

On Saturday evening she stayed in her apartment and watched the sixth program (hers) in the *Never Fear* series. She had not seen them all, but it was soon obvious why it was generally agreed that this was the best. It began with some predictable footage of creatures commonly feared—a snake, a rat, a bat, and a spider. Then Ed was on, explaining that less apparently disturbing creatures and experiences can induce phobias. He talked with that concise manner verging on curtness that she found so stimulating. In a series of short conversations with phobia sufferers, he coaxed some extraordinary information from them as coolly as if they were discussing the weather. He was shown at work with a patient, using the electrical-conductivity test, and then the program switched to Sarah's interview, and Ed's voice-over warned the audience that the film included an unscheduled incident.

She watched Ed more than she did herself. Hearing him repeat the questions he had asked her that morning in the lab, she felt the pulse beat in her neck and her lips went dry. She could not remember feeling like this at the time, but she saw now that it was a turning point. His questions were short and businesslike, but through them came the certainty that he cared. She could not have explained it to anyone else, but she knew. And that, more than anything, was why she had responded with confidence and fluency.

She needed him in her life.

The rest of the sequence, Rick Saville's accident with the case of *Tegenariae* and the business of recovering them, made no impact on Sarah. It might as well have been a commercial she had seen ten times before. She sat on her bed holding a pillow against her chest, biting the side of her hand as if it might stop the ache of her whole body for this one man in the world who understood her. She wanted his love. His touch.

Yet she was terrified of telling him, in case he became the psychiatrist, dismissing it as infatuation. Suddenly the credits were rolling and the phone was ringing. It startled her. She didn't get calls late in the evening. Of course—it had to be Ed, calling to make sure she was in a better frame of mind after seeing the program. They were entitled to indulge in some mutual congratulation.

In the split second before picking up the phone, she told herself this was not the moment to hammer him with the full force of her feelings. Not over the phone.

"Hi. Who is this?"

"Someone who just watched a superb TV show. Congratulations, Sarah. Terrific!" The voice was not Ed's.

She felt like hanging up. It was Don Rigden.

"I figured you were sure to be watching, only I didn't know if you would be home. Aren't you celebrating? You should be."

"You make it sound like a first night or something. It was just a TV documentary, Don."

"Hey, don't give me that! Starting tonight, you're in the big leagues. The papers are going to be full of you tomorrow."

"So what should I do—dance on the roof?"

"What *are* you doing?"

"As a matter of fact, I'm sitting on my bed, watching television."

"You're not even having a party?"

"Does it sound like it?"

"You're quite alone?"

"What is this—the Inquisition?"

"Sorry. I shouldn't have asked that. If you have company, I'll hang up. I just thought maybe—"

"Stupid!" said Sarah. "There isn't anyone with me." She was not answerable to Don for the company she kept, but she didn't want him making totally wrong assumptions.

"Really? Listen, I have an idea. You can't expect to go to sleep after watching yourself on TV? You need to shake the images out of your head. I'm going to pick you up in about a half hour and take you out."

"No," she said quickly. "It's nice of you, but—"

"Hold on. I haven't told you where we're going. You ever been to Legs, the disco near Broadway? It's the one place in

Manhattan where you should be tonight. Wait till you see the decor."

"I don't think so."

"It's cobwebs, Sarah. The whole place is festooned with them. The legs are spiders' legs. How about that?"

"I don't have anything to wear." As she said it, she thought of her April May outfit.

"For Christ's sake, don't insult me with that old line. Sarah, if you have a date already, just say so."

Before slamming down the phone she spat out four words: "Be here by midnight."

She had let herself be goaded into going, but he was right: sleep was out of the question for hours and hours. This ought to take her mind off Ed. She took a quick shower and put on the new outfit. It looked stunning. Perfect for the disco. She was risking getting it mussed before her TV appearance, but hell, clothes looked better for being worn a couple of times. She picked a perfume that was almost pure musk and used it liberally. Don was in for a jolt.

He buzzed at eleven-fifty and she came out to him, closing the door behind her.

He said, "Jesus!"

She walked past him and out to the cab without a word.

There was a notice outside Legs saying they were full, and it was reinforced by two uniformed security men.

"You wanna try someplace else?" asked the cab driver.

"No. This'll do." Don paid the fare and led Sarah up the steps. As one of the guards raised a hand, he said, "You know who this is? Miss Sarah Jordan, who was on TV tonight. The spider program. If there's a problem . . ."

There was no problem. The door was opened for them.

The heat and the heavy beat of the music hit them. It was big inside, but very crowded, and dark, except for strobe lights on the small dance area. He was right: it really was draped with huge webs and leggy spiders. They found two seats in a corner other people had overlooked or avoided under a furry eight-legged thing on a single line that stirred gently with the movement of dancers.

"What will you drink?"

"Champagne." She couldn't see his face too well, which was a pity. "Don't let them unload one of those 'sparkling wines' on you."

He went to order it and she watched the dancing. People were looking at her; the black sequins were flashing as the lights moved over her. Someone in a tuxedo and ruffled shirt approached. "It is Ms. Sarah Jordan? So nice to see you here. I'm Gil Borelli, the proprietor. You'll allow me to order you a drink, compliments of the management?"

"Thanks, but I have one coming."

"What was it? I'll have another brought over. Ms. Jordan, may I say what a sensational outfit you have on. You don't mind if our photographer gets a couple of pix?"

"That's okay."

"Marvelous. And the drink?"

"That was champagne."

A bottle of Dom Perignon arrived on a tray before Don returned, and the waiter poured her a glass. They took some pictures and then Don appeared. He stood back until she told him to come and be photographed. When the pictures were taken, they had a glass of the domestic champagne Don had bought, and then Sarah got up to dance. Don followed.

He was in a pale-gray lightweight suit and a dark-blue shirt with a white tie. He looked good and moved with the ease of a trained dancer. Sarah's dancing was restrained. She stayed in the same place, moving just enough to show that she was wearing nothing under the silk. It was pleasantly sensuous, reminding her of the courtship ritual of hunting spiders, the lycosid female, practically still, with the elegant male circling her, advancing and retreating, patiently parading. She was glad she had come.

They danced until nearly three A.M. and exchanged no more than a few short sentences, partly because the volume was so high, partly from a kind of understanding that the eloquence was all in the dancing—his, confident and expressive; hers, no less confident but reserved.

When they left, the proprietor thanked them for coming and got one of his staff to hail a cab.

As they drove through Central Park, Don rested his hand on Sarah's. She didn't move hers.

Outside her apartment building she said, "Coffee?" and he nodded and smiled. She led the way upstairs and unlocked the door. She said, "It's instant, I'm afraid. I don't have the real thing."

"That's okay by me."

"Kettle's through there. Would you mind? I should get out of this. It's my *Today* show ensemble."

She waited for him to go through the door of the kitchenette, then quickly took off the suit and got into a white bathrobe. On rapid inspection, there were no spots on the silk to bother about. She hung the suit in her closet. She slipped off her bikini pants and threw them in a drawer. Then she dabbed more perfume on her body.

She faced the prospect of sex coolly. She was not totally indifferent, as she had been with other men, but neither was she dizzy with desire. Any stirrings she felt were not especially for Don's body. They were inwardly derived, fueled by gorgeous clothes, dancing, and pampering. It amounted to a heightened sense of self. She was going to take him, just like the champagne, because it was gratification.

She called his name.

"Won't be a minute," he called back. "Kettle hasn't boiled."

"Switch it off and come here."

He was frowning slightly as he appeared in the doorway, but he said nothing.

"To me," said Sarah matter-of-factly.

He stopped a yard from her. "Yes?"

"I figure the coffee can wait, don't you?" She loosened the bathrobe and let it fall to the floor.

His eyes widened and dipped a fraction, but he made no move.

She took a half step forward. "I refuse to believe that Don Rigden is shy."

"You're extremely beautiful. Just looking at you . . ." He paused.

She raised her face to be kissed and their lips met, but he kept his hands off her body. It was a firm kiss, but it was saying something she refused to listen to. She turned from him and crossed the room. She threw the comforter on the floor and got on the bed. She cupped her left breast and looked at it. The sequins had left a faint mark on the skin. "I don't go in for the slow buildup. Just take off your things and give me what you came for."

"Like the coffee." He bent and picked the bathrobe off the floor.

"What does that mean?"

"Instant."

"Oh." She laughed to show that she took it as a joke. "That's the way I like it."

"I don't buy that." He approached the bed and dropped the robe beside her. "Put it back on, please."

She didn't move a muscle.

"Leave it, then." He shrugged and sat on the edge of the bed.

The humiliation erupted. "So now we know! The passionate Don Rigden has a problem. He can't get it up! Christ, wait till I tell all those sex-starved coeds hoping for a screw. Hey, it's the con of the century: half a university with hot pants over a guy with a limp cock if he has one at all! What a gas!" She grabbed the robe and covered her legs. "Why the hell did you come up here if you can't fuck?"

His eyes blazed. He grasped her right hand and pressed it over his crotch. "Just so you know. . . ." He got up from the bed. "Now, shut up and listen. I'm not willing to treat you as an easy lay. When you and I go to bed, I want us to make love, not screw. I want you, Sarah, more than you know. I want you forever, not one night when you're hyped up on success and champagne." He moved to the door. "You asked why I came up. It was to tell you what I just did—only I didn't figure it would be like this."

She looked straight ahead. "Yes, I can think of better scenarios."

He said, "It was nice at the disco. Let's remember that."

Sarah looked at him and said, "I'm sorry for those things I said. Won't you stay for that coffee?"

"No. If I see you like this a moment longer . . . The first time for us has to be different."

She said, "Come on," and rolled over on to her stomach so that she was naked again.

But the door slammed, and she was alone.

She cursed and reached for the light switch.

‡ ‡ ‡

She had her meeting with Ed on Sunday. It was sunny, so they walked in the park again. The heat of August had blanched the grass, and the smells of the zoo wafted across the mall. At the Bethesda Fountain, they stopped at a peddler's stand and he bought her a small enameled spider on a chain.

"It's a memento," he told her. "Whatever the media say, remember that Spider Girl was just a wild idea of Sloane's."

The media were saying plenty in the Sunday papers. The stories varied from accounts of the incident in *Never Fear* to news of her starring role in Havelock's show. They were supported by large pictures in the tabloids and quotes from her various interviews. 'I HATED THEM': SPIDER GIRL. The caption writers had really enjoyed themselves. SPIDER GIRL SARAH DROPS IN was typical, with such variations as SCARY SAREY and SHE'S OFF THE WALL. It was fun, but it didn't shake her conviction that Spider Girl could be a way of life.

"Ed, I wish you could see that it makes me a more positive person. It hasn't changed me and it won't. As you suggested, I simply identified areas of my personality that were spider-like."

"It isn't so simple. What we worked out was a way of thinking yourself into the character Sloane asked you to play. It was not a recipe for positive thinking. If you want to sort out your life, there are better ways of doing it."

"Like analysis?"

"It's not a dirty word, Sarah."

"To me it is."

"Well, if you want to keep analysts out of your life, don't indulge in dangerous fantasies."

"What's dangerous about it? I don't go along with this."

"It's a trap, Sarah. It limits your freedom. It cramps your thinking."

"That's where you're wrong. It gives a new dimension to my life."

"Television and publicity did that. Say whatever you like to them, only don't swallow it yourself. You are *not* like a spider."

"Tell me something new."

He took her arm and they walked in silence for a time. She was happy like this. They reached the Alice in Wonderland sculpture, and he glanced up at it. She said, "Don't you dare say a word about female fantasies."

He smiled. "Alice was a male fantasy. Freud could have had a field day with it."

"Are you a Freudian?"

"All psychoanalysts are, to a degree. He laid the foundations. Others are more illuminating to me."

"Who, for instance?"

"Jung, for one. He understood the role of the unconscious in fantasies and he recognized the dangers. There's a vivid passage in *Memories, Dreams, Reflections* where he describes the struggle to understand his fantasies. He faces them and analyzes them, but throughout he's afraid of losing command of himself and becoming—this was his own phrase—"a prey to the fantasies." He meant neurosis. Ultimately psychosis."

"I'm not scared of my fantasy, if that's what you think it is."

"But I am, Sarah."

"Does it really matter to you?" She spoke the question offhandedly, but it was momentous. She wanted him to say, in that forthright way of his, that he loved her.

"Would I keep on talking about it otherwise?"

"Tell me why it matters, Ed."

"Because I hold myself responsible. It was my suggestion that you look for spider tendencies in yourself. That was telling you to play with fire. I don't want you to get hurt."

"You really care about me?"

"I care about anyone in danger of psychological disturbance."

She turned to look at the sailboat lake. She would not let him see that her eyes had filled with tears.

He appeared not to notice. In a moment he said, "Did anyone you know see you on TV last night? I guess you got a lot of calls after it finished."

She turned. "Did you try me?"

"No, I was with friends."

It was another reminder that she was out in the cold. She didn't know a thing about his friends. They could be Bible readers or poker players.

She said, "Don Rigden called and took me out dancing."

"Nice. His idea?"

"Sure."

"He seems to be a nice guy."

"He can dance."

"You still resent him?"

"Why should I?"

"But you do."

"Okay, I admit it. I'm pretty mean to Don and I don't always want to be. He's nice to me. He's good-looking. Most girls would give their eye teeth to date him. But there's this hostility between us and it's all on my side. I guess it's a question of chemistry."

"No, it isn't that. There's a more obvious explanation."

Was he ready to admit that there was just one man she wanted in the world, and that was himself? "I'd like to hear it."

"No, you wouldn't. You'd accuse me of treating you like a patient again."

"Please."

"As you wish. On the most obvious level you resent Don because he's a rival and a threat. You were beautifully secure in your research project before he came along."

"I told you that myself."

"Exactly. You also told me something in your life that I

suspect is just as strong a cause of the resentment—your feelings about your dead brother."

"Marty?" She shook her head.

"Face facts, Sarah. You had reason enough to hate him. He was favored by your parents. His bad behavior was excused because he was superintelligent. They stopped your ballet dancing to pay for his private schooling. Each time you had a success, he topped it. You couldn't win. Then his accident happened, and you had nowhere to put all that resentment. He was still a winner. You couldn't bear a grudge against him now that he was dead. You turned it in on yourself and now you feel guilty. Right?"

She gave a shrug.

"But you succeeded in breaking out of that suffocating family where Marty had become a saint. You started building your own life at the university. It was a struggle, only this time you were winning. Then, out of nowhere came Don Rigden. Like Marty, he was younger than you and was said to be brilliant. Jerry Berlin treated him like he was the great white hope of the university. Your seniority and all your work were shoved aside, forgotten. What happened when Greg Laz arrived with his plans for TV? Don was brought in. It wasn't even mentioned to you. Hadn't it all happened before?"

"My feelings about Marty were transferred to Don?"

"Only this time the dice weren't loaded so much. You didn't need to sublimate your hostility. You could unload it on Don. And while you had been powerless against your parents, you were capable of fighting Jerry Berlin. You took them both on and you look like you're winning."

"If I keep my head?"

He smiled.

Sarah was stone-faced. It was not what she had hoped to hear, but she could not deny its basis in truth. She was taking revenge on Don for something he had had no part in. It was painful enough to be told things about her motives she had not deduced for herself, things that did her no credit, but to have them expounded by Ed was mortifying. He understood her too well.

"Does it figure?"

"Too well. I can't take too much of that. It makes me hate myself."

"Don't do that."

"Do you hate me?"

"Of course not."

"Dislike me?"

"On the contrary."

"Love me?"

He hesitated. "I'm not a young man, Sarah."

"That doesn't come into it."

"But it does. What you regard as love wouldn't fit my definition."

"I'm not speaking about sex."

He gave a faint smile. "You can if you like. I'm supposed to know something about it."

"It's not important to me."

He stopped and looked at her. "You really mean that?"

"I'm indifferent to it." She could see she had made an impression on him, but what was meant as reassurance obviously had him worried. She added, "Let's say I can take it or leave it. Only, Central Park on a Sunday isn't the place to chronicle my not too spectacular sexual adventures."

"Right." He smiled. "I guess it's time we looked for a cab."

"When will I see you again?"

"You're going to be busy these next few weeks."

"And you?"

"I'm ready for my vacation. A month in the Hamptons."

She felt abandoned.

"Jerry Berlin is throwing a party on September sixth. You're sure to be invited."

"I'm not much of a partygoer."

"It's to open the exhibition of webs from Havelock's production. It'll be a big occasion at the university." She watched him as she added, "Spider Girl's big night."

His face tightened. "Sarah, we've been over this. You've got to get this thing out of your head. It's finished."

If Spider Girl was finished, then so was their relationship. She was not going to let him go. He had admitted he felt responsible.

"It's not so simple, Ed. I can't turn it off. Anyway, you said you wanted to meet Spider Girl." She took hold of his arm with both hands.

"I saw enough in the TV studio. For God's sake, Sarah! You're a sweet girl, and this is poison. Leave it alone now."

" 'A sweet girl'! Who wants a label like that?"

He put a hand on her shoulder and gripped so hard that it hurt. "Is it psychotherapy you want from me?"

"I told you I didn't! You're hurting me."

"You're hurting yourself. Don't you think I know enough about you to judge the damage this can do to your personality?"

"Maybe the damage was done a long time back and is irreparable."

"I don't accept that." He relaxed his grip. "You really must put a higher value on yourself."

"That's what I've been doing. Spider Girl may be nasty, but she isn't cheap."

He sighed. "I don't think there's much point in going on with this."

She said, "If you think this is a gag, watch the *Today* show in the morning. I figure you'll be at that party on September sixth."

‡ ‡ ‡

Uncharacteristically, the interviewer was more nervous than Sarah. He had come in as a late substitute for Gene Shalit and he was new on the *Today* team. "I'm going to level with you. They brought me in because I'm the only available guy who saw the *Never Fear* program Saturday night," he explained as they got settled before the show. "The name's Sid—Sidney Berman. And naturally I've been reading the papers. They really have gone overboard for you, haven't they? You obviously touched a raw nerve with this spider thing. Now, I'll tell you how we handle this. No sweat—we'll keep it relaxed. I'm going to confess I'm a little jumpy about spiders, okay? Then I'll talk about *Never Fear*—we have a clip from the show—and that cues you in. I'll ask how you could bring yourself to handle spiders and we'll take it from there. You can be sure I won't miss the plug for Havelock Sloane's production. Any problems?"

"Not on my side."

"Great. That's a chic little number you're wearing, Sarah. Goes with the act, huh?"

"It's no act, Mr. Berman."

He twitched his mouth into a smile and looked at his clipboard. "Right—you're into research. Might be interesting to have some information about that, but keep it simple, right? Would you sit just there in the black chair? You're no stranger to NBC, of course."

She took her place opposite him and put her bag on the low table between them. The bag was black, tied at the top, and spotted with sequins.

Sid Berman eyed it. "Big enough for a fair-sized pet, huh?"

Sarah nodded and did not smile.

He gave another unhappy grin. "No surprises, please. We booked you, not the menagerie."

Across the studio, Tom Brokaw started the show and read an item about a Soviet defector.

Sid Berman fingered his tie and looked at the clock.

Sarah watched him without sympathy.

The first segment had run its course and now the cameras were on Sid Berman. "There was once a confident young lady by the name of Arachne, who lived in Ancient Greece, and she could handle a spinning wheel like nobody else in the land. Rashly, she decided to challenge the Goddess of Wisdom, Pallas Athene, to a spinning contest. The goddess didn't like that at all. She changed Arachne into a spider doomed to go on spinning for the rest of time. In the studio we have another young lady changed into a spider, by NBC. First, look at this clip from last Saturday's program *Never Fear.*"

On the monitor in front of them the spider case overturned once again and Sarah was seen picking up the fugitives.

"Meet Sarah Jordan," said Berman, "spider catcher and Spider Girl."

She looked into the camera.

"Speaking for myself," he went on, "in that situation, I would have been up the wall before the spiders. They scare me. How is it someone as pretty as you could actually do what you did in the film, Sarah—pick them up in your hands?"

She said, "Spiders are pretty."

Sid Berman put his hand to his face. "Well, that's an original idea. You really mean it?"

She looked him up and down. "Prettier than people."

"That's a little hard to take, but I believe you spend a lot of time studying their habits—spiders, not people. You're a doctoral candidate with a special interest in ecology. The clip we just saw was filmed in your lab. You had something to say about arachnophobia—the fear of spiders?"

"Yes. They scared me as a child. But I overcame it. Life is

like that—stages we go through. A spider has up to thirteen molts in its life. Each time it grows bigger."

"Sarah, this TV appearance has led to an exciting change in your life, I believe."

"That's right. I'm appearing in a major documentary feature about the life of a spider."

"Produced by Havelock Sloane, the two-time Emmy-winner. And he persuaded you to play the part of a spider. Would you tell me about that?"

"Sure. It's his idea to scale up the world of spiders to man size and use people to show how it functions."

"You move about on giant cobwebs?"

"Yes, it's fascinating to be a spider."

"It's not a part many girls would care to play."

"Don't make it sound like acting, Mr. Berman. This is documentary television. Anyway, why should it bother me?"

"Isn't the world of the spider pretty violent?"

"I don't find it so. There's killing for food, but there is in the human world, too. The fact that you have your killing done for you doesn't alter the fact that you feed on dead flesh."

Berman coughed into his hand. "That's a fair point, I guess. Turning to something more delicate—I believe you actually put the spider's mating ritual onto the screen."

"In simulation, yes."

"Tell us about that. I believe the male takes quite a risk."

"You mean slaughter by the female? It happens, but it's comparatively rare. They're pretty smart at getting away afterward. For me, the attraction of the mating is what happens before, when the male first gets on the female's web. He has to coax her by vibrating the lines, and several times she'll attack him for getting it wrong. It's very exciting. He has to convince her that he isn't prey. You should try it. After that, you'll never want a submissive female again."

"I'll take your word for that. You obviously enjoyed being Spider Girl."

"The enjoyment continues, Mr. Berman."

"The shooting hasn't finished?"

"It's finished, but Spider Girl is not."

"I don't understand."

"You wouldn't. There's no way you could find yourself on my web."

Berman grinned as well as he could. "You're implying that you're reorganizing your life to fit this image?"

"No. It's not a reorganization. More of an organic development. A molt." She smiled. "You break out of the old cuticle in which the body is enclosed. And you're bigger and more powerful."

He gave a laugh. "I wouldn't describe you as big or powerful."

"Not physically. Spider Girl is an attitude of mind. Mentally, I've grown."

"I'm still not too clear on this. Does it affect your behavior?"

"Naturally. I'm more decisive, more positive, and I don't tolerate invasions on my territory—from males or females. I watch and wait and attack."

"It sounds frightening."

"Spiders are—to most people."

"But fascinating, too."

"As I said."

"Sarah Jordan, Spider Girl, I'm not sure if you've just been stringing me along—" He stopped.

She had put out her hand to the bag on the table between them. The camera moved in. She appeared to be loosening the tie-string.

"—but I figure the viewers will make up their own minds."

Sarah reached into the bag and took out a Kleenex.

Sid Berman was no longer in his seat.

‡ ‡ ‡

After Sarah's *Today*-show appearance, the pace quickened. The papers and magazines that had interviewed her in the weeks before all chose this week to publish her story. *Time* magazine featured her on its "People" page with a photo taken at the Legs disco with the furry spider poised over her head and Don Rigden at her side. Don was not named; the caption read SARAH (SPIDER GIRL) JORDAN AND FRIEND. There were more press people wanting interviews. Harry Shakespeare sifted them. Small-circulation papers were out, and so were free-lancers. Big-name feature editors and column writers had a chance, but few others did. She had two long evenings of TV and radio interviews. She handled it all as she had the *Today* show, with total seriousness, and it was satisfying to find she was equal to every kind of challenge to her integrity. Flippant or sarcastic questions were simply turned back on the interviewers. The intellectual argument rarely arose, and when it did, she countered it with her own almost metaphysical assertions.

The publicity brought so many invitations—to parties, dinners, clubs, and colleges—that she had a card printed to decline them. She did attend a few campus parties, small affairs arranged by teaching staff and graduate students not on vacation. She wore April May gowns with the spider emblem, and she made a point of remaining in one corner of the room, watching and being watched and saying the minimum. She could depend on two or three men an evening trying their luck at making conversation, and it was no trouble putting them down. She always left early and alone.

One evening she was coming home from the Student Union building before midnight when she was conscious of someone not far behind. The steps were light and quick and gaining. She glanced back and saw that it was a girl, but the light was too poor to see if it was someone she knew.

Sarah stepped aside and looked in her bag, as if searching for a cigarette, and the girl caught up and said, "I want to talk to you."

"Do I know you?" Sarah asked.

"Meg Kellaway."

"Oh. I've seen you around."

"It's about Don."

"Of course! You're his dance partner."

"Not according to *Time* magazine."

Sarah laughed a little. "So you saw that. 'Spider Girl and friend.' It didn't say which was the friend—Don or the spider hanging over us. Shall we walk on? It gets cool standing still." She started walking again and Meg came with her. "What do you want, Meg?"

"I want to know how serious you are."

"Me? I'm serious all the time. I don't go for gags."

"About Don, I mean."

"Don? Is that it? You think you have exclusive rights or something?"

"I know that I haven't. He has plenty of dates."

"Do you check them all out?"

"You're different. You don't chase him."

"Do you?"

"There was a time when I did, just like the others. Then I found it worked better to let him do the running. He did, up to a point. He taught me to dance flamenco and I was happy, only he didn't want a full relationship. I couldn't work out why, until I heard he was dating you."

"Who told you this?"

"One of my friends saw you eating ice cream together."

"Deplorable!"

"One time he missed a rehearsal on account of some errand he had to make to you somewhere in the mountains. I couldn't understand what made him so interested in you. No offense, but he always said you were a man-hater, so I wasn't jealous of you working with him on research."

Sarah was irritated, yet intrigued enough to check her impulse to tear Meg Kellaway into small pieces.

"But on the night of the Amnesty International concert, when we danced the *seguidilla,* we had a bust-up and it was over you. He went to some bar to watch you on television. I'd done the damned dance with him and he didn't want to know me. I found him and gave him hell and walked out. We haven't spoken since."

"And now you miss him?"

"You guessed it."

"Why talk to me?"

"Don is nuts about you. If you want him, I mean really love him, he's yours and there's nothing I can do. If you don't, and you're just amusing yourself, I intend to fight you for him."

"Pistols at dawn?"

"Would you please be serious and tell me if you love Don?"

Sarah laughed out loud. *"Love?* What's that?"

"Are you sleeping with him?"

"Were you?"

"If you want to know, yes," said Meg. "And if you tell me he had dozens of girls before me, you're telling me nothing. I don't care about them. I care about now. You didn't answer my question."

"I don't intend to. It's my business—and Don's. Why don't you ask him?"

"I can't imagine what attracts him to you."

"Listening to you, I figure he was bored out of his skull," said Sarah.

"I can see why they call you Spider Girl. You're a man-eater, but I won't let you have Don."

"No?" said Sarah skeptically. "How would you like to learn a new dance to amuse Don, Miss Kellaway? Have you heard of the *tarantella?* If not, I suggest you get your ass around to the library in the morning and do some research. Then, if you care to take it further, stop me again some evening. Get along now. It's way past your bedtime."

11 In the last two weeks of August, the pressure eased enough for Sarah to think about research again. She knew the publicity would peak again in October, when Sloane's program was scheduled for airing, and she worked on her research for at least part of the time before then. On September 2, the Tuesday before Jerry's party, she arrived at the department building to find Bernice near to tears. "Jerry's a shit!" she told Sarah. "He *knew* the technicians would be here over the weekend putting up the webs for the exhibit, so what did he do? He arranged to go off on a fancy yacht for the Labor Day weekend. No one can reach him. They were calling *me* at home all Saturday and Sunday asking if it was all right to drill into the walls and the floor and the ceiling —as if I was responsible. I said you'd better do whatever is necessary, only don't leave a mess, and now the dean has just been in to say the cork floor in the main entrance is ruined and there's a crack in the ceiling and God knows what else he'll find as he walks around."

Sarah offered to take a look and, if necessary, to try to appease the dean. She was not acting out of loyalty to the department; personally, she agreed with Bernice's estimation of Jerry, who was dependable only in one respect: he vanished in the face of a crisis. What mattered to Sarah was to make sure no precipitate decision was made to cancel the exhibition. These were *her* webs.

As she anticipated, the problem had been exaggerated.

Given the size of the project, there was little damage. The dean's protest was a symptom of shock; the decision to mount the exhibit in the university buildings had been taken midway through the last semester, and the dean's memory was notoriously faulty. By the time Sarah caught up with him, he was reconciled to the change of scene.

It was spectacular. Now that they were out of that huge NBC studio and mounted in familiar settings, the webs looked markedly bigger and more sinister. The main lobby of the Administration building was dominated by a scaffold web. In the library a sheet web was slung from one side of the second-floor gallery to the other, above the readers' desks. Outside, an orb web ingeniously linked the campanile to one of the tallest lindens on fraternity row; the dean was convinced someone would be killed trying to climb it, so he was having the approach fenced off.

Sarah went looking for the orb web used for her main action sequences—the capture of the fly and the courtship ritual. A campus security officer told her to try the gym. She found a group of NBC people there, supervised by Rick Saville, still erecting the web. He spotted her at once and came over. "You timed it beautifully," he told her. "Who better to make the decision than Spider Girl? Look, we have to decide how to angle the web. You remember we had it almost horizontal in the studio and used an overhead camera, so you could move around freely? We figure we shouldn't do that here. We should go for accuracy and have it vertical. Only there's a problem: it's too big; or, to put it another way, the gym isn't high enough. All the other sites are taken. So what would you recommend —should we trim the web by lopping off a couple of spirals, or say the hell with fidelity to nature and have it tilted?"

"No problem," said Sarah. "You can tilt it as much as you like. The spider adapts the angle to suit the surroundings, and so can you. I've seen an orb web in the hollow of a large leaf, absolutely horizontal."

"I knew you'd have the answer." Rick hollered: "Okay, fellas, you hear that?" Then he said to Sarah, "They can go ahead now. They don't need me. How about coffee?"

She felt she couldn't refuse when Rick had apparently spent his weekend preparing an exhibit that was virtually in her honor. She still disliked what he confidently put across as charm, but she supposed it was understandable that a small man with a forgettable face should overcompensate, particularly working in television. This morning he was in a wine-colored velvet suit and pale-yellow silk shirt, open, naturally, to display the chain and ingot.

She preferred not to be seen with him in the main cafeteria, so she took him to the lab, where they kept a kettle and a jar of instant. No one else was around.

"The scene of my big moment on TV," commented Rick, looking around. "As I recall, you weren't overjoyed at the time, but when I knocked over that case of spiders, I also gave one hell of a push to your career as a TV personality."

"So I owe it all to you," said Sarah with irony. "And for thanks, all you got was insults. There's no justice."

"My reward is seeing you make it," said Rick. "I'm proud to have had a part in your success. You know, that blond guy your professor recommended really bombed. He was terrible."

"You mean Don." Sensing incipient rivalry behind Rick's remark, Sarah commented, "He's really nice. Just because people don't succeed on television, it doesn't consign them to outer darkness."

"Sorry. Saville screws up again. He's your guy, is he? I saw his picture in *Time* magazine."

Why did people keep making that assumption? "I just happened to go dancing with him one evening."

"You and he are not—"

"We work together. It's reasonable to meet socially from time to time."

"Sure. Why not? I take out girls from NBC. It's the civilized way to behave. They know I'm not serious. So what will you do now, Sarah? Talk to the spiders?"

"They don't have much small talk. I was thinking of going back to the gym to see if the web is in place. I'd like to be sure it's really safe. You know how it is in a gym. All the jocks will want to climb it. Come to think of it, I might climb up myself and see if I get lucky."

Rick Saville's eyes widened enough for Sarah to tell that her remark had made an impact. She had said it on impulse, and it was pure self-indulgence. Rick Saville held no attraction for her, but she found satisfaction in seeing him aroused.

When they got back to the gym, the job was done. The web was attached at the top to two of the beam supports at the center and anchored to the lowest rungs of the wall bars. Its white strands shimmered in the sunlight streaking through the windows on one side.

"Is it safe?" she asked.

"Try it. You're welcome," said one of the technicians.

She put her hand on one of the radii and tested the tension. The vibration traveled down her arm to her body. She felt a surge of energy like an electric charge. She reached for the outermost spiral and pulled herself up, kicking off her shoes in the same movement. She climbed swiftly to the center and stopped there for a moment, letting the web absorb the shock waves across its surface. It was good to have the pressure of the strands against her body again. It was not the same as when she wore the leotard, but even through the thicker denim the contact was stimulating.

"What's it like?" Rick called up.

"Just perfect. Why don't you try?"

"Now?"

"Come on up."

He hesitated, fingering the chain at his throat.

Someone broke the tension by saying, "There you go, Rick," and there were grins all around.

Rick had gone pink. "I, uh, figure there's no need to. I can see from here that the fellas fixed it okay."

Sarah smiled. "Pity. This may be your last chance."

‡ ‡ ‡

That afternoon she asked to see the guest list for the reception. Bernice was only too happy to produce it. "Is there someone in particular you want to check on?" she inquired.

"No. I'm just interested to see who's coming."

"It doesn't include people in the department," Bernice said archly. "They're automatically invited. That includes staff members and *all* graduate students."

"Fine." Sarah glanced through the list and verified that Dr. E. Cunningham was one of the names. "Do they have to confirm?"

"No. It's casual, but we know that Mr. Sloane and Mr. Laz will be here. If there's anyone else you would like added to the list, I could send out an extra invite, you know. Jerry leaves it up to me."

"Thanks, but there's no one." As she said it, she had a thought. "Wait. There is someone I'd like to be there. She's an undergraduate, but she's around, because I ran into her last week. Meg Kellaway."

Bernice was at a loss. "Meg—the girl who used to trail Don around. You want her to be there?"

"That's right."

"I thought you would come with Don."

"He hasn't mentioned it."

Bernice sighed. "Well, honey, I'll send an invite to Meg, if that's what you want. After all, it's your big night. Do you have something beautiful to wear?"

"Something I like."

‡ ‡ ‡

Ever since the night of the disco and its sequel, Don had made mental scenarios for his next meeting with Sarah. He had to expunge a nightmare. He was haunted by the image of Sarah stripped for sex, saying take off your clothes and give me what you came for. That was how clinical it had been. He had handled it ineptly, and he deserved every insult she had thrown at him. The one positive thing to be salvaged from that ruinous night was that she now knew he loved her. What her response would be, now that there had been time to reflect, he did not dare speculate on. He was left trying to contrive ways of meeting her that would give them both the chance of rebuilding confidence.

About nine Wednesday evening his phone rang. Sarah? He snatched it up. "Yes?"

"Is this Don Rigden?" A man's voice, goddammit.

"Speaking."

"My name's Cunningham, Ed Cunningham. I was on the TV team that visited you in the spring."

"I remember. You interviewed me."

"Yes. The shrink. This isn't about that, Mr. Rigden, not directly, anyway. It concerns Sarah Jordan. I believe you and she are friends."

"We work together."

"Of course. This is confidential, if you don't mind. I've seen

Sarah quite a few times since we made the *Never Fear* series."

"Is that so?" said Don coolly. It seemed unlikely. "Do you mean professionally?"

"Socially."

A man in his fifties? Don let him talk on.

"We had a couple of meals together, walked in Central Park a few times. I helped her find an agent. She also took my advice about her role as Spider Girl, and that's what concerns me, Mr. Rigden. You must know Sarah pretty well by now. Have you noticed any change in her behavior since she went to NBC?"

"I'm sorry," answered Don, "but I don't care to discuss Sarah over the phone with someone I hardly know."

"I respect that, Mr. Rigden. I'm not communicating as well as I'd like. Listen, I may be totally wrong, but I believe Sarah is approaching a crisis. As you know, she's been the focus of a lot of media interest lately. There has been heavy pressure. She's been through an exciting time as a TV star. And as Spider Girl she discovered a fantasy that released certain tensions deep in her personality. That needn't be harmful so long as she recognizes that it is only fantasy. My worry is that with all the pressure, she could lose her grip on reality."

"You claim to be her friend, Dr. Cunningham, but you're talking like her analyst."

"The two aren't incompatible. Would you tell me if you have seen Sarah lately? I believe you go hang-gliding sometimes."

"You seem to know a lot more about me than I do about you. No, we haven't gone hang-gliding since before the TV series. She's been too busy."

"But you've seen her?"

"Yes."

"And—it is important—was she acting normally?"

That image of Sarah naked flitted before his mind's eye. "I

thought I made it clear that I don't propose discussing her."

"I see. Maybe you'll let me give you my number. Then, if you feel she needs help at any time, you could contact me."

"If you like," said Don without enthusiasm. He took down the number.

"I respect your protective feelings toward Sarah," Cunningham added. "I feel a certain responsibility myself, and that's why I called you. I presume I'll see you Saturday night at your department's party. If you don't mind, we'll forget that this conversation took place."

"It didn't," said Don. "Good night."

He made himself some coffee and drank it black. Then he picked up the phone and dialed Sarah's number.

"It's Don. Isn't it time we talked?"

"I'm not sure what there is to say."

"Sarah, I'm not suggesting a post mortem on the other evening. You know the way I feel about you. I meant it. Would you let me take you to Jerry's party on Saturday?"

"Isn't that a little old-fashioned, Don? The modern girl doesn't get taken to parties. I have an invitation, same as you. I guess we'll see each other there."

"You're going with someone else?"

"I didn't say that, did I?"

"Cunningham—the shrink?"

There was a pause before she spoke. "Why do you mention him?"

"You've been seeing him a lot, haven't you—meals out, walks in Central Park?"

"What if I have? There's no law against it."

"You asked why I mentioned Cunningham, that's all."

"Have you been checking on my friends?"

"I happened to hear something. You hadn't mentioned he was your friend."

"I don't have to account to you for the people I meet. Has Bernice been gossiping again? That woman's a menace."

"Slow down, Sarah. This has nothing to do with Bernice. I'm sorry I mentioned Cunningham, but I'd appreciate it if you'd tell me right out whether you're going with him on Saturday."

"What makes you think I might be?"

"I happen to know he's very protective toward you. How you feel toward him I just don't know, but it's obvious he has a more than friendly interest in you."

"Why do you say that?"

"Because I heard him talk about you."

"When was this?"

"Never mind. But I think you should know about Cunningham. Just because he has silver hair, it doesn't mean he's decrepit. A lot of older guys go after girls in their twenties, and get 'em."

"I believe you're jealous."

"I'd just like to get things straight before Saturday. Do we have a date, or not?"

She answered in a controlled voice. "It's better if we don't. I don't blame you for anything and I'm not saying we can't be friends, but let's keep Saturday casual, shall we? I give you my word that I'm not going to the party with Ed. I don't even know for certain if he's going."

"He'll be there."

"Well, let's hope it's a nice evening, huh? And, Don, thanks for calling."

He immediately regretted having made the call. It had achieved nothing except to confirm that Cunningham really had been seeing her. This was pathetic, sweating over things said on the phone like some kid of sixteen. He could have any girl in the university he wanted. He could have had Sarah, only he wanted something more permanent than sex, and she, apparently, didn't.

The reason he loved her was that she was unique. To win her, he would have to forget what succeeded with other girls.

‡ ‡ ‡

The dress was from Saks and it was peacock blue. It had a small Oriental collar and a twist halter of two bands of silk crossing the breasts to a full, flowing skirt, leaving a bare back and midriff. Meg had never owned anything so lovely in her life, or spent so much on a dress. She had gone directly to Fifth Avenue on the morning she received the invitation, which could only have been sent at Don's personal request—Meg didn't know anyone else in the Ecology Department. What a brilliant way to make up: no embarrassing apologies, recriminations, promises. A simple invitation to a party. If she were still angry about the Amnesty concert, she could turn it down and no more need be said. But of course she wasn't angry; she wanted Don back, and here she was, arriving at the party in the most sensational dress she could find. The moment he saw her, he would know she was his.

She arrived soon after nine P.M. in the Senior Common Room, and it was thick with people she had never seen before. Someone took her coat and someone else put a glass of white wine in her hand and she was left with a group of television people asking who she was and what she did at the university. Don was not in sight, but there were so many tall men around, she could not see halfway across the room. She learned from the man monopolizing the conversation in her group that there would shortly be a tour of the campus to see the webs in their various locations. Don would have a chance to find her then.

‡ ‡ ‡

Havelock Sloane had already drunk more than was good for him. The moment Sarah had set foot in the Common Room, he had grabbed her, kissed her on both cheeks, and hauled her to the far end of the room to meet a group of NBC executives. She had no chance to see if Ed had arrived, but Don hovered nearby, clearly awaiting his chance to move in.

"Did I tell you there's a Spider Girl poster now?" said Havelock. Have you seen it, Sarah? We should have had it on display here. Give some of these guys a coronary just to look at you in a leotard."

"You haven't said if you like this outfit," said Sarah, straightening her jacket of black net with the April May spider motif in jet and sequins. It was worn over a sleeveless black crepe gown. The skirt consisted of the sheerest layers of the material cut to give glimpses of her legs as she moved.

"Sweetheart, it must be straight out of *Vogue.*"

It was. "Do you have a title yet for the program?" she asked.

"We do, and you'd better say you like it or I'll take your name off the credits," said Havelock. "It's *The Spinners.* Will it do?"

"I love it."

Over the babble of voices came one raised to make an announcement. Jerry Berlin was standing on a chair. "Friends, this isn't a speech, just a warm welcome from the university and my department in particular. Our excuse for this celebration is the opening of the exhibition of sets from Mr. Havelock Sloane's forthcoming NBC-TV production about the life of a spider, in which one of our graduate students, Sarah Jordan, is the narrator."

"And the star!" put in Havelock.

"He said he wouldn't make a speech," said Jerry.

"So did you," quipped Havelock.

"I'm here," Jerry continued, "to invite you good people to join me now in a short tour of the campus to see these quite sensational sets on display. Then I'm delighted to announce that NBC has arranged a closed-circuit preview of the program, which will be screened in the main lecture theater across the lawn from here. That's at ten-fifteen P.M. After that, we have dancing to music presented by disc jockey John Sutro. Have a great time, everyone."

Sarah slipped away from Sloane and his friends while they applauded Jerry's speech. She hoped she had also escaped from Don; she didn't look around to see if he was following. She zigzagged among bosoms, backs, and elbows, searching for Ed. She spotted Bernice with a pale, tense man, presumably the present husband or the next, and veered left to avoid them. People turned to stare at her and pointed her out to others as she moved past them, but she was used to that by now. She spotted the Kellaway girl in a blue dress, head turning like a radar scanner, as people started moving to the door.

Outside, someone put a hand around her waist and said, "Come on. You can't pass up the tour." It was Jerry. "I need your help. There are too many here to show around together. Would you act as guide if I divide the party into two? Most of them came to see you anyway."

In seconds she found herself leading a procession across the lawn to the campanile, where one of the orb webs was silhouetted against the evening sky. Inevitably, three or four trained tourists kept step with her and supplied a stream of questions. It meant there was no chance of finding Ed, but at least it insulated her from Don.

‡ ‡ ‡

Meg joined Professor Berlin's group, heading toward the gym. She hadn't come here to see Sarah Jordan playing to the crowd. She figured that Don was also likely to avoid Sarah since he had obviously come to his senses and decided Spider Girl was really venomous.

The group had not gone far along the cloistered way to the gym when some impulse caused Meg to turn. Standing alone by the Common Room door, looking quite desolate, was Don. She gathered her skirt and ran, calling his name, but she had not gone a few steps when she realized this was what she had vowed not to do: chase him around the park. She slowed to a judicious walk. She must not be so impetuous. That was the sure way to lose him forever.

He stood still, one hand clasped to the back of his neck, the other on his hip. He was in a beautiful gray suit, the first time she had seen him so formally dressed. Maybe that explained why she had failed to spot him before now.

"Hi," he said, sounding slightly surprised.

"Hi, Don. You look real smart."

"So do you. I couldn't believe it was you calling my name."

"You mean I don't always look smart?" she chided him, smiling.

"What I mean is I didn't expect to see you here."

"You thought I wouldn't come?"

"I didn't know you had any connection with the Ecology Department."

She smiled knowingly. If he wanted to be mysterious, so would she. Maybe he was too proud to admit he had sent the invitation. "I have my contacts. Aren't you going around the exhibition with the others?"

"I decided to skip it."

"You've seen enough spiders already, huh?"

He shrugged. "How about you? Don't let me hold you back. You were in Jerry Berlin's party."

"That was before I saw you."

"Yeah? I'm going to get another drink."

"That's a fine idea."

‡ ‡ ‡

When Sarah returned with her party, it was ten-ten, so she led them straight to the lecture theater for the screening of *The Spinners*. Inside, she rapidly scanned the faces of those already seated. Immediately she saw Ed between Greg Laz and Rick Saville. He must have arrived late and missed the tour. She felt a tingling rising to her skin.

Before she could go to him, someone took her arm. Havelock, swaying and breathing whiskey fumes in her face, said, "Spider Girl, I have a place reserved for you right here in the second row, next to me, only I can't find it. Would you help me to find our places? If some creep has parked his ass on my seat, I'm going to show him the door. This is my show and he can fuck off and get out."

"I'm sure there's no problem," she said, cursing her bad luck and steering him to the nearest available seats.

"That's a beautiful dress," said Havelock. He turned to the man on his right, a young assistant lecturer just appointed to the Ecology Department. "Isn't it a beautiful dress? Hey, don't look over there. You know who this lady is?"

"It's all right, Havelock," said Sarah in an effort to subdue him. There was no way she could get away from him without causing a scene.

Fortunately the program started on time and quieted Havelock. It opened in a way she would not have predicted—with a close-up of her face in profile. Nothing yet to suggest this was about spiders. Her memory picked up something Havelock had said weeks ago in the snack bar. *We're operating on another level of persuasion. We let them see you're pretty.* The focus · on her face softened. It sharpened instead on an orb web, glittering with minute drops of moisture that flashed with the changing colors of the spectrum. The web had been invisible between the camera and Sarah's face, and now it was diamond sharp. Then the trick was performed in reverse and the web vanished and her face filled the screen again. Slowly her head turned and the line of her hair moved across like a curtain. In the same shot the camera zoomed out to reveal her black-clothed body moving slowly and evenly across a web. The titles were superimposed and the electronic music increased in volume.

She heard her own voice say, "The orb web of the common garden spider is designed to last for a single day . . ." and there followed the sequence Greg Laz had filmed of a climber constructing a web inside the framework of a tower crane on the shoreline of the East River.

The audience was riveted for the entire fifty minutes. In its camerawork, direction, editing, there was no question that this was a landmark in documentary filmmaking. The shots were planned with a penetrating eye for the unexpected, yet the cutting permitted not a suggestion of self-indulgence. The commentary matched the visual content in sharpness of statement. Nothing was predictable or superfluous. Sloane had succeeded.

As the applause began and then mounted, Havelock leaned toward Sarah and said, "This is wrong. It's not theater. I'm not going to take a goddamned bow and neither are you." But people were leaving their seats to congratulate them.

For over ten minutes they could not move. Sarah was powerless to see whether Ed was still in the room. Havelock sat dully, allowing his hand to be shaken, until Greg Laz appeared and said a cab was waiting. Between them, they assisted Havelock outside. Jerry was standing by the car to pay his parting compliments to the great man. Havelock rested his hand on Jerry's shoulder and said, "Professor, you're a pain in the ass."

A voice close to Sarah said, "Good-bye to Berlin. How about a drink?" Rick Saville gave her his version of a winning smile.

She said, "Thanks, but I promised someone else. Would you excuse me?" She was gone before he could react.

‡ ‡ ‡

Meg had tried to persuade Don to miss the screening. "You don't want to give Sarah Jordan the satisfaction," she argued. "Stay out and let her see she doesn't have any hold on you. She's in there waiting to see if you come, like the spider she is."

He had said, "You don't know what you're talking about."

She had decided she had to make an issue of it. She hadn't come to the party for a repeat of that hateful putdown in Jax Bar. "Don, I'd better warn you. If you go in, don't expect to find me at your side."

His reply had been so casual that it hit harder than any insult. "See you around, then." And she was left at the bar. As simple as that.

She had stopped herself from running after him. She had ordered a gin and tonic. It gave her something to keep her there. The room had practically emptied as people left to see the program.

‡ ‡ ‡

Ed was outside the door of the Common Room talking to Greg Laz when Sarah finally found him.

"Little lady. We were talking about you. It was a knockout. Congratulations." He looked really happy for her.

"Well done," said Laz. "I claim a little of the glory for finding you. Will you let me get you a drink?"

"Thanks. Just a tomato juice."

"Ed? Your usual?"

"Great." As Laz left them, Ed said to Sarah, "That's a spectacular dress."

From the way he said it, she knew he didn't approve of the spider theme. "I'll never wear it again. It's pure *kitsch*. I'm going to stop dressing to please the media. Havelock didn't dress me in sequins and crepe."

"But you couldn't have come in a leotard," said Ed, "so what else could you wear? It's okay."

"If you think about it, the dress may be a good development," she said. "It could mean that I'm externalizing my spider feelings so they're just something I wear on the outside now."

"Now who's talking like a shrink?" he said, smiling. "Are you serious?"

If she was, she was not going to admit it. Until she was totally sure of Ed, she had to keep him in suspense about Spider Girl. The truth was that this evening was about reality. She wanted Ed for herself and he had never been featured in her spider fantasy. What she wanted from him was love. She said, "Could we get away from Greg when we've had the drinks? I'd like to talk to you alone."

Before he could answer, there was a movement behind her, and Don Rigden had joined them. "Hi, folks." He put his arm possessively around Sarah. "The elusive Spider Girl. How does anyone get to talk to you?"

She removed his hand from her waist. "Ed and I were speaking privately. Do you mind?"

"As it happens, I do. I've been waiting all evening to talk to you, and I think you know all about it."

Ed said, "I'll help Greg with the drinks," and he walked away before Sarah could think of a way to keep him there. She knew why he had gone: he still felt it was his duty to encourage her to be friendly with Don. It was so frustrating she could have wrung Don's neck.

She said, "You just screwed up my evening."

"He'll be back," said Don. "Listen, I want you to know that I didn't bring Meg Kellaway here. If you saw us together, it's because she was pursuing me."

"My heart bleeds for you."

"What's gotten into you, Sarah? Can't we get on the same wavelength? Haven't I made it clear I love you?"

"That doesn't give you any special rights. Maybe *he* loves me. Have you thought of that?"

"Cunningham? He's thirty years older than you. What can he do for you?"

"No less than you, apparently."

His face darkened. "Christ! Is that what this is about? Sarah, I thought I'd explained. I respect you. But if you really want—"

"I just want you off my back, Don. I arranged the invitation for Meg Kellaway."

"*You?*"

"Who else?"

"But why? What have I done?"

"I can't explain now. The feelings I have for you aren't what you imagine, Don. I was willing for you to screw me that evening in my room, but I could never love you. It's nothing personal. Now, would you leave me alone?"

"So you can go look for Cunningham?"

"Yes."

"You love him?"

"More than he or anyone knows. I'm sorry about Meg. Maybe if you went looking for her—"

"Maybe you should do that," said Don. "I don't mess around with people's lives." He walked away across the lawn.

She went into the Common Room to find Ed. The bar was at the far end. She had to edge through the dancers to get there. Greg Laz had only just been served, because there was a rush to get drinks while they lasted. The three of them found an empty table against the wall. She knew how it would be; for the next half hour people were stopping at the table to congratulate her on the program. Jerry; Bernice and her husband; Billie Shulman, the costume designer. For much of the time Ed was in conversation with Greg; there was nothing else he could do.

At last Sarah said, "This is ridiculous, Ed. I wanted to speak to you. Can we get out of here for some privacy?" She turned to Greg Laz. "Would you mind?"

It was cool outside and quite dark. She took Ed's arm and draped it around her shoulder, holding his hand tightly to keep it there.

‡ ‡ ‡

When the bar was filled again after the screening, Meg had decided to get her coat. "You're not leaving so early?" someone asked as she handed in her check. It was Bernice. Meg didn't want a conversation right now.

"Yes, I don't feel so great."

"Too bad, darling. Anything you need. Aspirin?"

"No, thanks."

"Don't you have anyone to take you home? Where do you live, sweetheart? I should remember; I addressed the invitation. You are Meg Kellaway, aren't you?"

"Yes. It's okay. I live nearby, in Gilmore Hall."

"Then it's no trouble for someone to walk there with you. How about Don Rigden? He's a friend of yours."

"No. Not Don. I'm fine by myself. Really." She picked up her coat. "Could you tell me something, please? Who was it that arranged for me to come to the party?"

Bernice helped her put on the coat. "I wouldn't bother your head about that, if I were you."

"I'd like to know. It wasn't Don, was it?"

"No, honey. It was a female."

Outside, Meg walked for maybe two minutes through the cloisters toward her dormitory. Then she stopped and sat on a bench against the wall of the Student Union, where she was alone and could think.

‡ ‡ ‡

Sarah told Ed, "I want you to take me home with you tonight."

"Just like that?"

"Ed, you've got to believe this. I've thought about it rationally. I'm twenty-three years old. That may seem young to you, but I'm old enough to know that this is not infatuation. And I'm not without experience. Nor am I drunk. I had one glass of wine and a tomato juice all evening."

"Hold on, little lady. I didn't suggest you were drunk."

"But you might. I can't leave anything to chance. I mean it, Ed. I really mean to share your bed tonight. No, don't start shaking your head. I'm not greedy for sex. I just want to know for certain that you care that much about me."

"Sarah, caring is one thing—"

She pressed her fingers against his mouth to stop him from speaking. "Will you hear me out, please? In the short time I've known you, I've told you just about everything important that ever happened in my life, but I know practically nothing about you—if you were married, divorced, widowed; if you have kids; what your childhood was like. I haven't asked. I won't ask. If you want to tell me, you will. All I want from you tonight is comfort, Ed. The comfort that will come when you let me through this invisible wall between us."

"You've got to put this out of your mind, Sarah."

"There you go again, blocking me out. How do I get through to you?"

"You have. You've made your intentions pretty clear."

"But you still treat me like I'm lying on your damned couch!" She pressed her face against his chest. "I'm sorry. I shouldn't have said that."

"It's okay. It's true. I use analytical techniques to keep that wall between us."

She stepped in front of him. They were under a tall tree at the edge of the East Lawn. "Why? Do you think my feelings about you are symptoms of some neurosis? Am I just a crazy with a crush on my analyst?"

"I've never suggested that. You're not crazy and I'm not your analyst."

"We're just two people who met?"

"I'll go along with that."

"Then would you treat me like a person, please? You have to admit I learned to control my fantasy. I haven't acted strangely this evening. All I'm asking is to be treated like a normal woman who has found the man she loves." She put her hands inside his jacket and around his back, pressing herself against him. "If you prefer, you could come to my place."

Quietly, but firmly, he said, "No."

She held him closer. "Sex isn't important. It's you I want."

"This can only hurt us both, Sarah. Let's leave it, huh?"

"If you wanted just to look at my body, maybe run your hands over it . . ."

Sharply he said, "Don't treat me like some impotent old man." He pushed her arms away. "Come on, we're going back inside." He took her arm, but there was no affection in the contact.

Sarah could not accept this. She had staked so much hope on this evening. Nothing had gone right. But if she had to fight, so be it. "I could ruin your career—do you know that? I'm famous, Ed. I say what I like to the papers and they print it. I could think up juicy stories about you and me, like how you forced me to believe I was a spider."

"Now you *are* talking like a neurotic." He walked faster. She was almost running to keep up.

"I mean it. I can get tough if you force me."

"It won't achieve what you want. Neither will the threat."

She realized they were heading in the direction of the parking lot behind the Senior Common Room. He intended to leave the party now.

"Why, Ed? Why won't you be kind to me?"

"You don't understand."

"For God's sake, help me."

He stopped. They were about thirty yards from the cars. Someone was watching them from there, hands in pockets, kicking the gravel.

"You see who that is?" asked Ed.

"Greg Laz? What does this have to do—"

"Why do you think he's waiting there?"

"I don't care. I'm not interested in Greg Laz."

"He's waiting for me," said Ed, and he spoke slowly, as if to a child. "I'm going to get into his automobile and he's going to drive me home to the apartment. My apartment and his. We live together, Greg and I. Do you understand?"

It was impossible. She couldn't accept it. She couldn't speak.

"I didn't want to hurt you," said Ed. "I'm not ashamed of my personal life, but I do keep it private, because other people react in ways they sometimes regret later. You're obviously shocked, and I'm sorry. I really thought until a moment ago that you need never know."

Suddenly it was cold and she wanted him to go. She took a step back from him.

"Sarah, will you be okay? We could give you a lift home."

Her belly started shaking and she took deep breaths. She was laughing in a strange, low voice.

He moved toward her, but she turned and ran back across the lawn, laughing hysterically.

Ed stood watching until she was lost in the darkness. Then he walked the rest of the way to the car.

"Shall we go?" asked Laz.

"We should never have come."

‡ ‡ ‡

She used her key to open the doors of the Department. There was no need for lights. She preferred the dark and she knew her way around. She opened the door of Bernice's office and took the key of the araneology lab off its hook above the filing cabinet. She glanced through the window to see if anyone was around, but they were all on the opposite side of the campus, where the dancing was still going on. Without stealth, she walked past the bulletin boards and schedules until she reached the door she wanted. She let herself in, leaving it open.

Then she began walking slowly between the benches, starting at the front end and progressing to the back, like an inspection officer reviewing the troops. Yet when Sarah had reached the last bench, she went back again, repeating the exercise in reverse. She was silent, absorbed in her thoughts. Again she turned and made the labyrinthine journey. She continued this way for a long time. No one observed her except possibly the inmates of the glass cases.

When she halted, it was at the case containing the Brazilian mygalomorph they called Pelé. The spider was in its nest, out of sight. Beside the case was a smaller cabinet containing Pelé's rations—large, live moths. She slipped back the lid enough to scoop one into her hand. Then she opened the top of Pelé's case and let the fluttering moth fall to the sand at the bottom.

She waited. The moth moved over the sand. After six minutes there was a movement under the stones forming the entrance to the nest. A pair of striped legs probed the outside. The spider emerged.

Sarah raised the top again and put her right hand in the case. She gripped Pelé's abdomen and lifted the spider out. The moth flew up and away.

‡ ‡ ‡

Meg Kellaway could not be certain how long she had sat on the bench by the Student Union. The air suddenly felt cold, and she shivered. She had to move. The faint strains of the dance music had stopped now. What time was it? She checked. Two-fifteen A.M.

She started walking along Busch Boulevard toward the dormitories, but she had not gone far when something to her left on the lawn outside the gym caught her attention. It looked like a mound of earth, but it was too large to have been made by a mole. She wondered if it was an animal in trouble and she went to look, but as she approached, it appeared to glitter darkly. She stopped and waited to see if it moved.

She went closer.

It was a black net jacket, neatly folded. It was decorated with black sequins. She lifted it and dropped it like a stone.

Underneath was the corpse of the largest spider she had ever seen.

She ran all the way to her room and locked herself in. She was violently sick.

‡ ‡ ‡

Sarah hung on the web and was comforted. She had asked for comfort and it had been denied; now she was claiming it in her own way. She had found the gym open and unlit. She had stepped forward in the pitch darkness with her hands probing the space ahead until they touched something. It was smooth and cordlike. That first contact as she slipped her fingers along the nylon rope was like a balm. She had never realized how powerful the tactile sense was as a source of comfort. The darkness intensified everything.

Now she rested on the spirals high under the gym roof, motionless, hunkered into a squat shape that covered the signal thread. She had discarded all her clothes except for her body stocking. She would not be wearing the April May clothes again. They were not only an encumbrance on the web; they were offensive to the dignity of Spider Girl. Havelock had been right: she hadn't needed dressing up. She had only to be herself.

Here in the dark she felt a stronger sense of self than she had ever experienced before. This was her web and she knew every radius and spiral. She drew strength from its resiliency, confidence from its symmetrical design. *While you are on that web, you have to become a spider.* It worked: her body felt different, less constricted. It was alive to new experiences, incredibly complex and beautiful vibrations. It reacted instinctively. And the force of instinctive reaction was so powerful that it annihilated rational thought. This was her refuge and she was entitled to it.

Time had no meaning on the web, so she had no idea how long she had been there when she thought she detected sounds below, as if someone had come into the gym and crossed the floor. She kept still, breathing evenly and lightly. She was not scared. This was the safest place in the world.

In a moment she felt a slight twitch on the signal thread. She tensed. There was a second twitch and then two or three convulsive jerks.

Someone had climbed on her web.

She waited for more signals. They did not come at once. There was an interval of almost half a minute. Then she felt a peculiarly faint movement, little more than you would make with a touch on one of the radial lines. It was followed by two more distinct pulsations, then another faint one. Two sharp. One faint.

The invader was signaling to her.

Her spine tingled and a pulse in her head began beating time with the rhythm on the signal thread. It was changing, becoming more intricate. Three sharp and fast. Two faint and slow. A pause. Three sharp and fast. At the same time a wrench on the web indicated a bigger movement, as if weight was being transferred to a higher spiral.

She was intrigued and her heartbeat quickened. The signals unerringly invited her to move down to the hub of the web. They were excitingly persuasive, so subtle that this had to be someone who knew the power of the signals. And their purpose.

Very well. Spider Girl would respond.

She waited for a pause in the vibrations. Without a sound she raced down the signal thread to the center.

There was a vigorous jerking as the visitor retreated. The web shook and then felt more resilient. She was alone on her web again.

She waited at the hub until all the vibrations stopped. She was acutely aroused. That pulse in her head was racing.

But the seconds passed and there was no fresh disturbance on the outer edge. She waited uncertainly for two minutes. Three.

Suddenly something hit the web with such an impact that she was almost thrown off. She gripped hard as the shock waves pitched her up and down. Before it calmed, she could tell from the stress on the lines where her would-be seducer was, below and to the right. He must have used one of the gym ropes to project himself onto the web with such force.

When she was quite still, the vibrations started again. She felt them with her hands and feet and the parts of her leg that touched the nylon lines. The rhythm was more gentle. It rippled over her flesh like shallow water on a safe beach. She luxuriated for a while, shifting her position to let it lap gently and evenly over her body. It made no demands. Sarah herself decided to move closer to the source because she wanted to feel the pulsations more intensely. She inched out along the radius.

The beat was heavier now and she was sure it had quickened. She strained to see ahead. She could make out a solid shape, but recognition was impossible. That was how it should be, she told herself. His rhythm was his identity. It said all that needed to be said. She was Spider Girl and she had a lover.

She crossed the spirals toward him and the vibrations got stronger. Her body throbbed with anticipation. It was the ultimate in experience, the most thrilling moment of her life.

She felt herself touched. His hand gripped her left wrist, then moved up the length of her arm, pressing it rhythmically and gently. It stroked her neck and buried itself in her hair. He was so close that she could feel his warmth, smell the vinegary tang of his body.

One of his hands covered one of hers and placed it on a line formed by a spiral, then slipped it gently across its width, and back.

The mating bridge.

She was ready. She drew the body stocking downward and eased it over her hips and legs, letting it drop into the void. Naked, she hitched her legs over the mating bridge with her knees bent and spread wide. She lay back on the steep-angled surface of the web, head toward the floor.

For him, this would be a difficult maneuver, but she was making no concessions. His technique had been faultless so far and she expected perfection.

He moved to a position higher on the web and put his hands on her knees. By degrees he moved them over her thighs and so down the length of her body. She moaned with pleasure.

He grasped the cord on either side of her head, and with one slow, exquisite thrust he penetrated her. The rhythm began and increased and came to its conclusion and Sarah learned the meaning of ecstasy.

He was breathing heavily from the combined effort of sex and literal suspense, but now that it was over, Sarah wanted to be free. She pushed at his chest. Her hand came into contact with a chain suspended from his neck. She followed it with her fingers until they rested on something small, angular, and heavy.

Rick Saville's ingot.

"Not bad, hey, Spider Girl?" he said as he eased himself aside. "Only next time we do it my way. In bed. Christ, I'm wiped."

It was intolerable. That cheap playboy she despised.

With an effort, she pulled herself up and freed her legs.

He was lying on his back on the web. Her web.

"But you have to admit I really had you in heat," he boasted. "I said I'd get it right. Remember?"

She was in no frame of mind to remember anything. Her web was being defiled.

"Hey," said Rick, "I like this now. It's like a hammock." He started the web swinging.

She moved toward him.

"Looking for more, huh?" said Rick. "Give me time, and you could be lucky."

She leaned over him and her hand felt for the silver ingot and gripped it tightly.

"Hey, passionate!" he chided her.

She forced his head downward and with her free hand grasped the stretch of nylon rope forming the spiral immediately above his head. She tugged at it and forced it under his chin.

Long hours on the web had taught her the strength of the recoil on those spiral lines.

As she moved aside and the rope tightened, she heard the snap of Rick Saville's neck. His body slipped down the web and crashed to the gym floor.

A spider will remove from its web anything that is of no further use.

‡ ‡ ‡

Ed Cunningham had taken off his shirt and was sitting in the apartment slumped over a chair back. "I'm bushed, Greg. Would you give me a massage?"

Laz moved behind him and began kneading his shoulders. "You still feel bad about Spider Girl?"

Irritated, Ed said, "I asked you not to call her that. Her name is Sarah."

"You figure it was a mistake to tell her about us?"

"I just wish it hadn't happened. It opens a whole can of worms."

Laz stopped massaging. "That's what you think about our relationship?"

"Greg, for Christ's sake, you know better than that. I'm talking about the girl. She took it hard. Now that I've told her, there's no way I can help her any more."

" 'Any more'?" echoed Laz with heavy irony.

"What do you mean?"

"Admit it, Ed—you really screwed that girl up. She has chronic delusions, not the least of which is that she could make it with you. That was all you had going with her. She didn't want you as her shrink. You were never in a position to help, because your relationship was based on a deception."

"Skip the lecture, would you?" said Ed. "Okay, I screwed it up. It's late. Let's hit the sack."

‡ ‡ ‡

When the phone rang, Don was showering, prior to getting into bed. He had drunk more straight scotches than he cared to count. He was still sober, but not from any intention on his part. He had wanted oblivion. It was his lot in life to be the guy who picked the drunks off the floor and helped them home. But his hangovers were as bad as theirs.

"Do you know what time it is?"

"Don?"

"Who is this?"

"Jerry Berlin."

"Jerry! What the hell—"

"Don, I'm speaking from my office. Would you come over here right away? Something terrible has happened, and we need your help. I can't discuss it. Just get here on the double."

‡ ‡ ‡

The light went on, and Laz was standing by the switch, in his shorts. "You're really in it now, shrink," he told Ed.

"What is it? I heard you talking. Must have slept through the phone."

"This'll wake you up. Your Spider Girl—sorry, Sarah—has gotten herself raped on that web by Rick Saville, and now he's dead."

"What?"

Laz crossed to the kitchen and poured a couple of drinks. He brought one in and handed it to Ed in a manner devoid of feeling.

Ed put down the glass, got out of bed, reached for his bathrobe, and wrapped it tightly around himself. "This is on the level?"

Laz nodded gravely.

"Hell—what time is it?"

"Just after three—if that makes any difference."

"Who called?"

"Berlin."

Ed picked up the drink and swallowed it in a gulp. "So what docs he want?"

Laz stared at him in amazement. "What do you think he wants, for God's sake? He's got a hysterical girl on his hands who's just been raped. He's got a dead body on the campus. He wants help. He wants you to take care of Sarah while we sort out what happened, and what to do about it. Start dressing."

Ed shook his head. "That isn't the way to handle this, Greg."

"Move your ass, man. They need us!"

"Will you listen to me? Sarah had a bad shock from me tonight, and she's had another from Saville. She doesn't need a third. I'm the last guy on earth she needs right now. I know what I'm talking about."

"You do? That girl was flinging herself at you a couple of hours ago, and now you say she doesn't want you to go to her?"

"How do I get through to you? She's in shock. If she saw me, it would reinforce the shock she had earlier."

There was still a baffled and angry look on Laz's face. "Ed, you must have *some* concern about the girl. She's been sexually attacked."

"Whose word do we have for that?"

Laz gave a shrug. "Professor Berlin's."

"Yeah—and who did he get it from?"

"Sarah, I guess. . . . Hey, what are you driving at?"

Ed poured himself a second drink. "I'm not sure if I buy it, that's all."

"Christ, you're a cold-hearted, cynical bastard."

"Thanks."

"Don't you have any conscience at all? I think I should drag you there."

Ed was tight-lipped. "If Sarah sees me, it will precipitate a crisis I won't be responsible for."

"The hell you won't! Who are you to talk about responsibility? You're abandoning that girl."

"For the sake of her sanity," said Ed. "Look, this isn't helping anyone. For God's sake, get dressed and go."

"And what do you suppose it will do for her sanity when she sees me?"

Ed picked up Laz's trousers and slung them toward him.

"You won't reinforce the shock. She isn't emotionally bound up with you. Go and see what state she's in, and if she needs a shrink, we can fix it, no problem."

Laz got into his clothes. "So what do I tell Berlin?"

"Whatever you like."

"And if the girl asks?"

"She won't," said Ed. "I know her."

"You won't ever see her again?"

"It's essential that I don't. She'll fasten on to someone else."

"Sure," said Laz, "and I hope for her sake he isn't a shit like you." He slammed the door.

‡ ‡ ‡

The office was thick with cigar smoke. The first person Don saw was Havelock Sloane, red-eyed and clutching a mug of black coffee, seated in Jerry's executive chair. He was wearing a yellow polo shirt and blue slacks. Greg Laz, in the suit he had worn earlier, was helping Jerry make more coffee. And in the armchair in the corner was Sarah, wrapped in a red blanket. She did not look up at Don.

"Don—thanks for coming so soon," said Jerry. He looked like a man under sentence. He handed Don a mug of coffee.

"This is Rigden, huh?" said Havelock. There was something different about the man. He had no hair. "Who's going to fill him in?"

Jerry said, "Take a seat, Don. Cigar?"

"No, thanks." There was only one chair unoccupied and that was the upright one beside the filing cabinet.

"Don, we have quite a problem on our hands," said Jerry. "It will help if we discuss it calmly." He glanced at the clock over the door. "Just over an hour ago one of the campus security officers was doing his rounds, and when he got near the gym he ran into Sarah wandering across the lawn. He asked if she was okay and she told him that there had been an accident and a guy was dead in there. The officer checked, and sure enough there was someone lying on the floor. It was pretty obvious his neck was broken. They called me and I got over pretty quick. I could see Sarah was very shaken, but she didn't want to talk except to tell me the dead guy's name was Rick Saville."

"He was my assistant on the *Never Fear* series," explained Laz. "And he worked on Havelock's project."

"I instructed the officer to stand guard while I talked to Sarah in the gym office," Jerry went on. "I noticed as soon as we got some lights on that the front of her body stocking was torn and she wasn't wearing shoes. Don, Sarah has been the victim of a sexual attack. Saville brought her to the gym on the pretext of showing her how he could move on the web. It seems he was jealous of the guys who were on the web with Sarah in Sloane's program. He was in charge of the crew that erected the webs earlier this week, and he had put in some practice. Sarah knew him from working on the production and she felt sorry for the guy. He obviously had some sort of personality problem, and she thought it wouldn't hurt to watch him showing off on the web." Jerry glanced Sarah's way. She had sat impassively through the account so far. "Saville persuaded Sarah to join him on the web and he tried to rape her."

"The lousy son of a bitch," muttered Havelock.

"Sarah knows that web better than Saville or anyone," said Jerry. "She put up a fight and managed to push him away. He lost his footing and fell. That's how he broke his neck."

"The idiot," said Laz. "He was always bothering women."

Don said, "Shouldn't the police be here?"

"We're coming to that," said Jerry tersely.

Sloane took over. "Don—if you don't mind first names—

we've been talking this over, Jerry and Greg and Sarah and me. We don't want to make a big production number out of this. It's a shabby little episode that could do a lot of harm to a whole lot of people. First there's Sarah. You know how it is with rape cases: the girl's ordeal isn't over when the son of a bitch gets off her. There's photographs. Statements to the cops. An autopsy. An inquest. Cross-examination. All kinds of shit. That's routine. Consider for a moment what Sarah faces. Spider Girl raped on her own web and killing the guy in self-defense. It's going to make headlines all over the world. Don, we'd like to spare her that."

"I agree, but I don't see how——"

"Hold on. We also have to think of the university."

"And the department," put in Jerry.

"This exhibit was staged to help you people," said Havelock. "My production unit wanted to show its gratitude for the help we got. A nice welcome to the freshmen and the students coming back for the new semester. Instead, what will they find? The campus crawling with cops. Half the staff under interrogation. A nice exhibit transformed into the scene of a crime. Are we going to have all that garbage dumped on this university?"

"Not if I can help it," said Jerry. "As soon as Sarah told me what happened, I saw how bad this could be for all of us, so I called Greg on the phone, figuring he was Saville's boss and he ought to be consulted."

"And Greg got me out of bed," said Havelock. "He knew I would want to be in on this. Don, there's a way to handle this that will get us all off the hook."

"Yeah?"

"It's simple. We don't mention Sarah to the cops. They look at the body and draw the correct conclusion: Saville slipped off the web and broke his neck. How did he get up there? He was drunk—Greg remembers seeing him knocking back straight vodkas early in the evening—and he climbed on the web because he was proud to have built it. He slipped. Simple accident."

"We don't owe anything to Rick, but it's nicer that way for his family," added Laz.

"What's more to the point," said Havelock, "it saves Sarah from all the heavy stuff. How do you feel now, sweetheart?"

"She doesn't want to talk," said Jerry. "But she'd be mighty grateful to have it handled this way."

"I'm not sure why you brought me in," Don said cautiously.

"You may be able to help in a small way," said Sloane. "First, do you agree that we shield Sarah from the rape story?"

He shrugged. "If you really think you can. How about the security man? He found Sarah. How do you keep him from talking to the cops?"

"It was Fred Holland," said Jerry. "You know him, Don? He's been here over twenty years. He's like a father to every coed on the campus. Believe me, Fred would go to the wall to keep Sarah out of this. He'll say he went in and found the body and reported it to me. Just like he did."

Don didn't like the way this had all been worked out before he'd arrived. "My brain isn't working at its sharpest, but don't you think the forensic people will find some evidence that Saville had a girl with him?"

"It's an accident, not a crime," said Havelock.

"Yeah, but if he was in the act of rape—"

"He had his pants unzipped, so we already adjusted his clothes."

"I see."

"But you're right about the forensic guys. They could find something we missed. A scratch on his face—though Sarah swears she didn't mark him—or maybe a hair on his shirt. It's possible—remote, but possible—that they could tell he was with a girl. No one saw Rick with Sarah. He stopped her outside, as she was leaving. So there's nothing to connect her with him. But just as a safeguard we decided she should have something to tell the cops. A kind of, uh—"

"Alibi?"

"Something like that."

"We want you to say you took Sarah back to her apartment," said Jerry. "Only if it comes up, of course."

"You two are friends. It's the most natural thing in the world," said Havelock.

"It's a lie," said Don.

"Look, this is no big deal," said Havelock. "There were plenty of girls at the party. Saville could have picked up any of them. You know, it's my guess that if they *did* suspect a girl was involved, but had no proof, they wouldn't press the investigation. They're human like us."

"Will you do this for Sarah's sake?" asked Jerry.

Don glanced at her, but she still seemed in a daze as to what was going on. "Is that what Sarah wants?"

She stared ahead as if she had not heard.

"She's in a state of shock, Don," said Jerry.

"Come on, fella—the girl needs help," said Havelock.

"She's not the only one," said Don.

"What do you mean?"

Quickly Jerry said, "He's right. The university needs help. Bad publicity will knock us hard."

"We've been over that," said Don. "I'm talking about Mr. Sloane's TV program. Isn't that what this is really about? NBC has invested a bundle in this. They won't be overjoyed to hear that the director's assistant tried to rape the star and got his neck broken. Isn't that what we're here to hush up?"

"Bullshit," said Havelock. "In hard commercial terms, a

thing like this would guarantee a massive viewing audience."

"Sure, but for the wrong reason. You're pitching for a third Emmy with this one. You don't want that kind of sensational publicity."

"Okay," said Havelock with a shrug. "Let's admit it: we all have a vested interest in this. Do we have your cooperation?"

While Don hesitated, Sarah unexpectedly said, "Don, would you do this for me, please?"

He turned to face her. He had never seen fear in her eyes before. "For you, yes."

Havelock heaved a massive sigh. "I knew we could rely on you, Don."

12 Classes began on Monday, September 8, with little to suggest the tragedy of early Sunday morning. Apart from a short paragraph in the *Daily News*, headed COBWEB DEATH MYSTERY, the only indication that anything had happened was the notice stating that the gym was closed to students. If there were detectives on the campus, it was hard to tell with so many new faces around. Bernice, who might have been expected to keep the department posted, was tight-lipped; all she would tell anyone was that the accident was being investigated and she was far too busy sorting registration forms to have noticed if the police had been in. The webs around the campus created the expected amount of interest for a few hours, and then people accepted them as part of the university scene. There were no reports of anyone climbing on them. Warning signs had made them strictly off limits.

It was early Tuesday morning when Jerry Berlin stopped by the lab to see Don.

"You alone?"

"Sure."

"Sarah?"

"I haven't seen her this week."

"I guess it'll take a few days. There's a slight problem. I just got a call from the police. There was an autopsy on Saville yesterday afternoon. They say his injuries aren't consistent with death by a fall from the web."

241

"What? We know he fell. Sarah told us."

"Right, but I can't tell them that, can I?"

"What's the trouble, exactly?"

"The lieutenant won't specify. He says he wants to interview everyone who was at the party. I've already asked Bernice to Xerox the guest list for him. So it's likely you'll be questioned. And Sarah."

Don shrugged. "I think I can handle it."

"It's purely routine," said Jerry, "and it'll take a few days, even if they have several cops taking statements. There were over eighty people here Saturday night. But it is important that you and Sarah agree what time you left the party."

"I must have left around twelve-thirty."

"Yes, but she was around until just before two-fifteen, when the body was found."

"Okay, if I'm asked, I'll say we left about two."

"Will you make sure Sarah says the same?"

"If I see her."

"You'd better call her. Tell her what's happening, but don't scare her. Just make sure you synchronize your statements. It wouldn't be wise for me to contact her. And, Don . . ."

"Yeah?"

"If you can manage it, say nothing to her about the autopsy report. We don't want to add to her anxieties at this stage."

Don doubted whether Sarah was the anxious type. Even after Saville's death, she had been well in control. But he agreed to do as Jerry suggested.

‡ ‡ ‡

This was the start of Meg's senior year. She knew how important the first classes would be, but there was no chance that she would get there for days to come. She was exhausted from lack of sleep. She kept the light on all night, and as soon as she closed her eyes and began to drift off, horrible images jerked her awake. Even if she had found the physical strength, she was terrified of going anywhere near the campus. In her own room she kept supposing she detected movements just at the edge of her vision, so how could she think of moving around the place where she had suffered the worst shock of her life? For her, the campus could be infested with giant spiders.

She had to hold on to her sanity. Distinguish facts from fears. There *had* been a sequined net jacket on the lawn outside the gym on the night of the party. It *had* been exactly like the jacket Sarah Jordan had been wearing. And there *had* been a huge dead spider under it. All facts.

She was not certain that it was Sarah's jacket. Or that there was any connection between Sarah and the dead spider. Fears.

Another fact: Bernice had said it was a girl who had fixed the invitation. Not Don. He had not expected to see Meg there. So it must have seemed to him that she had crashed the party with the aim of pursuing him all evening. Nothing could have been likelier to antagonize him. The way he had treated her, with polite, petrifying coolness, was understandable now.

The girl who had fixed the invitation could only have been Sarah. She had set her snare and lured Meg there, like prey.

Why?

It could only be to hurt her and destroy the last traces of her relationship with Don.

She had done it to get Don for herself.

‡ ‡ ‡

Don went out at lunchtime and called Sarah from a public phone booth.

"Yes?"

"This is Don."

"Oh." Her voice was toneless.

"How are you now?"

"Okay."

"We haven't seen you in the lab this week."

"No."

"I mean, no one's agitating. We expected you would need a few days to get over things."

"Things?"

She wasn't making this easy for him. "Saturday night."

"That's history. I've been redecorating my apartment."

So much for Jerry's theory about Sarah's state of anxiety. "So you really are okay?"

"Didn't I just say that? I'll show my face there later in the week. I hate the first week. All those kids straight out of high school."

It sounded as if she wanted everything settled before she made her entrance. "Sarah, Jerry asked me to call you. It's about the inquiries into what happened at the party. The police are interviewing everyone who was there. They're working through the list."

"So?"

"So they'll want to talk to you sometime."

"They'll have to wait. Tomorrow is my hang-gliding day." She sounded unconcerned. "You can come if you want."

"Thanks, but I'm tied up. Listen, we'd better make sure our stories tie in. Shall we say we left around two and took a cab back to your apartment, and I said good night and went home?"

"I'll buy that." Her voice had an edge of sarcasm.

He ignored it. "They'll probably ask if you spoke to Rick during the evening."

"That's a fair assumption."

"If Jerry wants to know when you can come in to make a statement, shall I tell him Thursday?"

"Whatever."

"Well, enjoy your hang-gliding tomorrow."

"I intend to."

" 'Bye, then."

She had already put down the phone.

Against all self-respect, all judgment, he still loved her.

‡ ‡ ‡

When he went to pick up the lab key from Bernice, she was taking an Alka-Seltzer. To make light of it, he made some remark implying she had been at Jerry's scotch bottle during the morning, but she said, "No, it's worry. It always gets me like this: I made a stupid mistake this morning, and I'm afraid to fix it up."

"Can I help?"

"Is that door closed? Well, Jerry asked me to photocopy the list of guests at the party on Saturday, because the police want to interview everyone. I did it right away, four copies, and put them on Jerry's desk. The police are already using them. Only I remembered just before lunch that there's a name missing from the list. Someone I invited after the list was drawn up. I did it as a kind of favor to someone in the department."

"Sarah?"

She was wide-eyed. "How did you know?"

"She told me. It's Meg Kellaway's name that's missing, isn't it?"

"That's right. What shall I do? I don't want to tell Jerry I added someone to his list."

"He must have seen her there."

"Yes, but Jerry's not that observant at parties. Besides, I

don't even think he knows her. He wouldn't have known if she was on the list. There was really no risk that he would find out."

"Does he have to?"

"What happens if someone mentions Meg's name in their statement? The police are going to ask Jerry why her name isn't on the list, and that blows it for me. I feel so stupid!"

"Can't you tell Jerry, appeal to his sense of chivalry by making a full confession?"

Bernice shook her head. "You don't know what Jerry's like just now. He's really uptight about the accident. He'll blow his stack."

"Would you like me to tell him?"

"No, I'll just have to sweat this out by myself. I figure there's a chance that Meg's name won't come up. But thanks anyway. You won't . . ."

"Of course not."

‡ ‡ ‡

Don's interview with the police was set for Thursday morning at eleven-thirty. He was leaving the Ecology building on Wednesday around five P.M. when a girl approached him and said, "Could I speak to you, please?" She looked Oriental and sounded like a New Yorker. She was pretty, but solemn-faced.

"Have we met?" As he said it, he remembered who she was: the girl he had seen a few times in conversation with Meg. Once, Sarah had mentioned that she seemed to be watching them.

"I'm Nancy Lim, but you don't know me. I'm majoring in math and I live in Gilmore Hall, where Meg Kellaway is."

"So it's about her."

She nodded.

"What is this?" said Don. "Is she sending messengers now?"

"No. She didn't ask me to see you. I came because some of us are very concerned about Meg. Did you know that she hasn't left her room since the weekend? She won't let anyone in. I have to talk to her through the door."

"Is she ill?"

"Physically she's okay, but she's very frightened."

"Frightened? Of what?"

"She won't say. She just says she had a terrifying experience."

He could understand that she had been upset at being left high and dry at the party, but he had tried to do it as gently as possible. To describe that as a terrifying experience was melodramatic, even by Meg's standards. "I'm sorry. You think I'm responsible, is that it?"

"No. I asked Meg if you had behaved badly to her. She said it was something else. She keeps her light on all night, and she's getting no sleep."

"Maybe she needs a doctor."

"We think she might talk to you."

"That's a little difficult. I'm trying to—"

"—cool her out? We know all about that. We don't want to interfere. It's just that none of us can get through to Meg. We're frightened, too, Don. We think she may be going out of her mind."

"Christ." He thought back to Saturday. Had it been so traumatic? He remembered that his prime concern had been to ditch her so that he could be with Sarah. He had not discovered how she had got invited to the party till Sarah had told him. Meg had come thinking she was his personal guest.

"Will you come?"

"I'll come, but I don't know if it will help."

When they got there, the door was locked.

"Meg, are you okay?" called Nancy.

No answer.

"Would you unlock the door, please? You have a visitor. It's Don."

They heard movements inside the room.

"Give her a moment to straighten up," said Nancy.

The door opened enough for Meg to peer out. She was pale and her eyes were red-rimmed. "Don?"

"I heard you weren't feeling so hot. Nancy suggested I might be able to help."

"You can come in."

She was wearing pajamas under a bathrobe. The room was devoid of furniture except for a bed, positioned in the center. She sat on it with her feet up. "There's a chair in the closet if you want to sit down."

He went to look. The closet was stuffed with items that must have furnished the room—pictures, books, two chairs, a tray, her desk. Even the curtains had been taken down and put there. He retrieved a chair.

"Don, I'm glad you came, so I can do some explaining."

He tried to be casual. "It doesn't bother me."

"I don't mean this. I mean at the party. I didn't understand at the time. You must have thought I crashed it. You see, I had this invitation."

"It's all right," he said. "I heard about it."

"She sent it."

"Yes. And you thought it came from me. I can see that I upset you badly. Like you, I didn't know about the invite."

"That isn't what frightened me. It was something that happened later, when I was on my way home." She described her discovery of the jacket and the dead spider outside the gym. "It was enormous, Don." She shuddered and closed her eyes. "You remember how even the smallest spiders scare me."

He couldn't make sense of what she had described. "Are you

sure of this, Meg? I mean, you've obviously been through a bad time. You don't think you could have imagined it?"

She said adamantly, "It happened."

"I don't disbelieve you, but shadows at night can do the strangest things, and if you're predisposed to be afraid of spiders, your eyes could make something out of some quite innocuous object. It's happened to all of us at one time or another."

"I tell you I saw the jacket she was wearing and I saw a dead spider the size of a tarantula. I know it doesn't make sense and I've been over it so many times trying to account for it, but I'm certain of what I saw."

"Why would she take off her jacket?"

"It was outside the gym. If she had taken it into her head to climb on that web thing . . ."

Was it possible Meg had not been told about Rick Saville's death? If so, it was better she didn't hear about it at this stage. But Don's brain pounded with possibilities. This story *had* to be the product of Meg's imagination. It was positively dangerous. If the police were led to believe Sarah's jacket had been seen outside the gym, they could draw really ugly conclusions.

"Don, has anything happened to her?"

"No, she's okay. It's you we have to worry about. Whatever happened, you had a bad shock."

"I need to know what happened, and why. If I could have it explained, I might get over this. As it is, I'm seeing spiders everywhere I look. I can't bear to pick anything up because of what might be underneath."

"It's your imagination, Meg."

"It wasn't on Saturday."

"It must have been."

"Would you do something for me? Check the lab to see if any of the big spiders are missing. If one is gone, we'll know it really happened. Please."

He gave a shrug. "If it will make you feel better."

"You will let me know?"

"Sure. Now, will you do something for me?" He opened the closet door and took a pair of jeans off a hanger. "Put these over those pajamas and walk down with me as far as the door. You can't stay in here forever."

"You'll hold my hand?"

"Of course."

She took the jeans and put them on.

‡ ‡ ‡

It was after seven in the evening when he entered the lab. He told himself he was doing this for Meg's peace of mind, but his heartbeat betrayed fears he would not yet admit to himself. He went straight to the cases at the far end containing the mygalomorphs. There were just five to check. If one *had* been missing since Saturday, it was possible that its disappearance would not be noticed, because they nested in tubes of silk out of sight under stones at the bottom of the case.

He saw at once that Pelé's food supply had not been touched, which was unusual for a spider that had long since gone through its full quota of molts. He lifted the lid and carefully raised the main stone that covered the nest. There was no spider.

Someone had taken Pelé from the case. There were not many people at the university capable of doing that.

He put the lid down and returned the lab key to the office. Then he walked quickly to the gym.

Somewhere on the lawn outside, Meg had found the spider under the jacket. Later, when Holland, the security man, had met Sarah at the door of the gym, she had been dressed, and she had shown him Saville's body. What had happened to the body of the spider?

Along the gym wall was a flower bed with various shrubs. He took a stick and started lifting the branches and probing the foliage. The light was poor now and he had to go in close to see anything at all.

After fifteen minutes or so he separated the leaves of a laurel quite close to the gym door and found a dark object lodged between the main stem and two branches. Carefully he lifted it out and examined it.

When he got back later that evening, he called Gilmore Hall. Meg came to the phone, and said she was feeling quite a lot better. He told her she was right about the spider.

He did not tell her its death wound was apparently made by a bite. From human teeth.

‡‡‡

Sarah drove back from Lake Pinecliff early Thursday morning, just as she had many times before. The gliding had been perfect—like California the previous summer. She had given herself totally to the experience, responding only to the laws of aerodynamics, functioning and mindless. At one with the birds and insects.

Conflicts that had disturbed and tormented her for years had lifted now. She could face the future calmly. She had recognized her need to let the deep, instinctive part of her personality express itself. Not permanently—there was no question of abandoning her rational self—but only when it pleased her. Obviously for sex. She knew now that Spider Girl was capable of fulfillment in sex that she, as Sarah, had not been near to experiencing. But it was more than a sexual fantasy. It was a refuge from so much that constrained her: pressures of family, the university, and the media; old wounds and new threats; moral implications; and conscience. When she wanted, she could block it all off.

She drove into the parking lot. Before she switched off the ignition, she was aware of someone beside the car. She lowered the window.

Don Rigden said, "Before you get out, can we talk?"

"Like this?"

"It's private."

She opened the passenger door and he got in and sat beside her.

He said, "I have my interview with the police at eleven-thirty."

"So?"

"Before I make my statement, I think I have a right to know what really happened on Saturday."

"What do you mean?"

"Sarah, I'd like to help you. Only you've got to do some explaining. The police don't know this yet, but your jacket was seen folded on the lawn outside the gym."

"Who saw it?"

"It doesn't matter. It's the truth, isn't it? And there was a dead spider under it. How did Pelé get killed, Sarah? You liked that spider."

"Has it been found?"

"I picked it out of a laurel bush myself. Someone had sunk their teeth into the poor thing. Why, for God's sake?"

"It's no loss," said Sarah evenly. "We're not using it in the research. It was just a pathetic old male. In its natural environment it would have been dead long before this. As for my jacket —sure, I covered the spider with it. I hated that damn jacket. I should never have worn it."

"But you must have picked it up later."

"Of course I did!" she said petulantly. "I saw it when I came out of the gym. I put it back on, and then I chucked the spider in the bushes before the campus cop found me."

"You admit you wanted to hide it?"

"Okay, I admit it. Now can we go in and start work?"

"Not yet." He gripped her by the wrist. "Don't you understand? This could link you with Saville's death. Maybe we can keep it from the police, but I have to know what happened."

With a curl of the lip, she said, "The full instant replay, huh? If you want to know, the party was a bad trip for me. I unloaded some of my anger by killing Pelé and covering him with that goddamned jacket. When I got in the gym, I took off my shoes and dress to go on the web. . . . Well, it's impossible in a skirt."

Don was incredulous. "You took off your clothes to join Saville on the web? Is it surprising he tried to have sex with you?"

"I didn't join him, as you put it. I was alone. He must have followed me."

"That isn't what you told Havelock Sloane and the others."

"It's unimportant."

"No, it's very important, Sarah. You were naked on that web and he came after you."

"If we're sticking to facts, I was wearing a body stocking. But only one fact matters in this: he fell off the web and was killed. If you want to subject me to the humiliation of telling all this to the police, you can. Some people get their kicks that way, I guess."

"For Christ's sake, let's not fight over this. There's something else you should know. The reason the police are interviewing everyone is that the autopsy showed Rick Saville's injuries weren't consistent with the theory that he just fell from the web."

A shiver went through her. "Who told you this?"

"They told Jerry. It's supposed to be confidential. I guess it means you must have marked him in some way, trying to fight him off." He paused. "It did happen like that, didn't it?"

"So they know someone was with him," said Sarah, ignoring the question. "Do you think they could trace me? Who was it who saw my jacket?"

"Don't worry. Someone who isn't on the list the police are using."

She couldn't tell why he was being so mysterious about this. "I'd like to know, please."

"It's better if you don't. Trust me."

Poor creep. He still cared. "What will you tell the police?"

"What we agreed, I guess. Someone has to make a positive statement that you were off the campus when it happened, or they're sure to be suspicious. It doesn't take Sherlock Holmes to link Spider Girl with a web."

"Will they want to talk to me?"

"You can count on it. Keep it simple, just like we said. I still think we can keep your name out of this." He opened the car door.

"Don."

"Yes."

"What did you do with Pelé's remains?"

"I put them back in the laurel bush."

"Maybe you could destroy them."

"I'll take care of it tonight."

"Thanks." She was not ungrateful. When this had blown over, she might even consider teaching him the courtship ritual. One male was as good as another.

‡ ‡ ‡

Now that there was a rational explanation for her nightmarish experience, Meg felt more in control. At Nancy Lim's suggestion, she came down for breakfast and had eggs and bacon. Nancy and the others had to get off to classes, so there wasn't much conversation. She didn't want to be fussed over.

When they had gone, she picked up a *Daily News* someone had left and took it back to her room to read. It took a few minutes before her eyes reached the inside page with the report headed

WEB DEATH: POLICE QUESTION PARTYGOERS

SEPT 10. The New York Police Department has mounted a full inquiry into the death of an assistant producer at NBC-TV, Rick Saville, following Monday's autopsy. Saville, 24, was found early Sunday morning with a broken neck at the foot of a giant nylon cobweb made for a forthcoming television documentary and rigged up in the gymnasium of Henry Hudson University, as part of an exhibition. The death occurred during a party held in connection with the exhibition. Lieutenant Thomas Flanagan stated that detectives would be questioning everyone who attended Saturday's party, and he appealed for assistance in tracing Saville's movements. The police had reached no firm conclusion yet on the circumstances surrounding the tragedy.

She dropped the paper. A man dead? Why hadn't they told her? Maybe the girls in the dorm had said nothing because they didn't want to add to her fears, but why had Don kept quiet about this? She had told him what she had seen outside the gym. Possibly it had some bearing on the case. Christ, was that why Don had kept quiet?

‡‡‡

Don's interview with the police was short and simple. He was seen in one of the small offices in the department by a young officer of Italian extraction whose name he didn't catch. "Did you know the deceased, Richard Saville?"

"By sight, yes. I met him when a TV program was being shot here in the araneology lab."

"The what?"

"Where the spiders are."

"Hm. Did you see Saville at the party?"

"Saw him, yes, during the TV showing. He was sitting next to Ed Cunningham, the shrink who worked on the first program."

"You didn't see him after that?"

"No."

"Did you go past the gym at any time that evening?"

"No."

"When did you leave the party?"

"Around two A.M."

"Alone?"

"I was with a friend. Sarah Jordan."

"The one they call Spider Girl?"

"Correct."

"You understand I have to get the details. Did you go back to your place?"

"Hers, on West Eighty-eighth. I said good night on the sidewalk and then went home."

"Too bad. Okay, we'll get this typed up and you can sign it. Would you come back after lunch?"

‡ ‡ ‡

Nancy Lim was back in the dorm at noon. Meg spotted her from her window coming across the front lawn. She hurried down to meet her.

"Could I join you for lunch today?"

"Sure. Feel free."

When they had filled their trays and found places at a quiet table against the window, Meg asked, "Why didn't anyone tell me about the guy who was killed at the party?"

Nancy answered in a level voice, "Because of your state of mind. We didn't want you any more scared than you were. Should we have told you?"

"Nancy, I've got a problem. The thing that scared me at the party may have a connection with the dead man." As calmly as she could, she went over the events of early Sunday morning.

"What a hideous experience!" said Nancy. "It's enough to blow anyone's mind."

"But do you see what I'm driving at? If Sarah Jordan's jacket was on the lawn outside the gym, it's more than likely she was inside."

"With the man who was killed?"

Meg nodded.

"On the web? I've heard of some weird ways of doing it, but . . ."

"She *is* weird, Nancy. She *believes* all that Spider Girl crap."

"If you're right, she must know how the man fell off the web, and she should have told the police by now."

Meg leaned forward. "But she hasn't. It says in this morning's paper they've reached no conclusion. They're appealing for information."

"I guess this would be bad for her image."

"Murder is bad for anyone's image."

Nancy gave Meg a long look and said, "Is there something else you know?"

"I thought it was common knowledge that after spiders have mated, the female kills her partner unless he's sharp enough to get away."

"God help us," said Nancy in a whisper.

"You don't buy it?"

"It's creepy. She'd have to be crazy."

"Isn't it crazy to kill a tarantula and take off your jacket to cover it?"

"Mm."

"What am I going to do?"

"You'll have to tell the police what you saw."

"Go to them?"

"They'll be seeing you. Everyone who was at that party is being questioned about what they saw."

"No one has asked to see me yet."

"They'll get around to you. But maybe you should volunteer a statement before they call you. If Sarah Jordan really did push that guy off the web, she's dangerous."

"Maybe I should talk to Don again. I told him what I saw."

"You did?" Nancy raised her eyebrows. "What did he say?"

"That it was my imagination. Only I asked him to check if there was a spider missing, and there was. He found its body in a bush near the gym."

"He should go to the police."

"I don't think Don would do anything to get Sarah Jordan in trouble. He's very attached to her. I told you before."

"I know. Has it occurred to you that he may be in danger? If she really has killed a man who tried to make love to her . . ."

"Oh, no! That's too horrible!"

"You must call the police and tell them what you saw."

‡ ‡ ‡

Don returned to the office after lunch to see if his statement was ready for signature and found Bernice close to hysteria. "It's no good coming in here asking for help. I'm incompetent! I'm a lousy typist with dangerous tendencies like talking to members of the staff and running the goddamn department single-handed when you-know-who is out, which is most of the time. My filing system is chaotic and I can't keep a secret and I leave a trail of Kleenex and paper cups wherever I go. That's just for openers. If you care to talk to Professor fucking Berlin, I'm sure he'll give you particulars of all my failings, including the fact that I don't put out like Della in the dean's office. The fact that I'm happily married—"

"Quiet down, Bernice. What's happened, for God's sake?"

"It's nothing." She ripped the sheet out of the typewriter, crushed it into a ball, and dropped it in the wastebasket. "Only this old crone carrying on as usual. Why don't you tell me I'm a stupid old bitch? He does. He's going to kick my ass from here to the main gate next time I let him down. Ask him— those were his words. That's the delicate turn of phrase he has for his confidential secretary after eight years' loyal service."

"Why? What was he pissed off about?"

"That goddamn guest list. I told you I left a name off."

"Yeah—Meg Kellaway."

"You know what happened? An hour ago the damn girl called the police and offered to talk to them. They checked the list and of course she wasn't on it. So they hauled in Jerry and twisted his vitals for twenty minutes and heaved him out so he could work me over. He did."

Don's head was reeling. Why had Meg done this, when it had all been going so well? He managed to say, "Don't take it so hard, Bernice. We all know what Jerry is like. It doesn't mean a thing. Can I get you some coffee?"

She shook her head. "Paper cups. I wouldn't dare. I'd better look busy. And I mustn't be seen fraternizing with research students, but thanks, I feel a little better for unloading some."

"Okay, I just came in to sign a statement."

"If it's done, it's in the tray by the door in a brown envelope."

He found it and slipped it quickly into his pocket. "So, is Meg Kellaway coming in to make a statement?"

'She's expected at three," said Bernice, "and if she walks in here . . ."

Don grinned and left, but before he was through the door the grin had vanished. He was in deep trouble. That statement in his pocket was false, and would shortly be proved so. If he signed it, he could face a criminal charge. He was going to have to go to the police and admit he had lied. At least he could stop Sarah from getting in similar trouble. She hadn't been seen by the police yet.

Sarah was in a room used for private study, copying some data recorded by her stand-in the previous semester. There were three freshmen students in there. He asked her to step outside, and mentioned that it was urgent. They walked out of the building and along one of the paths to the campanile before he told her what he had just learned. "I'll have to go back to the police and tell them I didn't take you home that night," he said. "I can say I wanted to shield you from all the questions and humiliations, which is true. Maybe when you make your statement, if you ask them to treat it in confidence—"

She tossed the hair off her shoulders and said lightly, "You won't change your statement. You'll let it stand."

"I can't, Sarah. Meg's about to blow it sky high."

"If we let her. You've got to stop her."

"How could I, for God's sake? She'll be walking through that door in just over forty minutes."

"She won't. You'll take care of it."

"What do you mean?"

"Make sure she doesn't get to see the police."

"Sarah, she phoned to say she is coming. They made an appointment."

"So she breaks it. They get hundreds of calls from nuts. They'll file it and forget it."

"They know who she is and they know she was at the party. If she doesn't come to them, they'll go to her."

"And she won't be there. End of problem."

He shook his head. "I just don't follow this line of reasoning."

Sarah's green eyes assessed him. "You said you love me. Is that still true, or was it, like, one of those things you say in bedrooms?"

"Of course I meant it. Only you told me—"

"—to forget it. That's right." She looked away at the orb web between the trees and the campanile. "Maybe I was a little hotheaded that night. You interrupted a conversation. It shocked me to see you so jealous of Ed Cunningham. I didn't like to see you like that and I guess I went overboard in some of the things I said." She gave an embarrassed laugh. "That's the nearest I'll ever get to an apology."

It broke over Don like a wave and lifted him high. "Oh, Sarah."

"Don't say any more. Words don't mean much to me. If you and I have any future, you must stop Meg Kellaway."

He frowned. "Stop her?"

"Silence her, then."

"How?"

She clicked her tongue impatiently. "Can't I leave that up to you?"

He shook his head. "It's not so easy. Meg is in a very nervous state of mind. Finding that spider under your jacket really upset her. She has a hatred of them bordering on arachnophobia. Now that she's got it into her head to go to the police, I don't think anything I can say—"

" 'Say'?" broke in Sarah. "It's too late to *say* things."

"Well, how else can I stop her, for Christ's sake?" He stopped. "Oh, no. If you think I would use force . . ."

"She knows exactly what she's doing," said Sarah. "She means to destroy me. Will you let her?"

This was a nightmare. "Sarah, let's be rational about this. If you have to admit you were attacked by Saville, it's rough, but there's no way it can destroy you. We can make damned sure the police treat this thing in confidence."

She said in a low voice, "Don Rigden, you'd better decide. If you won't take care of this, I'll do it myself, but don't ever come near me again."

"Sarah, will you listen to me? I just don't see the need—"

"You don't?" She nodded once. "That's all I wanted to know." She turned and walked away, fast, without looking back.

‡ ‡ ‡

"Are you sure you don't want me to come along? It's no trouble. I can work in the library while you talk to the police."

"Thanks, Nancy," said Meg, "but I'm a whole lot better now. And it's important to me to get on top of those fears I had. I'll take it calmly and quietly and prove to myself that the things I see I really do see, and it's not my imagination. See you later."

She walked to the end of the passage and stepped into the elevator. When she got out and was crossing the lobby to the front door, the dormitory superintendent called out to her from his desk.

"Message for you, Miss Kellaway. Someone called Bernice called just now from the Ecology Department. Said the location is changed and they're sending a car for you." He glanced out of his window. "That'll be it out front. A red Ford Pinto, she said."

The door of the Pinto was already open for her. She bent to say, "I'm Meg Kellaway."

The driver was wearing black clothes. And a crash helmet and shades. It was a girl's voice that said, "Check. Get in."

Meg took her seat and closed the door. The car moved out into the traffic. Fast. She began to understand the reason for the helmet.

She turned to take another look at the driver. And saw red-gold hair showing on the back of her neck where it was tucked under the helmet.

She said, "I know who you are. What is this?"

"Easy," said Sarah Jordan in a pacifying voice. "I offered to pick you up. We both have to go to the same place."

"Where?"

"Police headquarters. Downtown. It won't take long."

"I'd rather walk."

"You'd never make it. Relax."

"Let me out of here, please."

"What are you scared of?"

She didn't answer. She was telling herself not to panic. The police might well have decided to see her at headquarters, as her statement was volunteered. Maybe the detectives on campus were too busy seeing the people on their lists.

But why was Sarah Jordan going to the same place? Maybe the police had information already that she had been in the gym when the man had died. If they also wanted to talk to her at headquarters, it was reasonable that she should drive Meg there.

"Do you have an interview?" she asked as casually as she could.

"Sure."

"Mine is at three."

"That's why I'm driving fast."

They were going south on Broadway, past Lincoln Center,

snaking through traffic at a rate that had a chorus of horns
serenading them.

"Where is it?"

"Near City Hall."

"That's a long way."

"We'll make it."

The police could not possibly know that Meg had information linking Sarah with the man's death. She had said on the
phone that she wanted to volunteer a statement, no more than
that. The fact that she was getting a lift from the girl she was
about to implicate was pure coincidence. There was no sense
in getting disturbed about it. Sarah Jordan herself was not
aware of the information Meg was about to give the police.

They were approaching the Lower East Side now, past
Union Square and left onto Fourteenth Street. They turned
into one of the avenues and went a few blocks before turning
left again, still at a speed approaching fifty, which was faster
than Meg cared to be driving in a crowded area.

"You seem to know the way," she commented.

"I've been here before."

But as they drove deeper into the Lower East Side, and
derelict and burned-out buildings loomed on either side, whole
blocks abandoned to arsonists and looters and left as shells
surrounded by junk—abandoned cars, armchairs, bedsteads—
Meg's thin shell of confidence cracked.

"Would you please stop the car?"

"Why?"

"I want to get out."

"Don't be so dumb."

"There's no police headquarters down here. I'm getting
out."

Sarah Jordan spun the wheel violently and the car swung off
the street onto a vacant lot littered with the debris of the

gutted brownstone block overshadowing it. As they turned and Sarah decelerated, Meg jerked open the door and threw herself out.

She hit the ground hard, taking the impact with her right shoulder and hip and rolling over to try to break the fall. The pain was sharp and violent, but she got up and started running. She didn't care where—just away from the car and Sarah Jordan. Footsteps started behind her, but she didn't look back. She made for the building, sprinting over rubble that collapsed underfoot as it took her weight, threatening to wrench her ankle at each step.

With a spasm of terror she realized that the door she was trying to reach was barred. And the windows at ground level were boarded over. She couldn't change direction now without Sarah Jordan's cutting her off. She knew it would come to a fight and she was desperately weak from her fall and the strain of the past several days.

There was one chance: an ornate iron fire escape of the type common in old New York buildings, constructed in the shape of a series of Z's on end, the diagonal stepladders linking terraced platforms that reached up six floors. For security purposes, the lowest ladder worked on the drawbridge principle. By good fortune it had been let down to ground level.

She grasped the ironwork and hauled herself up to the first platform. She could see Sarah Jordan coming fast toward the ladder. With all the strength she could summon, Meg hauled it up, rung by rung, so that it homed into brackets on the railings of the platform and the one overhead. The last rung was secured by an iron clasp. She slammed it across and leaned back against the building, fighting for breath, surrendering to the pain in her shoulder, thigh, feet, and hands.

Sarah Jordan was fifteen feet below, unable to reach her. She stood looking up at Meg for a half minute at least, hands on hips. Then she took off the helmet, shook her hair loose, turned, and walked slowly back in the direction of the car, without a word having passed between them.

Meg sank to the platform floor and lay staring at the underside of the next landing, massaging her right hip. She couldn't think how she was going to get back from this godforsaken place, but she had to wait, anyway, for the sound of the car moving off.

It didn't happen.

When she turned her head to look again, after maybe six or seven minutes, the Pinto was still where it had stopped. The passenger door was still open. Her vantage point was too high for her to see if Sarah was inside. She sat up and scanned the refuse-littered area below. Not a movement. But she would not be tempted to let down the ladder while that car remained where it was.

She gave up trying to account for what had happened. The one thing she knew for certain was that she was in real danger from Sarah Jordan. If she had to wait all night, she would sit it out.

Ten minutes passed.

Twenty.

By now the police would be asking why she hadn't turned up. They might call the residence hall. With luck, the super would tell them she had left in a red Ford Pinto. But there was no reason for them to start a search. And no possibility they would come down here. Maybe by the evening Nancy Lim would notice she hadn't returned.

It occurred to her now—too late, of course—that the message the super had received was not from Bernice at all but from Sarah Jordan: a neat, nasty way of tricking her into the car. But it was still a mystery how Sarah had heard about her interview with the police. Unless Bernice had told her.

Even Bernice didn't know that the interview concerned Sarah's actions at the party. Only two people knew that: Nancy and Don.

She glanced at her watch. She had spent thirty-five minutes on the fire escape. The car hadn't moved.

She refused to depress herself by trying to account for what was happening. She had to find something to do. Climb to the top.

She checked that the ladder was secure and began slowly to mount the steps to the next landing. With each step a searing pain gripped her thigh, but she kept moving up.

There were broken windows on the second landing. She could not see much of the interior, because it had been blackened by fire. She went higher. If she could spot someone in the distance and attract his attention, she might get help. From the fifth landing all she could see was another block like this one, but shaded from the sun. It appeared to be uninhabited. She could not see the street they had driven along. She could not see a living thing.

Until she looked down through the small holes in the iron floor and noticed something black moving in silence across the landing below. She screamed and hurtled up the stairs to the top landing.

Sarah Jordan came after her.

There was a window with a gap wide enough between the frame and the sill for Meg to push her fingers under and force the frame upward. She swung her leg over the sill and saw just in time that she was about to step into a room with no floor, only a drop of perhaps thirty feet to another floor so burned out it was a death trap.

So she waited, straddling the sill. And Sarah Jordan came up the last stairs, smiling. In her left hand was a leather belt, in her right a broken bottle.

"Stay right there," she told Meg. "Don't move a muscle."

"If you touch me, I'll—"

"—scream? You just did. I don't see Batman and Robin yet." She came closer, holding the bottle with the jagged edges toward Meg's face. "I want you to put your other leg over the sill so you're facing the inside."

"There's no floor."

"Keep your ass on the sill then."

Meg hesitated, and the bottle was thrust closer. She obeyed. And prepared for the push that would send her into the chasm below.

"Get your hands off the woodwork and behind your back. Real close together, elbows touching."

She felt the strap being put around her forearms below the elbow and being tightened notch by notch. She cried out at the pain.

"Save it."

"I hurt my shoulder falling out of the car."

"Too bad. The butterfly injured her wing. Move now. Bring your legs over nice and slow and remember what I have in my right hand."

So with Meg leading, they went down the stairs. At the second landing she was ordered to stop. One of the windows there was open.

"Inside," she was told. "It's safe. To coin a phrase, this is where I came in."

In the building they made their way across a blackened floor to a doorway, then down some stairs and through a passage to the front. "It took me some time to find this way through," said Sarah. "Good of you to wait."

They returned to the car. Meg was ordered to lie on the backseat while her ankles were bound with rope. "We're not going far," Sarah told her, "but I'm taking no chances."

The journey took about four minutes, but every jolt and turn was like a stab. When they stopped, it was at a place little different from the first. More derelict blocks, silent and skeletal.

"What are we doing here?"

"Choosing a box for a butterfly."

"You're crazy."

"Would you like to crawl there?"

"I didn't mean that. I'm in a lot of pain."

The door was opened and her ankles untied. She was pushed, stumbling over rubble, toward the shell of a building.

"Lean against the door and it'll open."

They went inside.

"Straight ahead, then left and down to the basement."

"Would you please listen to me?" Meg asked as calmly as she was able. "I don't know why you want to hurt me, but—"

"Get down those stairs."

"I'm scared of cellars."

"You like being kicked?"

She went down as far as an open door.

Ahead it was pitch black. She could see three steps, then nothing. Her mind supplied impressions of what lay beyond. She was going to scream.

13

Before he left that evening, Don was called to Jerry's office. One of the detectives was there with Jerry. He looked and acted as if he was senior to the man who had taken the statement. The lieutenant. Probably in his fifties, he was dressed in a good blue suit. He was bald, with smiling eyes. He had a couple of gold teeth.

Don had decided the best way to get over the problem of the statement in his pocket was to admit he had lied to keep Sarah's name out of the investigation. With Jerry sitting in, it was going to be a rough ride.

The lieutenant didn't bring up the statement. He wanted to know about Meg. She had made an appointment to talk to the police, but she hadn't kept it. She had left her residence hall at two-forty P.M. and no one had seen her since.

Don tried to cover the kick of fear he felt in his stomach. He admitted he knew Meg, but he hadn't seen her that afternoon.

The lieutenant asked if Meg had discussed with him what she would tell the police. Don said he didn't know how much credence to give it, as Meg was undergoing a nervous crisis, but she had told him some things, yes. In response to more questions, he related the story of the jacket outside the gym and the dead spider.

Jerry stared at him blankly.

The lieutenant asked, "What do you make of this yourself, Mr. Rigden? Do you believe it?"

270

"I wasn't totally convinced when Meg told me, but later I checked the lab and one of our spiders was missing. I made a search and found its body under a shrub adjacent to the gym."

"So that much of the story appears to be true. Well, what do you know? A dead tarantula under a girl's jacket. How about the jacket—did you search for that?"

"No point. Sarah was wearing it when we—" Don stopped.

Jerry said, "Mr. Rigden has already made a statement to the effect that he escorted Miss Jordan home at the end of the party."

"Thanks, Professor, I'll handle this in my own way," the lieutenant said amicably but firmly. "If this really is true, it's important. Just for the record, we know the man Saville was not alone on the web. He had a woman with him and they had sex. There's no argument about that. Forensic found all the evidence they need, and plenty more. Seems like Miss Jordan was the woman, and your friend Miss Kellaway guessed as much from what she saw. I figure it's time I talked to these young ladies. I'm due to meet Sarah Jordan tomorrow morning at nine-thirty, but I'd like to take a statement from Miss Kellaway before that. Would you have any idea where she might be right now?"

"Sorry, but no."

"You see, you told me yourself that this is a girl in a nervous state. We don't want to alarm her any more by having a patrolman pick her up. If you could give it some thought, maybe talk to a few people, it might be the best way to handle this."

"I don't see the need for this," said Jerry thickly. "You've been given the salient facts. You know it was Sarah on the web with Saville. Why not talk to her?"

The lieutenant said slowly, spacing his words, "Richard Saville didn't die when he fell from the web. He was already dead."

"But he broke his neck, for Christ's sake."

"Correct. But the autopsy showed his feet hit the ground first. He had two fractured legs. The only mark on his head was an abrasion below the jaw, where the nylon rope had pressed into the flesh tissues. It jerked back the jaw with enough force to snap the spinal cord." He placed his finger crossways under his chin and pressed upward. "So."

Jerry screwed his face into horrified disbelief.

"The force was in the tension of the entire web," the lieutenant explained. "We did some tests."

"But why did it happen?"

"That's what I aim to ask Miss Jordan. She's not here or at home so we've put an APB out on her. But I still need that statement from Meg Kellaway."

‡ ‡ ‡

Maybe talk to a few people . . .

There was only one who could help: Sarah.

Don hadn't seen her since she had stormed off after their row over Meg. *If you won't take care of this, I'll do it myself.* And it seemed she had. Somehow she had stopped Meg from making that statement. Well, she was getting in deeper trouble than she could possibly know. She couldn't stand in the way of the police investigation.

She had also warned Don never to come near her again. So why was he bothering?

It was not too late to help her pull back. The lieutenant knew the score. Obviously he had talked to Jerry, established who in the department was closest to Meg on the principle that if the problem could be sorted out by the people concerned, it saved all the hassle of police inquiries. Maybe the lieutenant also

suspected Sarah had a hand in Meg's nonappearance. Whatever his thinking was, he evidently had no worries for Meg's
safety. Unlike Don.

Don was feeling increasingly responsible for Meg. Thanks to
him, she was in danger. He had let Sarah know what Meg had
seen. He had warned her that Meg had called the police. He
had been angered by Meg's decision to talk to them after it had
seemed she could be kept quiet, but really he had no right to
expect her silence. It was his duty now to help her, if she
needed it. And tell them both—Meg and Sarah—that the
police knew what Meg had seen outside the gym.

Duty was one thing; his feelings for Sarah were another. He
still cared about her, deeply and passionately. It was past ratio-
nality. She had told him and proved in a dozen ways that she
didn't love him. She had treated him with steady contempt. He
had started as her rival and never overcome it. She was not
prepared to treat him as an equal. He was allowed to get close
only on Sarah's terms: as a novice in hang-gliding, a dance
partner, or a stud. So why persist? It was because, against all
the evidence, he believed there was a warm, attractive, vulnerable side to Sarah. It could be an illusion, but he had not yet
persuaded himself that it was.

That evening after dinner, he called Gilmore Hall to check
whether Meg was back. She was not, but no one seemed
concerned. He called Sarah and got no answer. He tried both
places an hour later, with the same result.

About nine P.M. he went to Sarah's apartment. It was dark
by then, but there was no light from the windows. After trying
her intercom several times, he buzzed the people on the floor
below hers. It turned out that the man who answered owned
the building, and when Don said the police wanted to trace a
girl Sarah had been seen with, he reluctantly said he would
open up.

The only time Don had been in Sarah's apartment was the

disastrous night of the disco. It looked different, and he remembered she had said on the phone that she had been redecorating. She had painted everything white, the furniture as well as the walls and ceiling.

"Well, how about that?" said the owner. "I agreed she could paint the place, but this beats everything. Even the goddamn shades are white. And the quilt. You need shades to live in here."

Don had spotted a projector on the floor beside the bed. "She's got one of these. That's why she wanted it white. They're the latest thing in interior decoration. You have a rotating slide used in conjunction with a convex lens, and the color or pattern is projected all over the room. It's supposed to be relaxing."

"Let's see." The owner of the apartment switched it on.

Everything, walls, ceiling, even their faces, bore the slowly moving mesh of a cobweb.

"Hell, I couldn't live with that for long. It makes me itch all over. What kind of girl has a toy like this to relax with?"

Don didn't answer. He just said, "Would you call me at this number if she gets back tonight?" He handed the man a card.

"Ask her to call you?"

"No. Like I said."

"Okay. Let's turn this thing off and get out of here."

There was no call that evening. When Don phoned in the morning, he learned that Sarah hadn't been back all night. The same was true of Meg when he phoned Gilmore Hall.

He racked his brains trying to work out where they might have spent the night. He called Ed Cunningham on the phone. Sarah was not there, but when Don explained the problem, Cunningham sounded really alarmed, and suggested he come over at once.

"I want to give you all the help I can," Cunningham said as soon as Don stepped out of the elevator into his consulting room. "You must tell me everything that's happened since the party. I haven't seen anything of Sarah since then. It's best if I don't see her, and I'll explain why in a moment, but I do understand something about her state of mind, and if I can, I want to help prevent anything really tragic from happening."

The man was visibly concerned, and Don warmed to him as he had not before. He brought him fully up to date.

Then he heard from Cunningham how on the night of the party Sarah had pressed him to spend the night with her, until finally he had told her about his relationship with Greg Laz. "It broke her up," Cunningham said in a troubled voice.

Don had listened in amazement. "I can understand. She had a tremendous crush on you."

"I knew all about that. I tried everything I knew to deflect it, but this time it had to be faced. She demanded to know why I wasn't prepared to sleep with her. I knew the truth would shock her initially, but I figured that when she had time to reflect, she would understand the rejection wasn't personal."

"It's not easy to be so objective."

"You're telling me."

"I guess she was attracted to you as a father figure."

"Probably. Her own father is a nebulous character—no support at all. As a therapist I can deal with transference problems between patient and doctor, but my relationship with Sarah wasn't like that. She wouldn't let it be that way. So it was never within my control. I handled it ineptly."

"In what way?"

"I should have been tougher with her. She wouldn't admit it, but she wanted back-door analysis. Some bad experiences as a kid had turned her off to psychiatry, only she was desperate to see if it could help her, without facing anything so formal as analysis. She interested me, so I played along on the basis of friendship. I should never have done it."

"You think she needed formal psychotherapy?"

"She does now. She's the prisoner of her fantasies."

"Spider Girl?"

Cunningham nodded. "It's become a more potent self than her real one. Everyone has fantasies, needs them, uses them, but most of us recognize them for what they are. Sarah appears to have lost that capacity. Her Spider Girl identity cuts her off from reality. I've watched it develop without being in a position to check it. This latest development is very bad news."

"Why did she do it?"

"She must have been so shattered at learning I was a homosexual that she refused to come to terms with it. She switched to her spider self and turned her aggression onto Pelé."

"She destroyed you, in effect?"

"Right. Then I guess she took off her clothes to climb on the web. What happened after that—how Saville got to be there and was killed—I don't care to speculate."

Don said gravely, "It scares me."

"Fantasy divorced from reality is a terrifying thing, Don. It feeds on itself. It is destructive and dangerous, because the checks and balances of the real world don't apply. There is no sense of guilt, no reference to morality. While she is Spider Girl, she is omnipotent."

"Is there any way she can snap out of this?"

"It's not a permanent condition, yet, so far as I can judge. But if she was somehow responsible for Saville's death, as we both fear, she is unlikely to come to terms with it. She'll interpret it through her fantasy. In spider terms killing is natural and explicable; in human terms it's unthinkable, so she shuts off the human part of her personality."

"Can't anything be done to save her?"

"It's the other girl's safety we must think of first," said Cunningham.

"Meg? Do you think Sarah would—"

"Meg is a threat, so Sarah will deal with her as a spider does."

"Christ. By killing her?"

Cunningham shrugged. "You're the authority on spiders."

It was as much as Don could do to relate the behavior of a spider to Sarah. "She would trap her, bite her, bind her up, and, when she is ready, kill her. I can't believe this. It's pure—"

"—fantasy?" said Cunningham in a flat voice.

Don said, "You've got to help me find them. Where would they go?"

"Somewhere that fits the fantasy. Have you checked the webs around the university?"

"She wouldn't use them—too many people around."

"We must check them anyway."

"There's Lake Pinecliff," said Don, "where she goes hang-gliding. That's really remote. Listen, if I drive out there, could you check the webs on campus? Jerry will help. Should we tell the police, get a message out?"

"No. That could panic her. This has to be handled by people she knows."

‡ ‡ ‡

She could not tell how long she had lain there because she could not read her watch. She was bound from ankles to chest with nylon rope, wound around her body many times. Trussed and left like some mummified body in its tomb. The first hours had been the worst. After Sarah had finished tying her and left her lying with her head on a pile of coal, Meg had waited in horror for the first touch of a spider on her skin. A strip of adhesive tape prevented her from screaming. But in time she began to feel numb, physically and mentally. She may even have slept for a while. Now she no longer cared about anything, except the problem she had in breathing. She had tried dragging her face against the coal to lift the edges of the tape, but succeeded only in filling her ears and nostrils with dust.

She managed to squirm a yard or so across the floor, but it was impossible to loosen the rope. She would remain here till someone came or she no longer knew anything about it.

She definitely slept, because she was awakened by the bolt on the door being drawn. She tried to make noises. The door opened, admitting blinding light, and Sarah Jordan.

"Hi, Butterfly. How we doing?" She switched on a flashlight and came down the steps. "Didn't expect to see me again, huh? Surprise. I brought you a can of Seven-Up and some bagels for brunch. Let's look at you. Ugh—dirty."

Meg could not see her distinctly, because the light was shining in her face.

"Before I take off your gag, get this, Butterfly. You'll take your food and drink nicely, okay? If your table manners please me, I might let you go to the bathroom afterward. So keep it civilized, huh?"

She ripped off the plaster and it felt as if Meg's skin came with it, but that didn't matter. She could breathe. She gulped air.

"I'll loosen some of this rope," said Sarah.

"Why have you come back?"

"No questions."

The rope was loosened enough for her to sit up. Her wrists were untied. She moaned with pain as the blood coursed through her veins.

"I guess you want a drink first," said Sarah, popping the tab on the soda can. "Can you hold it?"

Her fingers didn't function yet, but she was able to hold the can between her palms and drink from it.

"Thanks," said Meg. "I don't know why you're doing this."

"Drink up. There's your food." She dropped a bag on Meg's lap.

"If you're not going to leave me to die, what do you intend to do with me?"

Sarah took one of the bagels from the bag, bit into it, and tossed it out of reach over the coal. From her look it was meant as a reprimand. She was not prepared to answer questions.

Meg was hungry. She ate the rest of what she was allowed in silence. Then her wrists were tied again and her legs freed. The "bathroom" was the deepest end of the cellar. She had to manage her clothes with her hands shackled. With no more privileges to lose, she asked, "Where are you taking me now?"

Sarah laughed. "Come here."

When Meg was close enough, Sarah pushed her in the chest, so that she fell back on the coal. "You're staying here, Butterfly, till I'm ready for you."

"You wouldn't kill me. You brought me food, so you want to keep me alive."

Sarah bound Meg's ankles with the rope and started winding it around her legs again.

"Why get yourself in trouble with the police?" Meg persisted. "If you let me out of here, we could see them together and explain what happened on the night of the party. They must know it was an accident, that guy falling off the web. There was nothing criminal in what you did. Can't you see—?"

Sarah covered Meg's mouth with adhesive tape again and continued securing the rope. With Meg silenced and helpless, she started to talk. They were not words of comfort. "Butterfly, you don't know a thing. Killing is nothing. I killed my own brother. Two years back. May fourth, 1978. You want to know why? Marty screwed up my life. He pulled the plug on everything I ever did. My parents doted on him. He was brilliant and handsome and charming. He was going to Yale, only he didn't get there because he crashed his bike on Highway Seventy. They said it was an accident, but nobody could say why it happened. The road was clear. The bike was in perfect condition. Now I'll tell you what really killed Marty. Imagine you're riding a motorcycle, one of those big Japanese machines. The road is straight and clear, so you open up. Eighty, ninety. Suddenly something is moving into your line of vision. It's a spider, not very big, but you don't know that, because it's on the inside of your crash helmet, crossing the visor an inch from your eye. You react, and at that speed it's fatal. Zap!" The charged quality in her voice changed to a giggle. "Want to know how I fixed it? Inside that crash helmet there was a strip of soft leather packed with fiberglass padding that lies across the forehead. It has a row of vents underneath. That was where the spider came from. I inserted an egg sac through the central vent into the fiberglass about ten days before Marty died. One egg sac contains anywhere up to eight hundred spiders, so even if plenty escaped or died, there was a good chance of one or two hatching and taking a walk across the visor sometime when Marty was on the road. You got to admit it was a cute idea. I guess, to be honest, I didn't expect him to get killed, but I sure as hell wanted to give him a good scare. It was on my conscience for a long time afterward. I had nightmares about it. But it doesn't bother me anymore."

She stood up and used the flashlight to check that the bindings were secure. "The reason I told you is so you know killing is no big deal. Telling you is a kind of commitment, too. It means I can't let you live. Too bad, huh?" She kicked the empty can out of reach. "That's something I'm working on. There's no hurry. See you, Butterfly."

The place was dark again, and the horrors came back.

‡‡‡

When Don returned from Lake Pinecliff without a shred of information about Sarah, he went straight to Jerry's office to see if any news had come in while he was away.

"Yeah," said Jerry. "Something came in." He tossed a newspaper across the desk.

It was an early edition of the *Post.* The headline ran WEB DEATH—SPIDER GIRL WAS THERE. Claiming an exclusive, the paper reported that Sarah "Spider Girl" Jordan was known to have been on the web at about the time Rick Saville was killed. An eyewitness was said to have told friends she had seen Sarah's jacket—recognizable for its black-sequin spider emblem—folded on the lawn outside the gym at around two A.M., the estimated time of Saville's death. The rest of the report was a rehash of information published earlier, except that it was stated that Miss Jordan was not available for comment and her present whereabouts were unknown.

"Someone talked, then," said Don calmly. "This stuff is secondhand. Nancy Lim, I guess. Is there any real news?"

"What do you want—another corpse?" said Jerry in a rising voice. "Isn't this enough? Havelock Sloane is raising hell. Every goddamned paper in America has been trying to call me all morning. The dean wants a meeting of the trustees and a full inquiry. And the police are all over the campus."

"We need them," said Don. "These girls haven't been seen in twenty-four hours. Was Cunningham here this morning?"

"I took him around the webs myself. No dice. I'm having the damned webs taken down this afternoon. They give people nasty ideas. Where you going now?"

"Police headquarters—see what's happening."

Downtown at headquarters, on Pearl Street, he was shown up to the detectives' squadroom. The lieutenant was there on the phone. He raised his hand to acknowledge Don. He covered the mouthpiece and said, "We found Miss Jordan's car."

A patrolman had spotted the red Ford Pinto on St. Mark's Place.

"We're making intensive inquiries at hotels in the area to see if she stayed there last night," the lieutenant said, "and naturally we're watching the car. Too bad we had to move in like this, but now that the story has broken, it could easily panic the girl. Do you know if she has any friends in the Village, or at NYU?"

"I've never heard of any. She doesn't talk much about friends."

"I heard you went out to Lake Pinecliff this morning. That's the place she goes hang-gliding, right?"

Don nodded. "The people at the motel saw her the day before yesterday, but she hasn't been there since. I scoured the area looking for the car and of course there was nothing."

"There's a lot of media interest in this, Mr. Rigden. This Spider Girl thing—is it just an act, would you say?"

"I'm afraid she may believe it, some of the time anyway. You might find it useful to talk to Dr. Edmund Cunningham about this."

"We already did. He says she's out of touch with reality. In my book, that's a psychopath."

"Does it matter what labels we use?"

"If she's dangerous, yes, sir. Things have moved on since we talked yesterday. We've been getting some background on Sarah Jordan and she's a very strange girl. She's on record as saying she has the characteristics of a spider. She admits she's aggressive. She actually sank her teeth in some guy's neck when he got on a web with her at NBC."

"Publicity," said Don. "If you get all your information from the papers—"

"We checked. It happened. In the last two hours we've had three unsolicited statements from people who say she is dangerous. That's not the press; that's so-called academics like yourself. They say she went to parties looking for guys who would share in her fantasies."

Don reddened. "That's a lie. What are you conducting—a search for two missing girls or a witch hunt?"

"I may be conducting a murder investigation, Mr. Rigden."

There was something like ice creeping down Don's spine. "You don't mean that."

"Add it up," said the lieutenant, and his eyes watched Don's face. "She took off her jacket to go on the web. Left it folded, so it was a voluntary action. She turns up afterward wearing all her clothes—which are now torn—and telling a story of attempted rape. Yeah, we've been digging. We know a whole lot of things now we didn't know last evening. The evidence won't support that story of rape. It looks like Miss Jordan was covering for something else." He gave a slight smile. "Maybe you reached the same conclusion. I notice you haven't signed the statement you made, saying you escorted Miss Jordan home that night. Did you think better of it?"

"I got it wrong," admitted Don. "I'd like to emend that statement."

"You left around midnight, alone?"

"Yeah. I'm sorry. I—"

"You wanted to keep her name out of this?"

Don nodded. "But before you reach any conclusions about what happened, you should give Sarah the chance to tell her story."

The lieutenant shook his head. "I can't wait. If she killed Saville—"

"*Killed?* Why would she want to kill him if he wasn't even attacking her?"

The lieutenant looked at Don for a moment in silence.

"Even an ignorant cop knows what happens to a male spider after sex, Mr. Rigden."

"That's a myth," said Don. "Well, it's a matter of dispute. Because it's been observed among laboratory spiders it doesn't mean it happens in the natural state. Most males are off the web immediately after mating."

"And if a male doesn't know he's in danger?"

"It's instinctive. They behave automatically."

"Spiders, yeah. How about men?"

Don hesitated.

The lieutenant said, "What if Saville didn't know the routine? What if he stayed on the web?"

The phone rang and he picked it up. He listened, made a couple of notes, and put it down. "Sarah Jordan spent last night at a small hotel on Christopher Street. Of course, she used a phony name. The manager had never seen her before. She checked out at eight-thirty this morning."

"What about Meg?"

"She wasn't mentioned, Mr. Rigden. Now, unless you can think of someplace she could be, I'd be glad if you would get the hell out of here."

Don was glad to go. He needed air. He was reeling from the lieutenant's assumptions. To hear Sarah labeled a psychopath and a killer was more than he could take. But deep inside, he knew it could not be ruled out as a possibility. There were things he couldn't explain or ignore, like the savage and pointless killing of Pelé. But whatever the truth might be, the police were treating her as a dangerous killer. That in itself was dangerous. Although Sarah liked to think she was independent, events had shown she was highly suggestible. She adapted herself to people's expectations. They had called her Spider Girl and she had convinced herself it was true. Now they were calling her a psychopath. If she was alerted to the police operation, had spotted them around the hotel and near her car, how would she react to it? If she were holding Meg somewhere, too scared to release her, the outcome could be tragic.

And the responsibility would be his. He had panicked Sarah by letting her know Meg was going to the police. If anything happened to Meg, it would be on his conscience. It was up to him to prevent the unthinkable from happening.

But how?

Find them.

She had left her car on St. Mark's Place. Stayed at a hotel on Christopher Street. Alone. Where was Meg?

Why downtown? Did Sarah seriously think she could hide there? There were plenty of places better for holing up. Cunningham had said she would go somewhere that fitted the fantasy. A small hotel in the Village? It made no sense.

He found a bar and ordered a beer. He would not go back to his apartment or to the campus until Meg and Sarah were found. They had to be somewhere at this end of town. Sarah, anyway. But it was pointless to stand waiting by the car or the hotel when the police were already there. He had to find Sarah now, before she walked into an ambush.

Somewhere that fitted the fantasy.

A spider would look for a place where it was safe. The underside of a stone. The inside of a cupboard. A lumber room. An attic. An empty house.

Months back, he had gone looking for Sarah in empty houses out in the wasteland of the Lower East Side. She had been studying the colonizing potential of spiders in a locality gutted by arsonists. She had missed a meeting they had arranged and he had gone looking for her, without success. Later she had come back, but she had never explained why she was away so long.

An empty house would be an ideal place to keep a hostage.

He left the bar and found a cab. The driver, hearing "Avenue C," treated him as if he were crazy, but agreed to make the trip for double the fare.

It was five-forty-five P.M. when he was dropped off on the blitzed street Sarah had once told him she was using as a location for research. It looked deserted. Blocks that had once housed hundreds stood waiting for demolition, stripped of anything salable, surrounded by rubble, smelling of decay.

He walked through an open doorway and shouted Sarah's name. And Meg's. He heard only the scuffle of vermin alarmed by the sound. He climbed the stairs and checked the upper floors.

There were more than thirty buildings, although some were shells only. For more than two hours he searched and shouted without result. It was past eight o'clock when he entered a building almost hollow inside and got the feeling at once that he was not alone. He couldn't say why. There was no sound. No response to his shouts. But when he looked up through the gaping levels to the roof, he saw a single rope suspended from one of the crossbeams. Obviously it had been put there by some kids. He had played games like that when he was eleven or twelve, except that the rope had been fixed to a tree over a stream in a California suburb.

"Anyone here?"

He picked his way over the debris toward the cellar. By now he knew the layout of these buildings better than the architect. The door was bolted, which was unusual. When the looters went through a place, they didn't stop to shut doors after them. He withdrew the bolt and noticed that the metal wasn't rusted like everything else. It had been used. Recently and often.

He repeated his question and got only the echo.

He started to go down the steps; then a thought stopped him. If there *was* someone hiding in the building, they had only to slam the door behind him and shoot the bolt to make him a prisoner.

So he came out and took another look. There was precious little cover for anyone there. The interior walls had practically all collapsed with the floors.

His eyes traveled upward, noting the charred stubs where joists had once supported floors with whole families and their possessions. Every window was smashed.

Then a movement caught his attention. The rope suspended from the roof was swinging very slightly, as if it had just been touched.

He would certainly have seen and heard anyone moving over the rubble. But there wasn't any wind strong enough to have disturbed the rope, unless the window spaces higher up provided a cross draft.

He went over and tested the rope. It was thick and heavy, no doubt pilfered from the docks along the East River. It was knotted in several places, where the kids had made hand- and footholds. He couldn't understand how it had moved. He looked up the fifty or so feet to where it was fixed. Was that where the movement had originated?

The building was flat-roofed, and he could see daylight in places up there. It didn't look safe, but the kids had got up there somehow to sling their rope from the beam.

He stepped outside to look at the iron fire escape. It went up five floors. There was no ladder connecting the top level with the roof. He decided to go up and take a look. It was dark now and sharply cooler as he mounted the stairs. He heard the sound of a vehicle moving somewhere in the neighboring streets, the first sure indication of life for hours.

On the top level of the fire escape he leaned through the empty window frame and called Sarah's name again. Then Meg's.

Silence.

He could see no way from here to the roof. The floor had gone except for one joist that jutted precariously into space.

"This is Don. Is anyone up here?"

Below in the street, about two blocks down, a police car had stopped. Its way was barred by rubble. They must have had a tail on him. He swore and climbed out of sight inside the building on a small ledge formed by the joist and the residue of the fallen floor.

"Sarah, if you're here, I want to help you. You need help."

Then he heard her voice say, "Get lost."

She was there, somewhere above him on the roof.

"Is Meg with you?"

No answer.

"She's okay, isn't she?"

"Who cares?"

It was vital to keep her talking. "How did you get up there, Sarah?"

No answer.

"I mean, I'd like to join you."

"What for?" Her voice was indifferent.

"I want to help you."

"I'm okay."

"Is Meg there?"

"Why go on about her? Is it me you want to see?"

"Sure."

"You're alone?"

From his place by the window he could hear faint voices below and the sound of another vehicle. He had to hope the sounds weren't carrying up to Sarah. "Yeah, I'm alone."

There was another pause before she said, "You still want me?"

"You bet."

"Love me, I mean?"

"I told you that before."

She considered it for a while. "Want to make love?"

"Here?" He covered that quickly by adding, "Just give me the chance." It was just too weird. He was interested only in finding the way up to where she was. "How do I get to you?"

"You see a beam jutting out to the center?"

"Christ, is it safe?"

"It's the way I came. When you're out far enough, you reach for the rope and climb up. You're not scared?"

"I guess if you did it, I can. Only it's getting dark in here."

"That's the exciting part." She made it sound as if she had done this before, and he remembered that Rick Saville must have climbed the web in the gym in darkness.

Somewhere below, a car door closed.

"What was that?" Sarah asked.

"Some door. I guess the wind blew it shut. When I get to the top of the rope, where will you be?"

"Waiting here. And, Don . . ."

"Yeah?"

"Let's keep it silent, huh. No talk. That's how I want it."

He didn't ask why. "Okay."

He felt the joist with his hands and put some weight on it. He sat astride it and began edging out from the ledge. The rope was some nine feet ahead, but the joist projected only about seven feet. It was too dark now to see the rubble he would hit seventy feet below if the joist collapsed.

He had moved as far out as he dared. With his arm and hand fully stretched he groped ahead for the rope and felt nothing.

Above him there was a small sound, and he heard breathing. Something touched him. He realized that she had climbed along the beam and started the rope swinging to bring it within his reach. As it came back to him for the second time, he caught it and got a grip on it. He reached as high as he was able, held on, brought his left foot up and rested it on the joist. He hauled himself into a standing position, reached higher up the rope, and swung clear.

Suspended there in almost total darkness, he thought, Why am I doing this? I am doing it for Sarah. Meg isn't up here.

He took a grip on the rope with his feet and pulled himself higher. Only a few feet more.

Suddenly the place lit up. The police had him in their searchlight and he saw his shadow, squat and menacing on the rafters above. A few feet above him he saw Sarah's face contorted with fury. She screamed, and it was a long, guttural scream, like no human sound.

"Sarah," he shouted. "It's okay! It's okay!"

But there was a flash of metal in the light and he saw she had a cleaver in her hand and she was hacking at the rope, hitting it with frenzied blows.

"For God's sake, Sarah!"

She was making no impression on the rope, so she reached farther down and took a wild swing at Don. The force of it tipped her off balance. Screaming, she plunged downward, so close to him that he felt the touch of her hair on his face.

The scream was stopped by a sickening thud.

Below, people were running toward the small, crumpled body.

Don's limbs began to shake. With an effort he hauled himself up to the beam from which Sarah had fallen, and rested there.

In a moment someone addressed him through a bullhorn. "You okay, Mr. Rigden? We found Miss Kellaway in the cellar. She's in bad shape, but she'll live."

"How about—?"

"This one? Didn't stand a chance."

‡ ‡ ‡

"It was like this," said Havelock Sloane. "I knew as soon as I heard she was dead that my documentary was dead, too. I'm not complaining. That's how it is in this business. I was sad about all that beautiful film we shot, that's all. I talked it over with Greg and he agreed it would be in bad taste to run the program, but while we were talking, I had this great idea. Shall I tell them, Greg?"

"Go ahead."

"It's a straight documentary of her life. It'll be unique—a study of the growth of a psychosis. You see, we got most of it on film. There's Ed's first interview with her when she talks about her fear of spiders as a kid. We can flesh that out by talking to her folks in Cherry Hill. There's that terrific action sequence with the spiders in the lab. Then the videorecording of the *Today*-show interview. And when you see that a second time, friends, I promise you you'll see the signs of what's to come—wouldn't you say, Ed?"

"It's there, certainly," Ed Cunningham confirmed.

"And that leaves all the footage I shot. How Spider Girl really took over when Sarah got on that web. Fascinating television. Which doesn't leave much for us to dramatize. We'll get an actress to stand in for the Kellaway girl in the cellar sequence. I heard she is going to be under sedation for some time, so we can't use her, even if we wanted to. But— you guessed it, Don—we'd like you to re-create the scene in the burned-out building. We don't need to show Sarah at all. Just a hand wielding a cleaver as you climb the rope, and then we drop a dummy from the roof and finish on one of the stills the police photographers took. Will you do it?"

Somehow Don kept his anger in check. "Sure," he said flatly. "I'll do it, with just a few conditions. I want the rest of the film shot and edited before I do any filming at all. And I want it to feature a few people you haven't mentioned who contributed in a major way. Okay, you're including her parents. Let's add Professor Jerry Berlin here, who made it all possible in the name of his department; Greg Laz, who first persuaded Sarah that she was star potential; Ed Cunningham, the kindly shrink so fascinated by her mind that he broke her heart. And you, Mr. Sloane, the guy who makes the big decisions, like putting that confused girl on a web and telling her to become a spider. When you're all on tape and I've seen it, I'll re-create her last moments, just like you said. It's another step forward in documentary TV. Might even win you that Emmy, Havelock."